A CHRISTMAS PROMISE

A Will and A Way

and

Home for Christmas

ANTHOLOGIES

From the Heart • *A Little Magic* • *A Little Fate*

Moon Shadows
(with Jill Gregory, Ruth Ryan Langan, and Marianne Willman)

The Once Upon Series
(with Jill Gregory, Ruth Ryan Langan, and Marianne Willman)
Once Upon a Castle • *Once Upon a Star* • *Once Upon a
Dream* • *Once Upon a Rose* • *Once Upon a Kiss* • *Once Upon
a Midnight*

Silent Night
(with Susan Plunkett, Dee Holmes, and Claire Cross)

Out of This World
(with Laurell K. Hamilton, Susan Krinard, and Maggie Shayne)

Bump in the Night
(with Mary Blayney, Ruth Ryan Langan, and Mary Kay McComas)

Dead of Night
(with Mary Blayney, Ruth Ryan Langan, and Mary Kay McComas)

Three in Death

Suite 606
(with Mary Blayney, Ruth Ryan Langan, and Mary Kay McComas)

In Death

The Lost
(with Patricia Gaffney, Ruth Ryan Langan, and Mary Blayney)

The Other Side
(with Mary Blayney, Patricia Gaffney, Ruth Ryan Langan,
and Mary Kay McComas)

Time of Death

The Unquiet
(with Mary Blayney, Patricia Gaffney, Ruth Ryan Langan,
and Mary Kay McComas)

Mirror, Mirror
(with Mary Blayney, Elaine Fox, Mary Kay McComas, and
R. C. Ryan)

Down the Rabbit Hole
(with Mary Blayney, Elaine Fox, Mary Kay McComas, and
R. C. Ryan)

ALSO AVAILABLE . . .

The Official Nora Roberts Companion
(edited by Denise Little and Laura Hayden)

A CHRISTMAS PROMISE

A Will and A Way

and

Home for Christmas

TWO NOVELS IN ONE

NORA ROBERTS

St. Martin's Paperbacks

This is a work of fiction. All of the characters, organizations, and events portrayed in this book are either products of the author's imagination or are used fictitiously.

Published in the United States by St. Martin's Paperbacks, an imprint of St. Martin's Publishing Group

A CHRISTMAS PROMISE: A WILL AND A WAY copyright © 1986 by Nora Roberts and HOME FOR CHRISTMAS copyright © 1986 by Nora Roberts.

For information, address St. Martin's Publishing Group, 120 Broadway, New York, NY 10271.

www.stmartins.com

ISBN: 978-1-250-84725-6

Our books may be purchased in bulk for promotional, educational, or business use. Please contact your local bookseller or the Macmillan Corporate and Premium Sales Department at 1-800-221-7945, ext. 5442, or by email at MacmillanSpecialMarkets@macmillan.com.

Printed in the United States of America

St. Martin's Paperbacks edition / October 2022

10 9 8 7 6 5 4 3 2 1

A Will and A Way

CHAPTER 1

One hundred fifty million dollars was nothing to sneeze at. No one in the vast, echoing library of Jolley's Folley would have dared. Except Pandora. She did so with more enthusiasm than delicacy into a tattered tissue. After blowing her nose, she sat back, wishing the antihistamine she had taken would live up to its promise of fast relief. She wished she'd never caught the wretched cold in the first place. More, she wished she were anywhere else in the world.

Surrounding her were dozens of books she'd read and hundreds more she'd never given a thought to, though she'd spent hours and hours in the library. The scent of the leather-bound volumes mixed with the lighter, homier scent of dust. Pandora preferred either to the strangling fragrance of lilies that filled three stocky vases.

In one corner of the room was a marble-and-ivory chess set, where she'd lost a great many highly disputed matches. Uncle Jolley, bless his round, innocent face and pudgy fingers, had been a compulsive and skilled cheat. Pandora had never taken a loss in stride. Maybe that's why he'd so loved to beat her, by fair means or foul.

Through the three arching windows the light shone dull

and a little gloomy. It suited her mood and, she thought, the proceedings. Uncle Jolley had loved to set scenes.

When she loved—and she felt this emotion for a select few who'd touched her life—she put everything she had into it. She'd been born with boundless energy. She'd developed iron-jawed stubbornness. She'd loved Uncle Jolley in her uninhibited, expansive fashion, acknowledging then accepting all of his oddities. He might have been ninety-three, but he'd never been dull or fussy.

A month before his death, they'd gone fishing—poaching actually—in the lake that was owned and stocked by his neighbor. When they'd caught more than they could eat, they'd sent a half-dozen trout back to the owner, cleaned and chilled.

She was going to miss Uncle Jolley with his round cherub's face, high, melodious voice and wicked humors. From his ten-foot, extravagantly framed portrait, he looked down at her with the same little smirk he'd worn whether he'd been making a million-dollar merger or handing an unsuspecting vice-president a drink in a dribble glass. She missed him already. No one else in her far-flung, contrasting family understood and accepted her with the same ease. It had been one more reason she'd adored him.

Miserable with grief, aggravated by a head cold, Pandora listened to Edmund Fitzhugh drone on, and on, with the preliminary technicalities of Uncle Jolley's will. Maximillian Jolley McVie had never been one for brevity. He'd always said if you were going to do something, do it until the steam ran out. His last will and testament bore his style.

Not bothering to hide her disinterest in the proceedings, Pandora took a comprehensive survey of the other occupants of the library.

To have called them mourners would have been just the sort of bad joke Jolley would have appreciated.

There was Jolley's only surviving son, Uncle Carlson, and his wife. What was her name? Lona—Mona? Did it matter? Pandora saw them sitting stiff backed and alert in matching shades of black. They made her think of crows on a telephone wire just waiting for something to fall at their feet.

Cousin Ginger—sweet and pretty and harmless, if rather vacuous. Her hair was Jean Harlow blond this month. Good old Cousin Biff was there in his black Brooks Brothers suit. He sat back, one leg crossed over the other as if he were watching a polo match. Pandora was certain he wasn't missing a word. His wife—was it Laurie?—had a prim, respectful look on her face. From experience, Pandora knew she wouldn't utter a word unless it were to echo Biff. Uncle Jolley had called her a silly, boring fool. Hating to be cynical, Pandora had to agree.

There was Uncle Monroe looking plump and successful and smoking a big cigar despite the fact that his sister, Patience, waved a little white handkerchief in front of her nose. Probably because of it, Pandora corrected. Uncle Monroe liked nothing better than to make his ineffectual sister uncomfortable.

Cousin Hank looked macho and muscular, but hardly more than his tough athletic wife, Meg. They'd hiked the Appalachian Trail on their honeymoon. Uncle Jolley had wondered if they stretched and limbered up before lovemaking.

The thought caused Pandora to giggle. She stifled it halfheartedly with the tissue just before her gaze wandered over to cousin Michael. Or was it second cousin Michael? She'd never been able to get the technical business straight. It seemed a bit foolish when you weren't talking blood relation anyway. His mother had been Uncle Jolley's niece by Jolley's son's second marriage. It was a complicated state of affairs, Pandora thought. But then Michael Donahue was a complicated man.

They'd never gotten along, though she knew Uncle Jolley had favored him. As far as Pandora was concerned, anyone who made his living writing a silly television series that kept people glued to a box rather than doing something worthwhile was a materialistic parasite. She had a momentary flash of pleasure as she remembered telling him just that.

Then, of course, there were the women. When a man dated centerfolds and showgirls it was obvious he wasn't interested in intellectual stimulation. Pandora smiled as she recalled stating her view quite clearly the last time Michael had visited Jolley's Folley. Uncle Jolley had nearly fallen off his chair laughing.

Then her smile faded. Uncle Jolley was gone. And if she was honest, which she was often, she'd admit that of all the people in the room at that moment, Michael Donahue had cared for and enjoyed the old man more than anyone but herself.

You'd hardly know that to look at him now, she mused. He looked disinterested and slightly arrogant. She noticed the set, grim line around his lips. Pandora had always considered Donahue's mouth his best feature, though he rarely smiled at her unless it was to bare his teeth and snarl.

Uncle Jolley had liked his looks, and had told Pandora so in his early stages of matchmaking. A hobby she'd made sure he'd given up quickly. Well, he hadn't given it up precisely, but she'd ignored it all the same.

Being rather short and round himself, perhaps Jolley had appreciated Donahue's long, lean frame, and the narrow intense face. Pandora might have liked it herself, except that Michael's eyes were often distant and detached.

At the moment he looked like one of the heroes in the action series he wrote—leaning negligently against the wall and looking just a bit out of place in the tidy suit and tie. His dark hair was casual and not altogether neat, as though he hadn't thought to comb it into place after riding with the top down. He looked bored and ready for action. Any action.

It was too bad, Pandora thought, that they didn't get along better. She'd have liked to have reminisced with someone about Uncle Jolley, someone who appreciated his whimsies as she had.

There was no use thinking along those lines. If they'd elected to sit together, they'd have been picking little pieces out of each other by now. Uncle Jolley, smirking down from his portrait, knew it very well.

With a half sigh she blew her nose again and tried to listen to Fitzhugh. There was something about a bequest to whales. Or maybe it was whalers.

Another hour of this, Michael thought, and he'd be ready to chew raw meat. If he heard one more *whereas* . . . On a long breath, Michael drew himself in. He was here for the duration because he'd loved the crazy old man. If the last thing he could do for Jolley was to stand in a room with a group of human vultures and listen to long rambling legalese, then he'd do it. Once it was over, he'd pour himself a long shot of brandy and toast the old man in private. Jolley had had a fondness for brandy.

When Michael had been young and full of imagination and his parents hadn't understood, Uncle Jolley had listened to him ramble, encouraged him to dream. Invariably on a visit to the Folley, his uncle had demanded a story then had settled himself back, bright-eyed and eager, while Michael wove on. Michael hadn't forgotten.

When he'd received his first Emmy for *Logan's Run,* Michael had flown from L.A. to the Catskills and had given the statuette to his uncle. The Emmy was still in the old man's bedroom, even if the old man wasn't.

Michael listened to the dry impersonal attorney's voice and wished for a cigarette. He'd only given them up two days before. Two days, four hours and thirty-five minutes. He'd have welcomed the raw meat.

He felt stifled in the room with all these people. Every one of them had thought old Jolley was half-mad and a bit of a nuisance. The one-hundred-fifty-million-dollar estate was different. Stocks and bonds were extremely sane. Michael had seen several assessing glances roaming over the library furniture. Big, ornate Georgian might not suit some of the streamlined lifestyles, but it would liquidate into very tidy cash. The old man, Michael knew, had loved every clunky chair and oversize table in the house.

He doubted if any of them had been to the big echoing house in the past ten years. Except for Pandora, he admitted grudgingly. She might be an annoyance, but she'd adored Jolley.

At the moment she looked miserable. Michael didn't believe he'd ever seen her look unhappy before—furious, disdainful, infuriated, but never unhappy. If he hadn't known better, he'd have gone to sit beside her, offer some comfort, hold her hand. She'd probably chomp it off at the wrist.

Still, her shockingly blue eyes were red and puffy. Almost as red as her hair, he mused, as his gaze skimmed over the wild curly mane that tumbled, with little attention to discipline or style, around her shoulders. She was so pale that the sprinkling of freckles over her nose stood out. Normally her ivory-toned skin had a hint of rose in it—health or temperament, he'd never been sure.

Sitting among her solemn, black-clad family, she stood out like a parrot among crows. She'd worn a vivid blue dress. Michael approved of it, though he'd never say so to Pandora. She didn't need black and crepe and lilies to mourn. That he understood, if he didn't understand her.

She annoyed him, periodically, with her views on his lifestyle and career. When they clashed, it didn't take long for him to hurl criticism back at her. After all, she was a bright, talented woman who was content to play around making outrageous jewelry for boutiques rather than taking advantage of her Master's degree in education.

She called him materialistic, he called her idealistic. She labeled him a chauvinist, he labeled her a pseudo-intellectual. Jolley had sat with his hands folded and chuckled every time they argued. Now that he was gone, Michael mused, there wouldn't be an opportunity for any more battles. Oddly enough, he found it another reason to miss his uncle.

The truth was, he'd never felt any strong family ties to anyone but Jolley. Michael didn't think of his parents very often. His father was somewhere in Europe with his fourth wife, and his mother had settled placidly into Palm Springs society with husband number three. They'd never understood their son who'd opted to work for a living in something as bourgeois as television.

But Jolley had understood and appreciated. More, much more important to Michael, he'd enjoyed Michael's work.

A grin spread over his face when he heard Fitzhugh drone out the bequest for whales. It was so typically Jolley. Several impatient relations hissed through their teeth. A hundred fifty thousand dollars had just spun out of their reach. Michael glanced up at the larger-than-life-size portrait of his uncle. You always said you'd have the last word, you old fool. The only trouble is you're not here to laugh about it.

"To my son, Carlson . . ." All the quiet muttering and whispers died as Fitzhugh cleared his throat. Without much interest Pandora watched her relatives come to attention. The charities and servants had their bequests. Now it was time for the big guns. Fitzhugh glanced up briefly before he continued. "Whose—aaah—mediocrity was always a mystery to me, I leave my entire collection of magic tricks in hopes he can develop a sense of the ridiculous."

Pandora choked into her tissue and watched her uncle turn beet red. First point Uncle Jolley, she thought and prepared to enjoy herself. Maybe he'd left the whole business to the ASPCA.

"To my grandson, Bradley, and my granddaughter by marriage, Lorraine, I leave my very best wishes. They need nothing more."

Pandora swallowed and blinked back tears at the reference to her parents. She'd call them in Zanzibar that evening. They would appreciate the sentiment even as she did.

"To my nephew Monroe who has the first dollar he ever made, I leave the last dollar I made, frame included. To my niece, Patience, I leave my cottage in Key West without much hope she'll have the gumption to use it."

Monroe chomped on his cigar while Patience looked horrified.

"To my grand-nephew, Biff, I leave my collection of matches, with the hopes that he will, at last, set the world on fire. To my pretty grand-niece, Ginger, who likes equally pretty things, I leave the sterling silver mirror purported to have been owned by Marie Antoinette. To my grand-nephew, Hank, I leave the sum of 3,528. Enough, I believe, for a life-time supply of wheat germ."

The grumbles that had begun with the first bequest continued and grew. Anger hovered on the edge of outrage. Jolley would have liked nothing better. Pandora made the mistake of glancing over at Michael. He didn't seem so distant and detached now, but full of admiration. When their gazes met, the giggle she'd been holding back spilled out. It earned her several glares.

Carlson rose, giving new meaning to the phrase controlled outrage. "Mr. Fitzhugh, my father's will is nothing more than a mockery. It's quite obvious that he wasn't in his right mind when he made it, nor do I have any doubt that a court will overturn it."

"Mr. McVie." Again Fitzhugh cleared his throat. The sun began to push its way through the clouds but no one seemed to notice. "I understand perfectly your sentiments in this matter. However, my client was perfectly well and lucid when this will was drawn. He may have worded it against my advice, but it is legal and binding. You are, of course, free to consult with your own counsel. Meanwhile, there's more to be read."

"Hogwash." Monroe puffed on his cigar and glared at everyone. "Hogwash," he repeated while Patience patted his arm and chirped ineffectually.

"Uncle Jolley liked hogwash," Pandora said as she balled her tissue. She was ready to face them down, almost hoped she'd have to. It would take her mind off her grief. "If he wanted to leave his money to the Society for the Prevention of Stupidity, it was his right."

"Easily said, my dear." Biff polished his nails on his lapel. The gold band of his watch caught a bit of the sun and gleamed. "Perhaps the old lunatic left you a ball of twine so you can string more beads."

"You haven't got the matches yet, old boy." Michael spoke lazily from his corner, but every eye turned his way. "Careful what you light."

"Let him read, why don't you?" Ginger piped up, quite pleased with her bequest. Marie Antoinette, she mused. Just imagine.

"The last two bequests are joint," Fitzhugh began before there could be another interruption. "And, a bit unorthodox."

"The entire document's unorthodox," Carlson tossed out, then harrumphed. Several heads nodded in agreement.

Pandora remembered why she always avoided family

gatherings. They bored her to death. Quite deliberately, she waved a hand in front of her mouth and yawned. "Could we have the rest, Mr. Fitzhugh, before my family embarrasses themselves any further?"

She thought, but couldn't be sure, that she saw a quick light of approval in the fusty attorney's eyes. "Mr. McVie wrote this portion in his own words." He paused a moment, either for effect or courage. "To Pandora McVie and Michael Donahue," Fitzhugh read, "the two members of my family who have given me the most pleasure with their outlook on life, their enjoyment of an old man and old jokes, I leave the rest of my estate, in entirety, all accounts, all business interests, all stocks, bonds and trusts, all real and personal property, with all affection. Share and share alike."

Pandora didn't hear the half-dozen objections that sprang out. She rose, stunned and infuriated. "I can't take his money." Towering over the family who sat around her, she strode straight up to Fitzhugh. The lawyer, who'd anticipated attacks from other areas, braced for the unexpected. "I wouldn't know what to do with it. It'd just clutter up my life." She waved a hand at the papers on the desk as if they were a minor annoyance. "He should've asked me first."

"Miss McVie . . ."

Before the lawyer could speak again, she whirled on Michael. "You can have it all. You'd know what to do with it, after all. Buy a hotel in New York, a condo in L.A., a club in Chicago and a plane to fly you back and forth, I don't care."

Deadly calm, Michael slipped his hands in his pockets. "I appreciate the offer, cousin. Before you pull the trigger, why don't we wait until Mr. Fitzhugh finishes before you embarrass yourself any further?"

She stared at him a moment, nearly nose to nose with him in heels. Then, because she'd been taught to do so at an early age, she took a deep breath and waited for her temper to ebb. "I don't want his money."

"You've made your point." He lifted a brow in the cynical, half-amused way that always infuriated her. "You're fascinating the relatives by the little show you're putting on."

Nothing could have made her find control quicker. She angled her chin at him, hissed once, then subsided. "All right then." She turned and stood her ground. "I apologize for the interruption. Please finish reading, Mr. Fitzhugh."

The lawyer gave himself a moment by taking off his glasses and polishing them on a big white handkerchief. He'd known when Jolley had made the will, the day would come when he'd be forced to face an enraged family. He'd argued with his client about it, cajoled, reasoned, pointed out the absurdities. Then he'd drawn up the will and closed the loopholes.

"I leave all of this," he continued, "the money, which is a small thing, the stocks and bonds, which are necessary but boring, the business interests, which are interesting weights around the neck. And my home and all in it, which is everything important to me, the memories made there, to Pandora and Michael because they understood and cared. I leave this to them, though it may annoy them, because there is no one else in my family I can leave what is important to me. What was mine is Pandora and Michael's now, because I know they'll keep me alive. I ask only one thing of each of them in return."

Michael's grip relaxed, and he nearly smiled again. "Here comes the kicker," he murmured.

"Beginning no more than a week after the reading of this document, Pandora and Michael will move into my home in the Catskills, known as Jolley's Folley. They will live there together for a period of six months, neither one spending more than two nights in succession under another roof. After this six-month period, the estate reverts to them, entirely and without encumbrance, share and share alike.

"If one does not agree with this provision, or breaks the terms of this provision within the six-month period, the estate, in its entirety, will be given over to all my surviving heirs and the Institute for the Study of Carnivorous Plants in joint shares.

"You have my blessing, children. Don't let an old, dead man down."

For a full thirty seconds there was silence. Taking advantage of it, Fitzhugh began straightening his papers.

"The old bastard," Michael murmured. Pandora would've taken offense if she hadn't agreed so completely. Because he judged the temperature in the room to be on the rise, Michael pulled Pandora out, down the hall and into one of the funny little parlors that could be found throughout the house. Just before he closed the door, the first explosion in the library erupted.

Pandora drew out a fresh tissue, sneezed into it, then plopped down on the arm of a chair. She was too flabbergasted and worn-out to be amused. "Well, what now?"

Michael reached for a cigarette before he remembered he'd quit. "Now we have to make a couple of decisions."

Pandora gave him one of the long lingering stares she'd learned made most men stutter. Michael merely sat across from her and stared back. "I meant what I said. I don't want his money. By the time it's divided up and the taxes dealt with, it's close to fifty million apiece. Fifty million," she repeated, rolling her eyes. "It's ridiculous."

"Jolley always thought so," Michael said, and watched the grief come and go in her eyes.

"He only had it to play with. The trouble was, every time he played, he made more." Unable to sit, Pandora paced to the window. "Michael, I'd suffocate with that much money."

"Cash isn't as heavy as you think."

With something close to a sneer, she turned and sat on the window ledge. "You don't object to fifty million or so after taxes I take it."

He'd have loved to have wiped that look off her face. "I haven't your fine disregard for money, Pandora, probably because I was raised with the illusion of it rather than the reality."

She shrugged, knowing his parents existed, and always had, mainly on credit and connections. "So, take it all then."

Michael picked up a little blue glass egg and tossed it from palm to palm. It was cool and smooth and worth several thousand. "That's not what Jolley wanted."

With a sniff, she snatched the egg from his hand. "He wanted us to get married and live happily ever after. I'd like to humor him. . . ." She tossed the egg back again. "But I'm not that much of a martyr. Besides, aren't you engaged to some little blond dancer?"

He set the egg down before he could heave it at her. "For someone who turns their pampered nose up at television, you don't have the same intellectual snobbery about gossip rags."

"I *adore* gossip," Pandora said with such magnificent exaggeration Michael laughed.

"All right, Pandora, let's put down the swords a minute." He tucked his thumbs in his pockets and rocked back on his heels. Maybe they could, if they concentrated, talk civilly with each other for a few minutes. "I'm not engaged to anyone, but marriage wasn't a term of the will in any case. All we have to do is live together for six months under the same roof."

As she studied him a sense of disappointment ran through her. Perhaps they'd never gotten along, but she'd respected

him if for nothing more than what she'd seen as his pure affection for Uncle Jolley. "So, you really want the money?"

He took two furious steps forward before he caught himself. Pandora never flinched. "Think whatever you like." He
said it softly, as though it didn't matter. Oddly enough, it
made her shudder. "You don't want the money, fine. Put that
aside a moment. Are you going to stand by and watch this
house go to the clan out there or a bunch of scientists studying Venus's-flytraps? Jolley loved this place and everything
in it. I always thought you did, too."

"I do." The others would sell it, she admitted. There wasn't
one person in the library who wouldn't put the house on the
market and run with the cash. It would be lost to her. All
the foolish, ostentatious rooms, the ridiculous archways.
Jolley might be gone, but he'd left the house like a dangling
carrot. And he still held the stick.

"He's trying to run our lives still."

Michael lifted a brow. "Surprised?"

With a half laugh, Pandora glanced over. "No."

* * *

Slowly she walked around the room while the sun shot
through the diamond panes of glass and lit her hair. Michael watched her with a sense of detached admiration.
She'd look magnificent on the screen. He'd always thought
so. Her coloring, her posture. Her arrogance. The five or ten
pounds the camera would add couldn't hurt that too angular,
bean-pole body, either. And the fire-engine-red hair would
make a statement on the screen while it was simply outrageous in reality. He'd often wondered why she didn't do
something to tone it down.

At the moment he wasn't interested in any of that—just
in what was in her brain. He didn't give a damn about the

money, but he wasn't going to sit idly by and watch everything Jolley had had and built go to the vultures. If he had to play rough with Pandora, he would. He might even enjoy it.

Millions. Pandora cringed at the outrageousness of it. That much money could be nothing but a headache, she was certain. Stocks, bonds, accountants, trusts, tax shelters. She preferred a simpler kind of living. Though no one would call her apartment in Manhattan primitive.

She'd never had to worry about money and that was just the way she liked it. Above or below a certain income level, there were nothing but worries. But if you found a nice, comfortable plateau, you could just cruise. She'd nearly found it.

It was true enough that a share of this would help her tremendously professionally. With a buffer sturdy enough, she could have the artistic freedom she wanted and continue the lifestyle that now caused a bit of a strain on her bank account. Her work was artistic and critically acclaimed but reviews didn't pay the rent. Outside of Manhattan, her work was usually considered too unconventional. The fact that she often had to create more mainstream designs to keep her head above water grated constantly. With fifty or sixty thousand to back her, she could . . .

Furious with herself, she blocked it off. She was thinking like Michael, she decided. She'd rather die. He'd sold out, turned whatever talent he had to the main chance, just as he was ready to turn these circumstances to his own financial advantage. She would think of other areas. She would think first of Jolley.

As she saw it, the entire scheme was a maze of problems. How like her uncle. Now, like a chess match, she'd have to consider her moves.

She'd never lived with a man. Purposely. Pandora liked running by her own clock. It wasn't so much that she minded sharing *things,* she minded sharing space. If she agreed, that would be the first concession.

Then there was the fact that Michael was attractive, attractive enough to be unsettling if he hadn't been so annoying. Annoying and easily annoyed, she recalled with a flash of amusement. She knew what buttons to push. Hadn't she always prided herself on the fact that she could handle him? It wasn't always easy; he was too sharp. But that made their altercations interesting. Still, they'd never been together for more than a week at a time.

But there was one clear, inarguable fact. She'd loved her uncle. How could she live with herself if she denied him a last wish? Or a last joke?

Six months. Stopping, she studied Michael as he studied her. Six months could be a very long time, especially when you weren't pleased with what you were doing. There was only one way to speed things up. She'd enjoy herself.

"Tell me, cousin, how can we live under the same roof for six months without coming to blows?"

"We can't."

He'd answered without a second's hesitation, so she laughed again. "I suppose I'd be bored if we did. I can tidy up loose ends and move in in three days. Four at the most."

"That's fine." When his shoulders relaxed, he realized he'd been tensed for her refusal. At the moment he didn't want to question why it mattered so much. Instead he held out a hand. "Deal."

Pandora inclined her head just before her palm met his. "Deal," she agreed, surprised that his hand was hard and a bit callused. She'd expected it to be rather soft and limp. After all, all he did was type. Perhaps the next six months would have some surprises.

"Shall we go tell the others?"

"They'll want to murder us."

Her smile came slowly, subtly shifting the angles of her face. It was, Michael thought, at once wicked and alluring. "I know. Try not to gloat."

When they stepped out, several griping relatives had spilled out into the hallway. They did what they did best together. They argued.

"You'd blow your share on barbells and carrot juice," Biff said spitefully to Hank. "At least I know what to do with money."

"Lose it on horses," Monroe said, and blew out a stream of choking cigar smoke. "Invest. Tax deferred."

"You could use yours to take a course in how to speak in complete sentences." Carlson stepped out of the smoke and straightened his tie. "I'm the old man's only living son. It's up to me to prove he was incompetent."

"Uncle Jolley had more competence than the lot of you put together." Feeling equal parts frustration and disgust, Pandora stepped forward. "He gave you each exactly what he wanted you to have."

Biff drew out a flat gold cigarette case as he glanced over at his cousin. "It appears our Pandora's changed her mind about the money. Well, you worked for it, didn't you, darling?"

Michael put his hand on Pandora's shoulder and squeezed lightly before she could spring. "You'd like to keep your profile, wouldn't you, cousin?"

"It appears writing for television's given you a taste for violence." Biff lit his cigarette and smiled. If he'd thought he could get in a blow below the belt . . . "I think I'll decline a brawl," he decided.

"Well, I think it's fair." Hank's wife came forward, stretching out her hand. She gave both Pandora and Michael a hearty shake. "You should put a gym in this place. Build yourself up a little. Come on, Hank."

Silent, and his shoulders straining the material of his suit, Hank followed her out.

"Nothing but muscles between the head," Carlson mumbled. "Come, Mona." He strode ahead of his wife, pausing long enough to level a glare at Pandora and Michael. The inevitable line ran though Michael's mind before Carlson opened his mouth and echoed it. "You haven't heard the last of this."

Pandora gave him her sweetest smile. "Have a nice trip home, Uncle Carlson."

"Probate," Monroe said with a grunt, and waddled his way out behind them.

Patience fluttered her hands. "Key West, for heaven's sake. I've never been south of Palm Beach. My, oh my."

"Oh, Michael." Fluttering her lashes, Ginger placed a hand on his arm. "When do you think I might have my mirror?"

He glanced down into her perfectly lovely, heart-shaped face. Her eyes were as pure a blue as tropical waters. He thanked God Jolley hadn't asked that he spend six months with Cousin Ginger. "I'm sure Mr. Fitzhugh will have it shipped to you as soon as possible."

"Come along, Ginger, we'll give you a ride to the airport." Biff pulled Ginger's hand through his arm, patted it and smiled down at Pandora. "I'd be worried if I didn't know you better. You won't last six days with Michael much less six months. Beastly temper," he said confidentially to Michael. "The two of you'll murder each other before a week's out."

"Don't spend the old man's money yet," Michael warned. "We'll make the six months if for no other reason than to spite you." He smiled when he said it, a chummy, well-meaning smile that took the arrogance from Biff's face.

"We'll see who wins the game." Straight backed, Biff turned toward the door. His wife walked out behind him without having said a word since she'd walked in.

"Biff," Ginger began as they walked out. "What are you going to do with all those matches?"

"Burn his bridges, I hope," Pandora muttered. "Well, Michael, though I can't say there was a lot of love before, there's nearly none lost now."

"Are you worried about alienating them?"

With a shrug of her shoulders, she walked toward a bowl of roses, then gave him a considering look. "Well, I've never had any trouble alienating you. Why is that, do you suppose?"

"Jolley always said we were too much alike."

"Really?" Haughty, she lifted a brow. "I find myself disagreeing with him again. You and I, Michael Donahue, have almost nothing in common."

"If that's so, we have six months to prove it." On impulse he moved closer and put a finger under her chin. "You know, darling, you might've been stuck with Biff."

"I'd've given the place to the plants first."

He grinned. "I'm flattered."

"Don't be." But she didn't move away from him. Not yet. It was an interesting feeling to be this close without snarling. "The only difference is you don't bore me."

"That's enough," he said with a hint of a smile. "I'm easily flattered." Intrigued, he flicked a finger down her cheek. It was still pale, but her eyes were direct and steady. "No, we won't bore each other, Pandora. In six months we might experience a lot of things, but boredom won't be one of them."

It might be an interesting feeling, she discovered, but it wasn't quite a safe one. It was best to remember that he didn't find her appealing as a woman but would, for the sake of his own ego, string her along if she permitted it. "I don't flatter easily. I haven't decided exactly what your reasons are for going through with this farce, but I'm doing it only for Uncle Jolley. I can set up my equipment here quite easily."

"And I can write here quite easily."

Pandora plucked a rose from the bowl. "If you can call those implausible scripts writing."

"The same way you call the bangles you string together art."

Color came back to her cheeks and that pleased him. "You wouldn't know art if it reached up and bit you on the nose. My jewelry expresses emotion."

His smile showed pleasant interest. "How much is lust going for these days?"

"I would have guessed you'd be very familiar with the cost." Pandora fumbled for a tissue, sneezed into it, then shut her bag with a click. "Most of the women you date have price tags."

It amused him, and it showed. "I thought we were talking about work."

"My profession is a time-honored one, while yours—yours stops for commercial breaks. And furthermore—"

"I beg your pardon."

Fitzhugh paused at the doorway of the library. He wanted nothing more than to be shed of the McVie clan and have a quiet, soothing drink. "Am I to assume that you've both decided to accept the terms of the will?"

Six months, she thought. It was going to be a long, long winter.

Six months, he thought. He was going to have the first daffodil he found in April bronzed.

"You can start counting the days at the end of the week," he told Fitzhugh. "Agreed, cousin?"

Pandora set her chin. "Agreed."

CHAPTER 2

It was a pleasant trip from Manhattan along the Hudson River toward the Catskills. Pandora had always enjoyed it. The drive gave her time to clear her mind and relax. But then, she'd always taken it at her own whim, her own pace, her own convenience. Pandora made it a habit to do everything just that way. This time, however, there was more involved than her own wants and wishes. Uncle Jolley had boxed her in.

He'd known she'd have to go along with the terms of the will. Not for the money. He'd been too smart to think she could be lured into such a ridiculous scheme with money. But the house, her ties to it, her need for the continuity of family. That's what he'd hooked her with.

Now she had to leave Manhattan behind for six months. Oh, she'd run into the city for a few hours here and there, but it was hardly the same as living in the center of things. She'd always liked that—being in the center, surrounded by movement, being able to watch and become involved whenever she liked. Just as she'd always liked long weekends in the solitude of Jolley's Folley.

She'd been raised that way, to enjoy and make the most of whatever environment she was in. Her parents loved to travel. Since they were wealthy, their trips were first class all the way.

Before she'd been fifteen, Pandora had been to more than thirty countries. She'd eaten sushi in Tokyo, roamed the moors in Cornwall, bargained in Turkish markets. A succession of tutors had traveled with them so that by her calculations, she'd spent just under two years in a classroom environment before college.

The exotic, vagabond childhood had given her a taste for variety—in people, in foods, in styles. And oddly enough the exposure to widely diverse cultures and mores had formed in her an unshakable desire for a home and a sense of belonging.

Though her parents liked to meander through countries, recording everything with pen and film, Pandora had missed a central point. Where was home? This year in Mexico, next year in Athens. Her parents made a name for themselves with their books and articles on the unusual, but Pandora wanted roots. She'd discovered she'd have to find them for herself.

She'd chosen New York, and in her way, Uncle Jolley.

Now, because her uncle and his home had become her central point, she was agreeing to spend six months living with a man she could hardly tolerate so that she could inherit a fortune she didn't want or need. Life, she'd discovered long ago, never moved in straight lines.

Jolley McVie's ultimate joke, she thought as she turned up the long drive toward his Folley. Well, he could throw them together, but he couldn't make them stick.

Still, she'd have felt better if she'd been sure of Michael. Was it the lure of the millions of dollars, or an affection for an old man that would bring him to the Catskills? She knew his *Logan's Run* was in its very successful fourth year, and that he'd had other lucrative ventures in television. But money was a seduction itself. After all, her Uncle Carlson had more than he could ever spend, yet he was already taking the steps for a probate of the will.

That didn't worry her. Uncle Jolley had believed in hiring the best. If Fitzhugh had drawn up the will, it was air-tight. What worried her was Michael Donahue.

Because of the trap she'd fallen into, she'd found herself thinking of him a great deal too much over the past couple of days. Ally or enemy, she wasn't sure. Either way, she was going to have to live with him. Or around him. She hoped the house was big enough.

By the time she arrived, she was worn-out from the drive and the lingering head cold. Though her equipment and supplies had been shipped the day before, she still had three cases in the car. Deciding to take one at a time, Pandora popped the trunk, then simply looked at Jolley's Folley.

He'd built it when he'd been forty, so the house was already over a half century old. It went in all directions at once, as if he'd never been able to decide where he wanted to start and where he wanted to finish. The truth about Jolley, she admitted, was that he'd never wanted to finish. The project, the game, the puzzle, was always more interesting to him before the last pieces were in place.

Without the wings, it might have been a rather somber and sedate late-nineteenth-century mansion. With them, it was a mass of walls and corners, heights and widths. There was no symmetry, yet to Pandora it had always seemed as sturdy as the rock it had been built on.

Some of the windows were long, some were wide, some of them were leaded and some sheer. Jolley had made up his mind then changed it again as he'd gone along.

The stone had come from one of his quarries, the wood from one of his lumberyards. When he'd decided to build a house, he'd started his own construction firm. McVie Construction, Incorporated was one of the five biggest companies in the country.

It struck her suddenly that she owned half of Jolley's share in the company and her mind spun at how many others. She had interests in baby oil, steel mills, rocket engines and cake mix. Pandora lifted the case and set her teeth. What on earth had she let herself in for?

From the upstairs window, Michael watched her. The jacket she wore was big and baggy with three vivid colors, blue, yellow and pink, patched in. The wind caught at her slacks and rippled them from thigh to ankle. She wasn't looking teary-eyed and pale this time, but grim and resigned. So much the better. He'd been tempted to comfort her during their uncle's funeral. Only the knowledge that too much sympathy for a woman like Pandora was fatal had prevented him.

He'd known her since childhood and had considered her a spoiled brat from the word go. Though she'd often been off for months at a time on one of her parents' journalistic safaris, they'd seen enough of each other to feed a mutual dislike. Only the fact that she had cared for Jolley had given Michael some tolerance for her. And the fact, he was forced to admit, that she had more honesty and humanity in her than any of their other relations.

There had been a time, he recalled, a brief time, during late adolescence that he'd felt a certain . . . stirring for her. A purely shallow and physical teenage hunger, Michael assured himself. She'd always had an intriguing face; it could be unrelentingly plain one moment and striking the next, and when she'd hit her teens . . . well, that had been a natural enough reaction. And it had passed without incident. He now preferred a woman with more subtlety, more gloss and femininity—and shorter fangs.

Whatever he preferred, Michael left the arranging of his own office to wander downstairs.

"Charles, did my shipment come?" Pandora pulled off her leather driving gloves and dropped them on a little round table in the hall. Since Charles was there, the ancient butler who had served her uncle since before she was born, she felt a certain pleasure in coming.

"Everything arrived this morning, miss." The old man would have taken her suitcase if she hadn't waved him away.

"No, don't fuss with that. Where did you have them put everything?"

"In the garden shed in the east yard, as you instructed."

She gave him a smile and a peck on the cheek, both of which pleased him. His square bulldog's face grew slightly pink. "I knew I could count on you. I didn't tell you before how happy I was that you and Sweeney are staying. The place wouldn't be the same without you serving tea and Sweeney baking cakes."

Charles managed to pull his back a bit straighter. "We wouldn't think about going anywhere else, miss. The master would have wanted us to stay."

But made it possible for them to go, Pandora mused. Leaving each of them three thousand dollars for every year of service. Charles had been with Jolley since the house was built, and Sweeney had come some ten years later. The bequest would have been more than enough for each to retire on. Pandora smiled. Some weren't made for retirement.

"Charles, I'd love some tea," she began, knowing if she didn't distract him, he'd insist on carrying her bags up the long staircase.

"In the drawing room, miss?"

"Perfect. And if Sweeney has any of those little cakes . . ."

"She's been baking all morning." With only the slightest of creaks, he made his way toward the kitchen.

Pandora thought of rich icing loaded with sugar. "I wonder how much weight a person can gain in six months."

"A steady diet of Sweeney's cakes wouldn't hurt you," Michael said from above her head. "Men are generally more attracted to flesh than bone."

Pandora spun around, then found herself in the awkward position of having to arch her neck back to see Michael at the top of the stairs. "I don't center my life around attracting men."

"I'd be the last one to argue with that."

He looked quite comfortable, she thought, feeling the first stirrings of resentment. And negligently, arrogantly attractive. From several feet above her head, he leaned against a post and looked down on her as though he was the master. She'd soon put an end to that. Uncle Jolley's will had been very clear. Share and share alike.

"Since you're already here and settled in, you can come help me with the rest of my bags."

He didn't budge. "I always thought the one point we were in perfect agreement on was feminism."

Pandora paused at the door to toss a look over her shoulder. "Social and political views aside, if you don't help me up with them before Charles comes back, he'll insist on doing it himself. He's too old to do it and too proud to be told he can't." She walked back out and wasn't surprised when she heard his footsteps on the gravel behind her.

She took a deep breath of crisp autumn air. All in all, it was a lovely day. "Drive up early?"

"Actually, I drove up late last night."

Pandora turned at the open trunk of her car. "So eager to start the game, Michael?"

If he hadn't been determined to start off peacefully, he'd have found fault with the tone of her voice, with the look in her eyes. Instead he let it pass. "I wanted to get my office set up today. I was just finishing it when you drove in."

"Work, work, work," she said with a long sigh. "You must put in slavish hours to come up with an hour of chase scenes and steam a week."

Peace wasn't all that important. As she reached for a suitcase, he closed a hand over her wrist. Later he'd think about how slim it was, how soft. Now he could only think how much he wished she were a man. Then he could've belted her. "The amount of work I do and what I produce is of absolutely no concern to you."

It occurred to Pandora, oddly, she thought, just how much she enjoyed seeing him on the edge of temper. All of her other relatives were so bland, so outwardly civilized. Michael had always been a contrast, and therefore of more interest. Smiling, she allowed her wrist to stay limp.

"Did I indicate that it was? Nothing, I promise you, could be further from the truth. Shall we get these in and have that tea? It's a bit chilly."

He'd always admired, grudgingly, how smoothly she could slip into the lady-of-the-manor routine. As a writer who wrote for actors and for viewers, he appreciated natural talent. He also knew how to set a scene to his best advantage. "Tea's a perfect idea." He hauled one case out and left the second for her. "We'll establish some guidelines."

"Will we?" Pandora pulled out the case, then let the trunk shut quietly. Without another word, she started back toward the house, holding the front door open for him, then breezing by the suitcase she'd left in the main hall. Because she knew Michael was fond of Charles, she hadn't a doubt he'd pick it up and follow.

The room she always took was on the second floor in the east wing. Jolley had let her decorate it herself, and she'd chosen white on white with a few startling splashes of color. Chartreuse and blazing blue in throw pillows, a long horizontal oil painting, jarring in its colors of sunset, a crimson waist-high urn stuffed with ostrich plumes.

Pandora set her case by the bed, noted with satisfaction that a fire had been laid in the small marble fireplace, then tossed her jacket over a chair.

"I always feel like I'm walking into *Better Homes*," he commented as he let her cases drop.

Pandora glanced down at them briefly, then at him. "I'm sure you're more at home in your own room. It's more—*Field and Stream*. I expect tea's ready."

He gave her a long, steady survey. Her jacket had concealed the trim cashmere sweater tucked into the narrow waist of her slacks. It reminded Michael quite forcibly just what had begun to attract him all those teenage years ago. For the second time he found himself wishing she were a man.

Though they walked abreast down the stairs, they didn't speak. In the drawing room, amid the Mideast opulence Jolley had chosen there, Charles was setting up the tea service.

"Oh, you lit the fire. How lovely." Pandora walked over and began warming her hands. She wanted a moment, just a moment, because for an instant in her room she thought she'd seen something in Michael's eyes. And she thought she'd felt the same something in response. "I'll pour, Charles. I'm sure Michael and I won't need another thing until dinner."

Casually she glanced around the room, at the flowing drapes, the curvy brocade sofas, the plump pillows and brass urns. "You know, this has always been one of my favorite rooms." Going to the tea set, she began to fill cups. "I was only twelve when we visited Turkey, but this room always makes me remember it vividly. Right down to the smells in the markets. Sugar?"

"No." He took the cup from her, plopped a generous slice

of cake on a dish, then chose a seat. He preferred the little parlor next door with its tidy English country air. This was the beginning, he thought, with the old butler and plump cook as witnesses. Six months from today, they'd all sign a document swearing that the terms of the will had been adhered to and that would be that. It was the time in between that concerned him.

"Rule number one," Michael began without preamble. "We're both in the east wing because it makes it easier for Charles and Sweeney. But—" he paused, hoping to emphasize his point "—both of us will, at all times, respect the other's area."

"By all means." Pandora crossed her legs and sipped her tea.

"Again, because of the staff, it seems fair that we eat at the same time. Therefore, in the interest of survival, we'll keep the conversations away from professional matters."

Pandora smiled at him and nibbled on cake. "Oh yes, let's do keep things personal."

"You're a nasty little package—"

"See, we're off to a perfect start. Rule number two. Neither of us, no matter how bored or restless, will disturb the other during his or her set working hours. I generally work between ten and one, then again between three and six."

"Rule number three. If one of us is entertaining, the other will make him or herself scarce."

Pandora's eyes narrowed, only for a moment. "Oh, and I so wanted to meet your dancer. Rule number four. The first floor is neutral ground and to be shared equally unless specific prior arrangements are made and agreed upon." She tapped her finger against the arm of the chair. "If we both play fair, we should manage."

"I don't have any trouble playing fair. As I recall, you're the one who cheats."

Her voice became very cool, her tone very rounded. "I don't know what you're talking about."

"Canasta, poker, gin."

"That's absurd and you have absolutely no proof." Rising, she helped herself to another cup of tea. "Besides, cards are entirely different." Warmed by the fire, soothed by the tea, she smiled at him. As Michael recalled, that particular smile was lethal. And stunning. "Are you still holding a grudge over that five hundred I won from you?"

"I wouldn't if you'd won it fairly."

"I won it," she countered. "That's what counts. If I cheated and you didn't catch me, then it follows that I cheated well enough for it to be legal."

"You always had a crooked sense of logic." He rose as well and came close. She had to admire the way he moved. It wasn't quite a swagger because he didn't put the effort into it. But it was very close. "If we play again, whatever we play, you won't cheat me."

Confident, she smiled at him. "Michael, we've known each other too long for you to intimidate me." She reached a hand up to pat his cheek and found her wrist captured a second time. And a second time she saw and felt that same dangerous something she'd experienced upstairs.

There was no Uncle Jolley as a buffer between them now. Perhaps they'd both just begun to realize it. Whatever was between them that made them snarl and snap would have a long, cold winter to surface.

Perhaps neither one of them wanted to face it, but both were too stubborn to back down.

"Perhaps we're just beginning to know each other," Michael murmured.

She believed it. And didn't like it. He wasn't a posturing fool like Biff nor a harmless hulk like Hank. He might be a cousin by marriage only, but the blood between them had

always run hot. There was violence in him. It showed sometimes in a look in his eyes, in the way he held himself. As
though he wouldn't ward off a blow but counter it. Pandora
recognized it because there was violence in her, as well. Perhaps that was why she always felt compelled to shoot darts at
him, just to see how many he could boomerang back at her.

They stood as they were a moment, gauging each other,
reassessing. The wise thing to do was for each to acknowledge a hit and step aside. Pandora threw up her chin. Michael set for the volley. "We'll go to the mat another time,
Michael. At the moment, I'm a bit tired from the drive. If
you'll excuse me?"

"Rule number five," he said without releasing her. "If one
of us takes potshots at the other, they'll damn well pay the
consequences." When he freed her arm, he went back for his
cup. "See you at dinner, cousin."

* * *

Pandora awoke just past dawn fully awake, rested and
bursting with energy. Whether it had been the air in the
mountains or the six hours of deep sleep, she was ready
and eager to work. Breakfast could wait, she decided as she
showered and dressed. She was going out to the garden shed,
organizing her equipment and diving in.

The house was perfectly quiet and still dim as she made
her way downstairs. The servants would sleep another hour
or two, she thought as she stuck her head in the pantry and
chose a muffin. As she recalled, Michael might sleep until
noon.

They had made it through dinner without incident. Perhaps they'd been polite to each other because of Charles
and Sweeney or perhaps because both of them had been too
tired to snipe. Pandora wasn't sure herself.

They'd dined under the cheerful lights of the big chandelier and had talked, when they'd talked, about the weather and the food.

By nine they'd gone their separate ways. Pandora to read until her eyes closed and Michael to work. Or so he'd said.

Outside the air was chill enough to cause Pandora's skin to prickle. She hunched up the collar of her jacket and started across the lawn. It crunched underfoot with the early thin frost. She liked it—the absolute solitude, the lightness of the air, the incredible smell of mountain and river.

In Tibet she'd once come close to frostbite because she hadn't been able to resist the snow and the swoop of rock. She didn't find this slice of the Catskills any less fascinating. The winter was best, she'd always thought, when the snow skimmed the top of your boots and your voice came out in puffs of smoke.

Winter in the mountains was a time for the basics. Heat, food, work. There were times Pandora wanted only the basics. There were times in New York she'd argue for hours over unions, politics, civil rights because the fact was, she loved an argument. She wanted the stimulation of an opposing view over broad issues or niggling ones. She wanted the challenge, the heat and the exercise for her brain. But . . .

There were times she wanted nothing more than a quiet sunrise over frost-crisped ground and the promise of a warm drink by a hot fire. And there were times, though she'd rarely admit it even to herself, that she wanted a shoulder to lay her head against and a hand to hold. She'd been raised to see independence as a duty, not a choice. Her parents had the most balanced of relationships, equal to equal. Pandora saw them as something rare in a world where the scales tipped this way or that too often. At age eighteen, Pandora had decided she'd never settle for less than a full partnership. At age twenty, she decided marriage wasn't for her. Instead she put all her passion, her energy and imagination into her work.

Straight-line dedication had paid off. She was successful, even prominent, and creatively she was fulfilled. It was more than many people ever achieved.

Now she pulled open the door of the utility shed. It was a big square building, as wide as the average barn, with hardwood floors and paneled walls. Uncle Jolley hadn't believed in the primitive. Hitting the switch, she flooded the building with light.

As per her instructions, the crates and boxes she'd shipped had been stacked along one wall. The shelves where Uncle Jolley had kept his gardening tools during his brief, torrid gardening stage had been packed away. The plumbing was good, with a full-size stainless-steel sink and a small but more than adequate bath with shower enclosed in the rear. She counted five workbenches. The light and ventilation were excellent.

It wouldn't take her long, Pandora figured, to turn the shed into an organized, productive workroom.

It took three hours.

Along one shelf were boxes of beads in various sizes— jet, amethyst, gold, polished wood, coral, ivory. She had trays of stones, precious and semiprecious, square cut, brilliants, teardrops and chips. In New York, they were kept in a safe. Here, she never considered it. She had gold, silver, bronze, copper. There were solid and hollow drills, hammers, tongs, pliers, nippers, files and clamps. One might have thought she did carpentry. Then there were scribes and drawplates, bottles of chemicals, and miles of string and fiber cord.

The money she'd invested in these materials had cost her every penny of an inheritance from her grandmother, and a good chunk of savings she'd earned as an apprentice. It had been worth it. Pandora picked up a file and tapped it against her palm. Well worth it.

She could forge gold and silver, cast alloys and string impossibly complex designs with the use of a few beads or shells. Metals could be worked into thin, threadlike strands or built into big bold chunks. Pandora could do as she chose, with tools that had hardly changed from those used by artists two centuries earlier.

It was and always had been both the sense of continuity and the endless variety that appealed to her. She never made two identical pieces. That, to her, would have been manufacturing rather than creating. At times, her pieces were elegantly simple, classic in design. Those pieces sold well and allowed her a bit of artistic freedom. At other times, they were bold and brash and exaggerated. Mood guided Pandora, not trends. Rarely, very rarely, she would agree to create a piece along specified lines. If the lines, or the client, interested her.

She turned down a president because she'd found his ideas too pedestrian but had made a ring at a new father's request because his idea had been unique. Pandora had been told that the new mother had never taken the braided gold links off. Three links, one for each of the triplets she'd given birth to.

At the moment, Pandora had just completed drafting the design for a three-tiered necklace commissioned to her by the husband of a popular singer. Emerald. That was her name and the only requirement given to Pandora. The man wanted lots of them. And he'd pay, Pandora mused, for the dozen she'd chosen just before leaving New York. They were square, three karats apiece and of the sharp, sharp green that emeralds are valued for.

This was, she knew, her big chance, professionally and, most importantly, artistically. If the necklace was a success, there'd not only be reviews for her scrapbook, but acceptance. She'd be freer to do more of what she wanted without compromise.

The trick would be to fashion the chain so that it held like steel and looked like a cobweb. The stones would hang from each tier as if they'd dripped there.

For the next two hours, she worked in gold.

Between the two heaters at each end of the shed and the flame from her tools, the air became sultry. Sweat rolled down under her sweater, but she didn't mind. In fact, she barely noticed as the gold became pliable. Again and again, she drew the wire through the drawplate, smoothing out the kinks and subtly, slowly, changing the shape and size. When the wire looked like angel hair she began working it with her fingers, twisting and braiding until she matched the design in her head and on her drawing paper.

It would be simple—elegantly, richly simple. The emeralds would bring their own flash when she attached them.

Time passed. After careful, meticulous use of drawplate, flame and her own hands, the first thin, gold tier formed.

She'd just begun to stretch out the muscles in her back when the door of the shed opened and cool air poured in. Her face glowing with sweat and concentration, she glared at Michael.

"Just what the hell do you think you're doing?"

"Following orders." He had his hands stuffed in his jacket pockets for warmth, but hadn't buttoned the front. Nor, she noticed, had he bothered to shave. "This place smells like an oven."

"I'm working." She lifted the hem of the big apron she wore and wiped at her brow. It was being interrupted that annoyed her, Pandora told herself. Not the fact that he'd walked in on her when she looked like a steelworker. "Remember rule number three?"

"Tell that to Sweeney." Leaving the door ajar, he wandered in. "She said it was bad enough that you skipped breakfast, but you're not getting away with missing lunch." Curious, he poked his finger into a tray that held brilliant colored stones. "I have orders to bring you back."

"I'm not ready."

He picked up a tiny sapphire and held it to the light. "I had to stop her from tramping out here herself. If I go back alone, she's going to come for you. Her arthritis is acting up again."

Pandora swore under her breath. "Put that down," she ordered, then yanked the apron off.

"Some of this stuff looks real," he commented. Though he put the sapphire back, he picked up a round, winking diamond.

"Some of this stuff is real." Pandora crouched to turn the first heater down.

The diamond was in his hand as he scowled down at her head. "Why in hell do you have it sitting out like candy? It should be locked up."

Pandora adjusted the second heater. "Why?"

"Don't be any more foolish than necessary. Someone could steal it."

"Someone?" Straightening, Pandora smiled at him. "There aren't many someones around. I don't think Charles and Sweeney are a problem, but maybe I should worry about you."

He cursed her and dropped the diamond back. "They're your little bag of tricks, cousin, but if I had several thousand dollars sitting around that could slip into a pocket, I'd be more careful."

Though under most circumstances she fully agreed, Pandora merely picked up her jacket. After all, they weren't in Manhattan but miles away from anyone or anything. If she locked everything up, she'd just have to unlock it again every time she wanted to work. "Just one of the differences between you and me, Michael. I suppose it's because you write about so many dirty deeds."

"I also write about human nature." He picked up the sketch of the emerald necklace she had drawn. It had the sense of scale that would have pleased an architect and the flair and flow that would appeal to an artist. "If you're so into making bangles and baubles, why aren't you wearing any?"

"They get in the way when I'm working. If you write about human nature, how come the bad guy gets caught every week?"

"Because I'm writing for people, and people need heroes."

Pandora opened her mouth to argue, then found she agreed with the essence of the statement. "Hmm," was all she said as she turned out the lights and went out ahead of him.

"At least lock the door," Michael told her.

"I haven't a key."

"Then we'll get one."

"*We* don't need one."

He shut the door with a snap. "*You* do."

Pandora only shrugged as she started across the lawn. "Michael, have I mentioned that you've been more crabby than usual?"

He pulled a piece of hard candy out of his pocket and popped it into his mouth. "Quit smoking."

The candy was lemon. She caught just a whiff. "So I noticed. How long?"

He scowled at some leaves that skimmed across the lawn. They were brown and dry and seemed to have a life of their own. "Couple weeks. I'm going crazy."

She laughed sympathetically before she tucked her arm into his. "You'll live, darling. The first month's the toughest."

Now he scowled at her. "How would you know? You never smoked."

"The first month of anything's the toughest. You just have to keep your mind occupied. Exercise. We'll jog after lunch."

"We?"

"And we can play canasta after dinner."

He gave a quick snort but brushed the hair back from her cheek. "You'll cheat."

"See, your mind's already occupied." With a laugh, she turned her face up to his. He looked a bit surly, but on him, oddly, it was attractive. Placid, good-natured good looks had always bored her. "It won't hurt you to give up one of your vices, Michael. You have so many."

"I like my vices," he grumbled, then turned his head to look down at her. She was giving him her easy, friendly smile, one she sent his way rarely. It always made him forget just how much trouble she caused him. It made him forget he wasn't attracted to dramatically bohemian women with wild red hair and sharp bones. "A woman who looks like you should have several of her own."

Her mouth was solemn, her eyes wicked. "I'm much too busy. Vices take up a great deal of time."

"When Pandora opened the box, vices popped out."

She stopped at the back stoop. "Among other miseries. I suppose that's why I'm careful about opening boxes."

Michael ran a finger down her cheek. It was the sort of gesture he realized could easily become a habit. She was right, his mind was occupied. "You have to lift off the lid sooner or later."

She didn't move back, though she'd felt the little tingle of tension, of attraction, of need. Pandora didn't believe in moving back, but in plowing through. "Some things are better off locked up."

He nodded. He didn't want to release what was in their private box any more than she did. "Some locks aren't as strong as they need to be."

They were standing close, the wind whistling lightly between them. Pandora felt the sun on her back and the chill on her face. If she took a step nearer, there'd be heat. That she'd never doubted and had always avoided. He'd use whatever was available to him, she reminded herself. At the moment, it just happened to be her. She let her breath come calmly and easily before she reached for the doorknob.

"We'd better not keep Sweeney waiting."

CHAPTER 3

The streets are almost deserted. A car turns a corner and disappears. It's drizzling. Neon flashes off puddles. It's garish rather than festive. There's a gray, miserable feel to this part of the city. Alleyways, cheap clubs, dented cars. The small, neatly dressed blonde walks quickly. She's nervous, out of her element, but not lost. Close-up on the envelope in her hands. It's damp from the rain. Her fingers open and close on it. Tires squeal offscreen and she jolts. The blue lights of the club blink off and on in her face as she stands outside. Hesitates. Shifts the envelope from hand to hand. She goes in. Slow pan of the street. Three shots and freeze.

Three knocks sounded at the door of Michael's office. Before he could answer, Pandora swirled in. "Happy anniversary, darling."

Michael looked up from his computer. He'd been up most of the night working the story line out in his mind. It was nine in the morning, and he'd only had one cup of coffee to prime him for the day. Coffee and cigarettes together were too precious a memory. The scene that had just jelled in his mind dissolved.

"What the hell are you talking about?" He reached his

hand into a bowl of peanuts and discovered he'd already eaten all but two.

"Two full weeks without any broken bones." Pandora swooped over to him, clucked her tongue at the disorder, then chose the arm of a chair. It was virtually the only free space. She brushed at the dust on the edge of the table beside her and left a smear. "And they said it wouldn't last."

She looked fresh with her wild mane of red pulled back from her face, comfortable in sweater and slacks that were too big for her. Michael felt like he'd just crawled out of a cave. His sweatshirt had ripped at the shoulder seam two years before, but he still favored it. A few weeks before, he'd helped paint a friend's apartment. The paint smears on his jeans showed her preference for baby pink. His eyes felt as though he'd slept facedown in the sand.

Pandora smiled at him like some bright, enthusiastic kindergarten teacher. She had a fresh, clean, almost woodsy scent. "We have a rule about respecting the other's work space," he reminded her.

"Oh, don't be cranky." It was said with the same positive smile. "Besides, you never gave me any schedule. From what I've noticed in the past couple of weeks, this is early for you."

"I'm just starting the treatment for a new episode."

"Really?" Pandora walked over and leaned over his shoulder. "Hmm," she said, though she wondered who had shot whom. "Well, I don't suppose that'll take long."

"Why don't you go play with your beads?"

"Now you're being rude when I came up here to invite you to go with me into town." After brushing off the sleeve of her sweater, she sat on the edge of the desk. She didn't know exactly why she was so determined to be friendly. Maybe it was because the emerald necklace was nearly finished and was exceeding even her standards. Maybe it was because in the past two weeks she'd found a certain enjoyment in Michael's company. Mild enjoyment, Pandora reminded herself. Nothing to shout about.

Suspicious, Michael narrowed his eyes. "What for?"

"I'm going in for some supplies Sweeney needs." She found the turtle shell that was his lampshade intriguing, and ran her fingers over it. "I thought you might like to get out for a while."

He would. It had been two weeks since he'd seen anything but the house and grounds. He glanced back at the page on his computer. "How long will you be?"

"Oh, two, three hours I suppose." She moved her shoulders. "It's an hour's round trip to begin with."

He was tempted. Free time and a change of scene. But the half-blank page remained on his computer. "Can't. I have to get this fleshed out."

"All right." Pandora rose from the desk a bit surprised by the degree of disappointment she felt. Silly, she thought. She loved to drive alone with the radio blaring. "Don't strain your fingers."

He started to growl something at her back, then because his bowl of nuts was empty, thought better of it. "Pandora, how about picking me up a couple pounds of pistachios?"

As she stopped at the door, she lifted a brow. "Pistachios?"

"Real ones. No red dye." He ran a hand over the bristle on his chin and wished for a pack of cigarettes. One cigarette. One long deep drag.

She glanced at the empty bowl and nearly smiled. The way he was nibbling, he'd lose that lean, rangy look quickly. "I suppose I could."

"And a copy of the *New York Times*."

Her brow rose. "Would you like to make me a list?"

"Be a sport, will you? Next time Sweeney needs supplies, I'll go in."

She thought about it a moment. "Very well then, nuts and news."

"And some pencils," he called out.

She slammed the door smartly.

Nearly two hours passed before Michael decided he deserved another cup of coffee. The story line was bumping along just as he'd planned, full of twists and turns. The fans of *Logan's Run* expected the gritty with occasional bursts of color and magic. That's just the way it was panning out.

Critics of the medium aside, Michael enjoyed writing for the small screen. He liked knowing his stories would reach literally millions of people every week and that for an hour, they could involve themselves with the character he had created.

The truth was, Michael liked Logan—the reluctant but steady heroism, the humor and the flaws. He'd made Logan human and fallible and reluctant because Michael had always imagined the best heroes were just that.

The ratings and the mail proved he was on target. His writing for Logan had won him critical acclaim and awards, just as the one-act play he'd written had won him critical acclaim and awards. But the play had reached a few thousand at best, the bulk of whom had been New Yorkers. *Logan's Run* reached the family of four in Des Moines, the steelworkers in Chicago and the college crowd in Boston. Every week.

He didn't see television as the vast wasteland but as the magic box. Michael figured everyone was entitled to a bit of magic.

Michael switched off the laptop so that the screen died. For a moment he sat in silence. He'd known he could work at the Folley. He'd done so before, but never long-term. What he hadn't known was that he'd work so well, so quickly or be so content. The truth was, he'd never expected to get along half so well with Pandora. Not that it was any picnic, Michael mused, absently running the stub of a pencil between his fingers.

They fought, certainly, but at least they weren't taking chunks out of each other. Or not very big ones. All in all he enjoyed the evenings when they played cards if for no other reason than the challenge of trying to catch her cheating. So far he hadn't.

Also true was the odd attraction he felt for her. That hadn't been in the script. So far he'd been able to ignore, control or smother it. But there were times . . . There were times, Michael thought as he rose and stretched, when he'd like to close her smart-tongued mouth in a more satisfactory way. Just to see what it'd be like, he told himself. Curiosity about people was part of his makeup. He'd be interested to see how Pandora would react if he hauled her against him and kissed her until she went limp.

He let out a quick laugh as he wandered to the window. Limp? Pandora? Women like her never went soft. He might satisfy his curiosity, but he'd get a fist in the gut for his trouble. Even that might be worth it. . . .

She wasn't unmoved. He'd been sure of that since the first day they'd walked back together from her workshop. He'd seen it in her face, heard it, however briefly in her voice. They'd both been circling around it for two weeks. Or twenty years, Michael speculated.

He'd never felt about another woman exactly the way he felt about Pandora McVie. Uncomfortable, challenged, infuriated. The truth was that he was almost always at ease around women. He liked them—their femininity, their peculiar strengths and weaknesses, their style. Perhaps that was the reason for his success in relationships, though he'd carefully kept them short-term.

If he romanced a woman, it was because he was interested in her, not simply in the end result. True enough he was interested in Pandora, but he'd never considered romancing her. It surprised him that he'd caught himself once or twice considering seducing her.

Seducing, of course, was an entirely different matter than romancing. But all in all, he didn't know if attempting a casual seduction of Pandora would be worth the risk.

If he offered her a candlelight dinner or a walk in the moonlight—or a mad night of passion—she'd come back with a sarcastic remark. Which would, inevitably, trigger some caustic rebuttal from him. The merry-go-round would begin again.

In any case, it wasn't romance he wanted with Pandora. It was simply curiosity. In certain instances, it was best to remember what had happened to the intrepid cat. But as he thought of her, his gaze was drawn toward her workshop.

They weren't so very different really, Michael mused. Pandora could insist from dawn to dusk that they had nothing in common, but Jolley had been closer to the mark. They were both quick-tempered, opinionated and passionately protective of their professions. He closed himself up for hours at a time with a laptop. She closed herself up with tools and torches. The end result of both of their work was entertainment. And after all, that was . . .

His thoughts broke off as he saw the shed door open. Odd, he hadn't thought she was back yet. His rooms were on the opposite end of the house from the garage, so he wouldn't have heard her car, but he thought she'd drop off what she'd picked up for him.

He started to shrug and turn away when he saw the figure emerge from the shed. It was bundled deep in a coat and hat, but he knew immediately it wasn't Pandora. She moved fluidly, unselfconsciously. This person walked with speed and wariness. Wariness, he thought again, that was evident in the way the head swiveled back and forth before the door was closed again. Without stopping to think, Michael dashed out of the room and down the stairs.

He nearly rammed into Charles at the bottom. "Pandora back?" he demanded.

"No, sir." Relieved that he hadn't been plowed down, Charles rested a hand on the rail. "She said she might stay in town and do some shopping. We shouldn't worry if—"

But Michael was already halfway down the hall.

With a sigh for the agility he hadn't had in thirty years, Charles creaked his way into the drawing room to lay a fire.

The wind hit Michael the moment he stepped outside, reminding him he hadn't stopped for a coat. As he began to race toward the shed, his face chilled and his muscles warmed. There was no one in sight on the grounds. Not surprising, he mused as he slowed his pace just a bit. The woods were close at the edge, and there were a half a dozen easy paths through them.

Some kid poking around? he wondered. Pandora would be lucky if he hadn't pocketed half her pretty stones. It would serve her right.

But he changed his mind the minute he stood in the doorway of her workshop.

Boxes were turned over so that gems and stones and beads were scattered everywhere. Balls of string and twine had been unraveled and twisted and knotted from wall to wall. He had to push some out of his way to step inside. What was usually almost pristine in its order was utter chaos. Gold and silver wire had been bent and snapped, tools lay where they'd been carelessly tossed to the floor.

Michael bent down and picked up an emerald. It glinted

sharp and green in his palm. If it had been a thief, he decided, it had been a clumsy and shortsighted one.

"Oh, God!" Pandora dropped her purse with a thud and stared.

When Michael turned, he saw her standing in the doorway, ice pale and rigid. He swore, wishing he'd had a moment to prepare her. "Take it easy," he began as he reached for her arm.

She shoved him aside forcibly and fought her way into the shed. Beads rolled and bounced at her feet. For a moment there was pure shock, disbelief. Then came a white wall of fury. "How could you?" When she turned back to him, she was no longer pale. Her color was vivid, her eyes as sharp as the emerald he still held.

Because he was off guard, she nearly landed the first blow. The air whistled by his face as her fist passed. He caught her arms before she tried again. "Just a minute," he began, but she threw herself bodily into him and knocked them both against the wall. Whatever had been left on the shelves shuddered or fell off. It took several moments, and a few bruises on both ends, before he managed to pin her arms back and hold her still.

"Stop it." He pressed her back until she glared up at him, dry-eyed and furious. "You've a right to be upset, but putting a hole in me won't accomplish anything."

"I knew you could be low," she said between her teeth. "But I'd never have believed you could do something so filthy."

"Believe whatever the hell you want," he began, but he felt her body shudder as she fought for control. "Pandora," and his voice softened. "I didn't do this. Look at me," he demanded with a little shake. "Why would I?"

Because she wanted to cry, her voice, her eyes were hard. "You tell me."

Patience wasn't one of his strong points, but he tried again. "Pandora, listen to me. Try for common sense a minute and just listen. I got here a few minutes before you. I saw someone coming out of the shed from my window and came down. When I got here, this is what I found."

She was going to disgrace herself. She felt the tears backing up and hated them. It was better to hate him. "Let go of me."

Perhaps he could handle her anger better than her despair. Cautiously Michael released her arms and stepped back. "It hasn't been more than ten minutes since I saw someone coming out of here. I figured they cut through the woods."

She tried to think, tried to clear the fury out of her head. "You can go," she said with deadly calm. "I have to clean up and take inventory."

Something hot backed up in his throat at the casual dismissal. Remembering his own reaction when he'd opened the shed door, he swallowed it. "I'll call the police if you like, but I don't know if anything was stolen." He opened his palm and showed her the emerald. "I can't imagine any thief leaving stones like this behind."

Pandora snatched it out of his hand. When her fingers closed over it, she felt the slight prick of the hoop she'd fastened onto it only the day before. The emerald seemed to grow out of the braided wire.

Her heart was thudding against her ribs as she walked to her worktable. There was what was left of the necklace she'd been fashioning for two weeks. The deceptively delicate tiers were in pieces, the emeralds that had hung gracefully from them, scattered. Her own nippers had been used to destroy it. She gathered up the pieces in her hands and fought back the urge to scream.

"It was this, wasn't it?" Michael picked up the sketch from the floor. It was stunning on paper—at once fanciful and bold. He supposed what she had drawn had some claim to art. He imagined how he'd feel if someone took scissors to one of his scripts. "You'd nearly finished."

Pandora dropped the pieces back on the table. "Leave me alone." She crouched and began to gather up stones and beads.

"Pandora." When she ignored him, Michael grabbed her by the shoulders and shook. "Dammit, Pandora, I want to help."

She sent him a long, cold look. "You've done enough, Michael. Now leave me alone."

"All right, fine." He released her and stormed out. Anger and frustration carried him halfway across the lawn. Michael stopped, swore and wished bitterly for a cigarette. She had no right to accuse him. Worse, she had no right to make him feel responsible. The guilt he was experiencing was nearly as strong as it would have been if he'd actually vandalized her shop. Hands in his pockets, he stood staring back at the shed and cursing her.

She really thought he'd done that to her. That he was capable of such meaningless, bitter destruction. He'd tried to talk to her, soothe her. Every offer of help had been thrown back at him. Just like her, he thought with his teeth gritted. She deserved to be left alone.

He nearly started back to the house again when he remembered just how shocked and ill she'd looked in the doorway of the shed. Calling himself a fool, he went back.

When he opened the door of the shed again, the chaos was just as it had been. Sitting in the middle of it on the floor by her workbench was Pandora. She was weeping quietly.

He felt the initial male panic at being confronted with feminine tears and surprise that they came from Pandora who never shed them. Yet he felt sympathy for someone who'd been dealt a bull's-eye blow. Without saying a word, he went to her and slipped his arms around her.

She stiffened, but he'd expected it. "I told you to go away."

"Yeah. Why should I listen to you?" He stroked her hair.

She wanted to crawl into his lap and weep for hours. "I don't want you here."

"I know. Just pretend I'm someone else." He drew her against his chest.

"I'm only crying because I'm angry." With a sniff, she turned her face into his shirt.

"Sure." He kissed the top of her head. "Go ahead and be angry for a while. I'm used to it."

She told herself it was because she was weakened by shock and grief, but she relaxed against him. The tears came in floods. When she cried, she cried wholeheartedly. When she was finished, she was done.

Tears dry, she sat cushioned against him. Secure. She wouldn't question it now. Along with the anger came a sense of shame she was unaccustomed to. She'd been filthy to him. But he'd come back and held her. Who'd have expected him to be patient, or caring? Or strong enough to make her accept both. Pandora let out a long breath and kept her eyes shut for just a moment. He smelled of soap and nothing else.

"I'm sorry, Michael."

She was soft. Hadn't he just told himself she wouldn't be? He let his cheek brush against her hair. "Okay."

"No, I mean it." When she turned her head, her lips skimmed across his cheek. It surprised them both. That kind of contact was for friends—or lovers. "I couldn't think after I walked in here. I—" She broke off a moment, fascinated by his eyes. Wasn't it strange how small the world could become if you looked into someone's eyes? Why hadn't she ever noticed that before? "I need to sort all this out."

"Yeah." He ran a fingertip down her cheek. She was soft. Softer than he'd let himself believe. "We both do."

It was so easy to settle herself in the crook of his arm. "I can't think."

"No?" Her lips were only an inch from his—too close to ignore, too far to taste. "Let's both not think for a minute."

When he touched his mouth to hers, she didn't draw away but accepted, experimented with the same sense of curiosity that moved through him. It wasn't an explosion or a shock, but a test for both of them. One they'd both known would come sooner or later.

She tasted warm, and her sweetness had a bite. He'd known her so long, shouldn't he have known that? Her body felt primed to move, to act, to race. Soft, yes, she was soft, but not pliant. Perhaps he'd have found pliancy too easy. When he slipped his tongue into her mouth, hers met it teasingly, playfully. His stomach knotted. She made him want more, much more of that unapologetically earthy scent, the taut body. His fingers tangled in her hair and tightened.

He was as mysterious and bold as she'd always thought he would be. His hands were firm, his mouth giving. Sometimes she'd wondered what it would be like to meet him on these terms. But she'd always closed her mind before any of the answers could slip through. Michael Donahue was dangerous simply because he was Michael Donahue. By turns he'd attracted and alienated her since they'd been children. It was more than any other man had been able to do for more than a week.

Now, as her mouth explored his, she began to understand why. He was different, for her. She didn't feel altogether safe in his arms, and not completely in control. Pandora had always made certain she was both those things when it came to a man. The scrape of his unshaved cheek didn't annoy her as she'd thought it would. It aroused. The discomfort of the hard floor seemed suitable, as was the quick rush of cold air through the still-open door.

She felt quietly and completely at home. Then the quick nip of his teeth against her lip made her feel as though she'd just stepped on uncharted land. New territory was what she'd been raised on, and yet, in all her experience, she'd never explored anything so unique, so exotic or so comfortable.

She wanted to go on and knew she had to stop.

Together they drew away.

"Well." She scrambled for composure as she folded her hands in her lap. Be casual, she ordered herself while her pulse thudded at her wrists. Be careless. She couldn't afford to say anything that might make him laugh at her. "That's been coming for a while, I suppose."

He felt as though he'd just slid down a roller coaster without a cart. "I suppose." He studied her a moment, curious and a bit unnerved. When he saw her fingers twist together, he felt a small sense of satisfaction. "It wasn't altogether what I'd expected."

"Things rarely are." Too many surprises for one day, Pandora decided, and rose unsteadily to her feet. She made the mistake of looking around and nearly sunk to the floor again.

"Pandora—"

"No, don't worry." She shook her head as he rose. "I'm not going to fall apart again." Concentrating on breathing evenly, she took one long look at her workshop. "It looks like you were right about the locks. I suppose I should be grateful you haven't said I told you so."

"Maybe I would if it applied." Michael picked up the emeralds scattered on her table. "I'm no expert, cousin, but I'd say these are worth a few thousand."

"So?" She frowned as her train of thought began to march with his. "No thief would've left them behind." Reaching down, she picked up a handful of stones. Among them were two top-grade diamonds. "Or these."

As was his habit, he began to put the steps together in a sort of mental scenario. Action and reaction, motive and result. "I'd wager once you've inventoried, you won't be missing anything. Whoever did this didn't want to risk more than breaking and entering and vandalism."

With a huff, she sat down on her table. "You think it was one of the family."

"'They said it wouldn't last,'" he quoted, and stuck his hands in his pockets. "You may've had something there, Pandora. Something neither of us considered when we were setting out the guidelines. None of them believed we'd be able to get through six months together. The fact is, we've gotten through the first two weeks without a hitch. It could make one of them nervous enough to want to throw in a complication. What was your first reaction when you saw all this?"

She dragged her hand through her hair. "That you'd done it for spite. Exactly what our kith and kin would expect me to think. Dammit, I hate to be predictable."

"You outsmarted them once your mind cleared."

She sent him a quick look, not certain if she should thank him or apologize again. It was best to do neither. "Biff," Pandora decided with relish. "This sort of low-minded trick would be just up his alley."

"I'd only vote for Biff if you find a few rocks missing." Michael rocked back on his heels. "He'd never be able to resist picking up a few glitters that could be liquidated into nice clean cash."

"True enough." Uncle Carlson—no, it seemed a bit crude for his style. Ginger would've been too fascinated with the sparkles to have done any more than fondle. Pulling a hand through her hair, she tried to picture one of her bland, civilized relations wielding a pair of nippers. "Well, I don't suppose it matters a great deal which one of them did it. They've put me two weeks behind on my commission." Again she picked up pieces of thin gold. "It'll never be quite the same," she murmured. "Nothing is when it's done over."

"Sometimes it's better."

With a shake of her head, she walked over to a heater. If he gave her any more sympathy now, she wouldn't be able to trust herself. "One way or the other I've got to get started. Tell Sweeney I won't make it in for lunch."

"I'll help you clean this up."

"No." She turned back when he started to frown. "No, really, Michael, I appreciate it. I need to be busy. And alone."

He didn't like it, but understood. "All right. I'll see you at dinner."

"Michael . . ." He paused at the doorway and looked back. Amid the confusion she looked strong and vivid. He nearly closed the door and went back to her. "Maybe Uncle Jolley was right."

"About what?"

"You may have one or two redeeming qualities."

He smiled at her then, quick and dashing. "Uncle Jolley was always right, cousin. That's why he's still pulling the strings."

Pandora waited until the door shut again. Pulling the strings he was, she mused. "But you're not playing matchmaker with my life," she mumbled. "I'm staying free, single and unattached. Just get that through your head."

She wasn't superstitious, but Pandora almost thought she heard her uncle's high, cackling laugh. She rolled up her sleeves and got to work.

CHAPTER 4

Because after a long, tedious inventory Pandora discovered nothing missing, she vetoed Michael's notion of calling in the police. If something had been stolen, she'd have seen the call as a logical step. As it was, she decided the police would poke and prod around and lecture on the lack of locks. If the vandal had been one of the family—and she had to agree with Michael's conclusion there—a noisy, official investigation would give the break-in too much importance and undoubtedly too much publicity.

Yes, the press would have a field day. Pandora had already imagined the headlines. "Family vs. family in the battle of eccentric's will." There was, under her independent and straightforward nature, a prim part of her that felt family business was private business.

If one or more of the members of the family were keeping an eye on Jolley's Folley and the goings-on there, Pandora wanted them to think that she'd brushed off the vandalism as petty and foolish. As a matter of pride, she didn't want anyone to believe she'd been dealt a stunning blow. As a matter of practicality, she didn't want anyone to know that she had her eyes open. She was determined to find out who had broken into her shop and how they'd managed to pick such a perfect time for it.

Michael hadn't insisted on calling the police because his thoughts had run along the same lines as Pandora's. He'd managed, through a lot of maneuvering and silence, to keep his career totally separate from his family. In his business, he was known as Michael Donahue, award-winning writer, not Michael Donahue, relative of Jolley McVie, multimillionaire. He wanted to keep it that way.

Stubbornly, each had refused to tell the other of their reasons or their plans for some personal detective work. It wasn't so much a matter of trust, but more the fact that neither of them felt the other could do the job competently. So instead, they kept the conversation light through one of Sweeney's four-star meals and let the vandalism rest. More important, they carefully avoided any reference that might trigger some remark about what had happened on a more personal level in Pandora's workshop.

After two glasses of wine and a generous portion of chicken fricassee, Pandora felt more optimistic. It would have been much worse if any of her stock or tools had been taken. That would have meant a trip into Manhattan and days, perhaps weeks of delay. As it was, the worst crime that she could see was the fact that she'd been spied on. Surely that was the only explanation for the break-in coinciding so perfectly with her trip to town. And that would be her first order of business.

"I wonder," Pandora began, probing lightly, "if the Saundersons are in residence for the winter."

"The neighbors with the pond." Michael had thought of the Saunderson place himself. There were certain points on that property where, with a good set of binoculars, someone could watch the Folley easily. "They spend a lot of time in Europe, don't they?"

"Hmm." Pandora toyed with her chicken. "He's in hotels, you know. They tend to pop off here or there for weeks at a time."

"Do they ever rent the place out?"

"Oh, not that I know of. I'm under the impression that they leave a skeleton staff there even when they fly off. Now that I think of it, they were home a few months ago." The memory made her smile. "Uncle Jolley and I went fishing and Saunderson nearly caught us. If we hadn't scrambled back to the cabin—" She broke off as the thought formed.

"Cabin." Michael picked up where she'd left off. "That old two-room wreck Jolley was going to use as a hunting lodge during his eat-off-the-land stage? I'd forgotten all about it."

Pandora shrugged as though it meant nothing while her mind raced ahead. "He ended up eating more beans than game. In any case, we caught a bundle of trout, ate like pigs and sent the rest along to Saunderson. He never sent a thank-you note."

"Poor manners."

"Well, I've heard his grandmother was a barmaid in Chelsea. More wine?"

"No, thanks." He thought it best to keep a clear head if he was going to carry out the plans that were just beginning to form. "Help yourself."

Pandora set the bottle down and sent him a sweet smile. "No, I'm fine. Just a bit tired really."

"You're entitled." It would clear his path beautifully if he could ship her off to bed early. "What you need is a good night's sleep."

"I'm sure you're right." Both of them were too involved with their own moves to notice how excruciatingly polite the conversation had become. "I'll just skip coffee tonight and go have a bath." She feigned a little yawn. "What about you? Planning to work late?"

"No—no, I think I'll get a fresh start in the morning."

"Well then." Pandora rose, still smiling. She'd give it an hour, she calculated, then she'd be out and gone. "I'm going up. Good night, Michael."

"Good night." Once the light in her room was off, he decided, he'd be on his way.

* * *

Pandora sat in her darkened room for exactly fifteen minutes and just listened. All she had to do was get outside without being spotted. The rest would be easy. Opening her door a crack, she held her breath, waited and listened a little longer. Not a sound. It was now or never, she decided and bundled into her coat. Into the deep pockets, she shoved a flashlight, two books of matches and a small can of hair spray. As good as mace, Pandora figured, if you ran into something unfriendly. She crept out into the hall and started slowly down the stairs, her back to the wall.

An adventure, she thought, feeling the familiar pulse of excitement and anxiety. She hadn't had one since Uncle Jolley died. As she let herself out one of the side doors, she thought how much he'd have enjoyed this one. The moon was only a sliver, but the sky was full of stars. The few clouds that spread over them were hardly more than transparent wisps. And the air—she took a deep breath— was cool and crisp as an apple. With a quick glance over her shoulder at Michael's window, she started toward the woods.

The starlight couldn't help her there. Though the trees were bare, the branches were thick enough to block out big chunks of sky. She dug out her flashlight and, turning it side to side, found the edges of the path. She didn't hurry. If she rushed, the adventure would be over too soon. She walked slowly, listened and imagined.

There were sounds—the breeze blew through pine needles and scattered the dry leaves. Now and again there was a skuttle in the woods to the right or left. A fox, a raccoon, a bear not quite settled down to hibernate? Pandora liked not being quite certain. If you walked through the woods alone, in the dark, and didn't have some sense of wonder, it was hardly worth the trip.

She liked the smells—pine, earth, the hint of frost that would settle on the ground before morning. She liked the sense of being alone, and more, of having something up ahead that warranted her attention.

The path forked, and she swung to the left. The cabin wasn't much farther. She stopped once, certain she'd heard something move up ahead that was too big to be considered a fox. For a moment she had a few uncomfortable thoughts about bears and bobcats. It was one thing to speculate and another to have to deal with them. Then there was nothing. Shaking her head, Pandora went on.

What would she do if she got to the cabin, and it wasn't dusty and deserted? What would she do if she actually found one of her dear, devoted relatives had set up housekeeping? Uncle Carlson reading the *Wall Street Journal* by the fire? Aunt Patience fussing around the rocky wooden table with a dust cloth? The thought was almost laughable. Almost, until Pandora remembered her workshop.

Drawing her brows together, she walked forward. If someone was there, they were going to answer to her. In moments, the shadow of the cabin loomed up before her. It looked as it was supposed to look, desolate, deserted, eerie. She kept her flashlight low as she crept toward the porch, then nearly let out a scream when her own weight caused the narrow wooden stair to creak. She held a hand to her heart until it no longer felt as though it would break her ribs. Then slowly, quietly, stealthily, she reached for the doorknob and twisted it.

The door moaned itself open. Wincing at the sound, Pandora counted off ten seconds before she took the next step. With a quick sweep of her light, she stepped in.

When the arm came around her neck, she dropped the flashlight with a clatter. It rolled over the floor, sending an erratic beam over the log walls and brick fireplace. Even as she drew the breath to scream, she reached in her pocket for the hair spray. After she was whirled around, she found herself face-to-face with Michael. His fist was poised inches from her face, her can inches from his. Both of them stood just as they were.

"Dammit!" Michael dropped his arm. "What are you doing here?"

"What are you doing here?" she tossed back. "And what do you mean by grabbing me that way? You may've broken my flashlight."

"I almost broke your nose."

Pandora shook back her hair and walked over to retrieve her light. She didn't want him to see her hands tremble. "Well, I certainly think you should find out who someone is before you throw a headlock on them."

"You followed me."

She sent him a cool, amused look. It helped to be able to do so when her stomach was still quaking. "Don't flatter yourself. I simply wanted to see if something was going on out here, and I didn't want you to interfere."

"Interfere." He shone his own light directly in her face so that she had to throw up a hand in defense. "And what the hell were you going to do if something was going on? Overpower them?"

She thought of how easily he'd taken her by surprise. It only made her lift her chin higher. "I can take care of myself."

"Sure." He glanced down at the can she still held. "What have you got there?"

Having forgotten it, Pandora looked down herself, then had to stifle a chuckle. Oh, how Uncle Jolley would've appreciated the absurdity. "Hair spray," she said very precisely. "Right between the eyes."

He swore, then laughed. He couldn't have written a scene so implausible. "I guess I should be glad you didn't get a shot off at me."

"I look before I pounce." Pandora dropped the can back into her pocket. "Well, since we're here, we might as well look around."

"I was doing just that when I heard your catlike approach." She wrinkled her nose at him, but he ignored her. "It looks like someone's been making themselves at home." To prove his point, Michael shone his light at the fireplace. Half-burnt logs still smoldered.

"Well, well." With her own light, Pandora began to walk around the cabin. The last time she'd been there, the chair with the broken rung had been by the window. Jolley had sat there himself, keeping a lookout for Saunderson while she'd opened a tin of sardines to ward off starvation. Now the chair was pulled up near the fire. "A vagrant, perhaps."

Watching her, Michael nodded. "Perhaps."

"But not likely. Suppose they'll be back?"

"Hard to say." The casual glance showed nothing out of place. The cabin was neat and tidy. Too tidy. The floor and table surfaces should have had a film of dust. Everything had been wiped clean. "It could be they've done all the damage they intend to do."

Disgruntled, Pandora plopped down on the bunk and dropped her chin in her hands. "I'd hoped to catch them."

"And what? Zap them with environmentally safe hair spray?"

She glared up at him. "I suppose you had a better plan."

"I think I might've made them a bit more uncomfortable."

"Black eyes and broken noses." She made an impatient sound. "Really, Michael, you should try to get your mind out of your fists."

"I suppose you just wanted to talk reasonably with whichever member of our cozy family played search and destroy with your workshop."

She started to snap, caught herself, then smiled. It was the slow, wicked smile Michael could never help admiring. "No," she admitted. "Reason wasn't high on my list. Still, it appears we've both missed our chance for brute force. Well, you write the detective stories—so to speak—shouldn't we look for clues?"

His lips curved in something close to a sneer. "I didn't think to bring my magnifying glass."

"You can almost be amusing when you put your mind to it." Rising, Pandora began to shine her light here and there. "They might've dropped something."

"A name tag?"

"Something," she muttered, and dropped to her knees to look under the bunk. "Aha!" Hunkering down, she grabbed at something.

"What is it?" Michael was beside her before she'd straightened up.

"A shoe." Feeling foolish and sentimental, she held it in both hands. "It's nothing. It was Uncle Jolley's."

Because she looked lost, and more vulnerable than he'd expected, Michael offered the only comfort he knew. "I miss him, too."

She sat a moment, the worn sneaker in her lap. "You know, sometimes it's as though I can almost feel him. As though he's around the next corner, in the next room, waiting to pop up and laugh at the incredible joke he's played."

With a quick laugh, Michael rubbed a hand over her back. "I know what you mean."

Pandora looked at him, steady, measuring. "Maybe you do," she murmured. Briskly she set the sneaker on the bunk and rose. "I'll have a look in the cupboards."

"Let me know if you find any cookies." He met the look she tossed over her shoulder with a shrug. "In the early stages of nonsmoking, you need a lot of oral satisfaction."

"You ought to try chewing gum." Pandora opened a cupboard and shone her light over jars and cans. There was peanut butter, chunky, and caviar, Russian. Two of Jolley's favorite snacks. She passed over taco sauce and jumbo fruit cocktail, remembering that her ninety-three-year-old uncle had had the appetite of a teenager. Then reaching in, she plucked out a can and held it up.

"Aha!"

"Again?"

"Tuna fish," Pandora announced waving the can at Michael. "It's a can of tuna."

"Right you are. Any mayo to go with it?"

"Don't be dense, Michael. Uncle Jolley hated tuna."

Michael started to say something sarcastic, then stopped. "He did, didn't he?" he said slowly. "And he never kept anything around he didn't like."

"Exactly."

"Congratulations, Sherlock. Now which of the suspects has an affection for canned fish?"

"You're just jealous because I found a clue and you didn't."

"It's only a clue," Michael pointed out, a little annoyed

at being outdone by an amateur, "if you can do something with it."

He'd never give her credit, she thought, for anything, not her craft, her intelligence and never her womanhood. There was an edge to her voice when she spoke again. "If you're so pessimistic, why did you come out here?"

"I was hoping to find someone." Restless, Michael moved his light from wall to wall. "As it is all we've done is prove someone was here and gone."

Pandora dropped the can of tuna in disgust. "A waste of time."

"You shouldn't've followed me out."

"I didn't follow you out." She shone her light back at him. He looked too male, too dangerous in the shadows. She wished, only briefly, that she had the spectacular build and stunning style that would bring him whimpering to his knees. Their breath came in clouds and merged together. "For all I know, you followed me."

"Oh, I see. That's why I was here first."

"Beside the point. If you'd planned to come out here tonight, why didn't you tell me?"

He came closer. But if he came too close to her, he discovered, he began to feel something, something like an itch along the skin. Try to scratch it, he reminded himself, and she'd rub you raw in seconds. "For the same reason you didn't tell me. I don't trust you, cousin. You don't trust me."

"At least we can agree on something." She started to brush by him and found her arm captured. In one icy movement, she tilted her head down to look at his hand, then up to look at his face. "That's a habit you should try to break, Michael."

"They say when you break one habit, you pick up another."

The ice in Pandora's voice never changed, but her blood was warming. "Do they?"

"You're easier to touch than I'd once thought, Pandora."

"Don't be too sure, Michael." She took a step back, not in retreat, she told herself. It was a purely offensive move. Still, he moved with her.

"Some women have trouble dealing with physical attraction."

The temper that flared in her eyes appealed to him as much as the passion he'd seen there briefly that afternoon. "Your ego's showing again. This dominant routine might work very well with your centerfolds, but—"

"You've always had an odd fascination with my sex life." Michael grinned at her, pleased to see frustration flit over her face.

"The same kind of educated fascination one has with the sex lives of lower mammals." It infuriated her that her heart was racing. And not from anger. She was too honest to pretend it was anger. She'd come looking for an adventure, and she'd found one. "It's getting late," she said, using the tone of a parochial schoolteacher to a disruptive student. "You'll have to excuse me."

"I've never asked about your sex life." When she took another step away, he boxed her neatly into a corner. Pandora's hand slipped into her pocket and rested on the can of hair spray. "Let me guess. You prefer a man with a string of initials after his name who philosophizes about sex more than he acts on it."

"Why, you pompous, arrogant—"

Michael shut her mouth the way he'd once fantasized. With his own.

The kiss was no test this time, but torrid, hot, edging toward desperate. Whatever she might feel, she'd dissect later. Now she'd accept the experience. His mouth was warm, firm, and he used it with the same cocky male confidence that would have infuriated her at any other time. Now she met it with her own.

He was strong, insistent. For the first time Pandora felt herself body to body with a man who wouldn't treat her delicately. He demanded, expected and gave a completely un-inhibited physicality. Pandora didn't have to think her way through the kiss. She didn't have to think at all.

He'd expected her to rear back and take a swing at him. Her instant and full response left him reeling. Later Michael would recall that nothing as basic and simple as a kiss had made his head spin for years.

She packed a punch, but she did it with soft lips. If she knew just how quickly she'd knocked him out, would she gloat? He wouldn't think of it now. He wouldn't think of anything now. Without a moment's hesitation, he buried his consciousness in her and let the senses rule.

The cabin was cold and dark without even a single stream of moonlight for romance. It smelled of dying smoke and settling dust. The wind had kicked up enough to moan grumpily at the windows. Neither of them noticed. Even when they broke apart, neither of them noticed.

He wasn't steady. That was something else he'd think about later. At least he had the satisfaction of seeing she wasn't steady, either. She looked as he felt, stunned, off balance and unable to set for the next blow. Needing some equilibrium, he grinned at her.

"You were saying?"

She wanted to slug him. She wanted to kiss him again until he didn't have the strength to grin. He'd expect her to fall at his feet as other women probably did. He'd expect her to sigh and smile and surrender so he'd have one more victory. Instead she snapped, "Idiot."

"I love it when you're succinct."

"Rule number six," Pandora stated, aiming a killing look. "No physical contact."

"No physical contact," Michael agreed as she stomped toward the doorway, "unless both parties enjoy it."

She slammed the door and left him grinning.

* * *

When two people are totally involved in their own projects, they can live under the same roof for days at a time and rarely see each other. Especially if the roof is enormous and the people very stubborn. Pandora and Michael brushed together at meals and otherwise left each other alone. This wasn't out of any sense of politeness or consideration. It was simply because each of them was too busy to heckle the other.

Separately, however, each felt a smug satisfaction when the first month passed. One down, five to go.

When they were into their second month, Michael drove into New York for a day to handle a problem with a script that had to be dealt with personally. He left, cross as a bear and muttering about imbeciles. Pandora prepared to enjoy herself tremendously in his absence. She wouldn't have to keep up her guard or share the Folley for hours. She could do anything she wanted without worrying about anyone coming to look over her shoulder or make a caustic remark. It would be wonderful.

She ended up picking at her dinner, then watching for his car through the heavy brocade drapes. Not because she missed *him,* she assured herself. It was just that she'd become used to having someone in the house.

Wasn't that one of the reasons she'd never lived with anyone before? She wanted to avoid any sense of dependence. And dependence, she decided, was natural when you shared the same space—even when it was with a two-legged snake.

So she waited, and she watched. Long after Charles and Sweeney had gone to bed, she continued to wait and watch. She wasn't concerned, and certainly not lonely. Only restless. She told herself she didn't go to bed herself because she wasn't tired. Wandering the first floor, she walked into Jolley's den. Game room would have been a more appropriate name. The decor was a cross between video arcade and disco lounge with its state-of-the-art components and low, curved-back sofas.

She turned on the huge, fifty-four-inch television, then left it on the first show that appeared. She wasn't going to *watch* it. She just wanted the company.

There were two pinball tables where she passed nearly an hour trying to beat the high scores Jolley had left behind. Another legacy. Then there was an arcade-size video game that simulated an attack on the planet Zarbo. Under her haphazard defense system, the planet blew up three times before she moved on. There was computerized chess, but she thought her mind too sluggish to take it on. In the end she stretched out on the six-foot sofa in front of the television. Just to rest, not to watch.

Within moments, she was hooked on the late-night syndication of a cop show. Squealing tires and blasting bullets. Head pillowed on her arms, one leg thrown over the top of the sofa, she relaxed and let herself be entertained.

When Michael came to the doorway, she didn't notice him. He'd had a grueling day and had hit some nasty traffic on the drive back. The fact was he'd considered staying in the city overnight—the sensible thing to do. He'd found himself making a dozen weak excuses why he had to go back instead of accepting the invitation of the assistant producer—a tidily built brunette with big brown eyes.

He'd intended to crawl upstairs, fall into his bed and

sleep until noon, but he'd seen the lights and heard the racket. Now, here was Pandora, self-proclaimed critic of the small screen, sprawled on a sofa watching reruns at one in the morning. She looked suspiciously as though she were enjoying herself.

Not a bad show, Michael mused, recognizing the series. In fact, he'd written a couple of scripts for it in his early days. The central character had a sly sort of wit and a fumbling manner that caused the perpetrator to spill out enough information for an arrest by the end of the show.

Michael watched Pandora as she shifted comfortably on the couch. He waited until the commercial break. "Well, how the mighty have fallen."

She nearly did, rolling quickly to look back toward the doorway. She sat up, scowled and searched her mind for a plausible excuse. "I couldn't sleep," she told him, which was true enough. She wouldn't add it was because he hadn't been home. "I suppose television is made for the insomniac. Valium for the mind."

He was tired, bone tired, but he realized how glad he was she'd had a comeback. He came over, plopped down beside her and propped his feet on a coffee table made out of a fat log. "Who done it?" he asked, and sighed. It was good to be home.

"The greedy business partner." She was too pleased to have him back to be embarrassed. "There's really very little challenge in figuring out the answers."

"This show wasn't based on the premise of figuring out who did the crime, but in how the hero maneuvers them into betraying themselves."

She pretended she wasn't interested, but shifted so that she could still see the screen. "So, how did things go in New York?"

"They went." Michael pried off one shoe with the toe of the other. "After several hours of hair tearing and blame casting, the script's intact."

He looked tired. Really tired, she realized, and unbent enough to take off his other shoe. He merely let out a quick grunt of appreciation. "I don't understand why people would get all worked up about one silly hour a week."

He opened one eye to stare at her. "It's the American way."

"What's there to get so excited about? You have a crime, the good guys chase the bad guys and catch them before the final credits. Seems simple enough."

"I can't thank you enough for clearing that up. I'll point it out at the next production meeting."

"Really, Michael, it seems to me things should run fairly smoothly, especially since you've been on the air with this thing for years."

"Know anything about ego and paranoia?"

She smiled a little. "I've heard of them."

"Well, multiply that with artistic temperament, the ratings race and an escalating budget. Don't forget to drop in a good dose of network executives. Things haven't run smoothly for four years. If *Logan* goes another four, it still won't run smoothly. That's show biz."

Pandora moved her shoulders. "It seems a foolish way to make a living."

"Ain't it just," Michael agreed, and fell sound asleep.

She let him doze for the next twenty minutes while she watched the sly, fumbling cop tighten the ropes on the greedy business partner. Satisfied that justice had been done, Pandora rose to switch off the set and dim the lights.

She could leave him here, she considered as she watched Michael sleep. He looked comfortable enough at the moment. She thought about it as she walked over to brush his hair from his forehead. But he'd probably wake up with a stiff neck and a nasty disposition. Better get him upstairs into bed, she decided, and shook his shoulder.

"Michael."

"Mmm?"

"Let's go to bed."

"Thought you'd never ask," he mumbled, and reached halfheartedly for her.

Amused, she shook him harder. "Never let your reach exceed your grasp. Come on, cousin, I'll help you upstairs."

"The director's a posturing idiot," he grumbled as she dragged him to his feet.

"I'm sure he is. Now, see if you can put one foot in front of the other. That's the way. Here we go." With an arm around his waist, she began to lead him from the room.

"He kept screwing around with my script."

"Of all the nerve. Here come the steps."

"Said he wanted more emotional impact in the second act. Bleaches his hair," Michael muttered as she half pulled him up the steps. "Lot he knows about emotional impact."

"Obviously a mental midget." Breathlessly she steered him toward his room. He was heavier than he looked. "Here we are now, home again." With a little strategy and a final burst of will, she shoved him onto the bed. "There now, isn't that cozy?" Leaving him fully dressed, she spread an afghan over him.

"Aren't you going to take my pants off?"

She patted his head. "Not a chance."

"Spoilsport."

"If I helped you undress this late at night, I'd probably have nightmares."

"You know you're crazy about me." The bed felt like heaven. He could've burrowed in it for a week.

"You're getting delirious, Michael. I'll have Charles bring you some warm tea and honey in the morning."

"Not if you want to live." He roused himself to open his eyes and smile at her. "Why don't you crawl in beside me? With a little encouragement, I could show you the time of your life."

Pandora leaned closer, closer, until her mouth was inches from his. Their breath mixed quickly, intimately. She hovered there a moment while her hair fell forward and brushed his cheek. "In a pig's eye," she whispered.

Michael shrugged, yawned and rolled over. "'Kay."

In the dark, Pandora stood for a moment with her hands on her hips. At least he could've acted insulted. Chin up, she walked out—making sure she slammed the door at her back.

CHAPTER 5

Tier by painstaking tier, Pandora had completed the emerald necklace. When it was finished, she was pleased to judge it perfect. This judgment pleased her particularly because she was her own toughest critic. Pandora didn't feel emotionally attached or creatively satisfied by every piece she made. With the necklace, she felt both. She examined it under a magnifying glass, held it up in harsh light, went over the filigree inch by inch and found no flaws. Out of her own imagination she'd conceived it, then with her own skill created it. With a kind of regret, she boxed the necklace in a bed of cotton. It wasn't hers any longer.

With the necklace done, she looked around her workshop without inspiration. She'd put so much into that one piece, all her concentration, her emotion, her skill. She hadn't made a single plan for the next project. Restless, wanting to work, she picked up her pad and began to sketch.

Earrings perhaps, she mused. Something bold and chunky and ornate. She wanted a change after the fine, elegant work she'd devoted so much time to. Circles and triangles, she thought. Something geometric and blatantly modern. Nothing romantic like the necklace.

Romantic, she mused, and sketched strong, definite lines. She'd been working with a romantic piece; perhaps that's why she'd nearly made a fool of herself with Michael. Her emotions were involved with her work, and her work had been light and feminine and romantic. It made sense, she decided, satisfied. Now, she'd work with something strong and brash and arrogant. That should solve the problem.

There shouldn't be a problem in the first place. Teeth gritted, she flipped a page and started over. Her feelings for Michael had always been very definite. Intolerance. If you were intolerant of someone, it went against the grain to be attracted to him.

It wasn't real attraction in any case. It was more some sort of twisted . . . curiosity. Yes, curiosity. The word satisfied her completely. She'd been curious, naturally enough, to touch on the sexuality of a man she'd known since childhood. Curious, again naturally, to find out what it was about Michael Donahue that attracted all those poster girls. She'd found out.

So he had a way of making a woman feel utterly a woman, utterly involved, utterly willing. It wasn't something that had happened to her before nor something she'd looked for. As Pandora saw it, it was a kind of skill. She decided he'd certainly honed it as meticulously as any craftsman. Though she found it difficult to fault him for that, *she* wasn't about to fall in with the horde. If he knew, if he even suspected, that she'd had the same reaction to him that she imagined dozens of other women had, he'd gloat for a month. If he guessed that from time to time she'd wished—just for a moment— that he'd think of her the way he thought of those dozens of other women, he'd gloat for twice as long. She wouldn't give him the pleasure.

Individuality was part of her makeup. She didn't want to be one of his women, even if she could. Now that her curiosity had been satisfied, they'd get through the next five months without any more . . . complications.

Just because she'd found him marginally acceptable as a human being, almost tolerable as a companion wouldn't get in the way. It would, if anything, make the winter pass a bit easier.

And when she caught herself putting the finishing touches on a sketch of Michael's face, she was appalled. The lines were true enough, though rough. She'd had no trouble capturing the arrogance around the eyes or the sensitivity around the mouth. Odd, she realized; she'd sketched him to look intelligent. She ripped the sheet from her pad, crumpled it up in a ball and tossed it into the trash. Her mind had wandered, that was all. Pandora picked up her pencil again, put it down, then dug the sketch out again. Art was art, after all, she told herself as she smoothed out Michael's face.

* * *

He wasn't having a great deal of success with his own work. Michael sat at his desk and typed like a maniac for five minutes. Then he stared into space for fifteen. It wasn't like him. When he worked, he worked steadily, competently, smoothly until the scene was set.

Leaning back in his chair, he picked up a pencil and ran his fingers from end to end. Whatever the statistics said, he should never have given up smoking. That's what had him so edgy. Restless, he pushed away from the desk and wandered over to the window. He stared down at Pandora's workshop. It looked cheerful under a light layer of snow that was hardly more than a dusting. The windows were blank.

That's what had him so edgy.

She wasn't what he'd expected. She was softer, sweeter. Warmer. She was fun to talk to, whether she was arguing and snipping and keeping you on the edge of temper, or whether she was being easy and companionable. There wasn't an overflow of small talk with Pandora. There weren't any trite conversations. She kept your mind working, even if it was in defense of her next barb.

It wasn't easy to admit that he actually enjoyed her company. But the weeks they'd been together at the Folley had gone quickly. No, it wasn't easy to admit he liked being with her, but he'd turned down an interesting invitation from his assistant producer because . . . Because, Michael admitted on a long breath, he hadn't wanted to spend the night with one woman when he'd known his thoughts would have been on another.

Just how was he going to handle this unwanted and unexpected attraction to a woman who'd rather put on the gloves and go a few rounds than walk in the moonlight?

Romantic women had always appealed to him because he was, unashamedly, a romantic himself. He enjoyed candlelight, quiet music, long, lonely walks. Michael courted women in old-fashioned ways because he felt comfortable with old-fashioned ways. It didn't interfere with the fact that he was, and had been since college, a staunch feminist. Romance and sociopolitical views were worlds apart. He had no trouble balancing equal pay for equal work against offering a woman a carriage ride through the park.

And he knew if he sent Pandora a dozen white roses, she'd complain about the thorns.

He wanted her. Michael was too much a creature of the senses to pretend otherwise. When he wanted something, he worked toward it in one of two ways. First, he planned out the best approach, then took the steps one at a time, maneuvering subtly. If that didn't work, he tossed out subtlety and went after it with both hands. He'd had just as much success the first way as the second.

As he saw it, Pandora wouldn't respond to patience and posies. She wouldn't go for being swept off her feet, either. With Pandora, he might just have to toss his two usual approaches and come up with a whole new third.

An interesting challenge, Michael decided with a slow smile. He liked nothing better than arranging and rearranging plot lines and shifting angles. And hadn't he always thought Pandora would make a fascinating character? So, he'd work it like a screenplay.

Hero and heroine living as housemates, he began. Attracted to each other but reluctant. Hero is intelligent, charming. Has tremendous willpower. Hadn't he given up smoking—five weeks, three days and fourteen hours ago? Heroine is stubborn and opinionated, often mistakes arrogance for independence. Hero gradually cracks through her brittle shield to their mutual satisfaction.

Michael leaned back in his chair and grinned. He might just make it a play. A great deal of the action would be ad-lib, of course, but he had the general theme. Satisfied, and looking forward to the opening scene, Michael went back to work with a vengeance.

Two hours breezed by with Michael working steadily. He answered the knock at his door with a grunt.

"I beg your pardon, Mr. Donahue." Charles, slightly out of breath from the climb up the stairs, stood in the doorway.

Michael gave another grunt and finished typing the paragraph. "Yes, Charles?"

"Message for you, sir."

"Message?" Scowling, he swiveled around in the chair. If there was a problem in New York—as there was at least once a week—the phone was the quickest way to solve it. "Thanks." He took the message, but only flapped it against his palm. "Pandora still out in her shop?"

"Yes, sir." Grateful for the chance to rest, Charles expanded a bit. "Sweeney is a bit upset that Miss McVie missed lunch. She intends to serve dinner in an hour. I hope that suits your schedule."

Michael knew better than to make waves where Sweeney was concerned. "I'll be down."

"Thank you, sir, and if I may say, I enjoy your television show tremendously. This week's episode was particularly exciting."

"I appreciate that, Charles."

"It was Mr. McVie's habit to watch it every week in my company. He never missed an episode."

"There probably wouldn't have been a *Logan's Run* without Jolley," Michael mused. "I miss him."

"We all do. The house seems so quiet. But I—" Charles reddened a bit at the thought of overstepping his bounds.

"Go ahead, Charles."

"I'd like you to know that both Sweeney and I are pleased to remain in your service, yours and Miss McVie's. We were glad when Mr. McVie left you the house. The others . . ." He straightened his back and plunged on. "They wouldn't have been suitable, sir. Sweeney and I had both discussed resigning if Mr. McVie had chosen to leave the Folley to one of his other heirs." Charles folded his bony hands. "Will there be anything else before dinner, sir?"

"No, Charles. Thank you."

Message in hand, Michael leaned back as Charles went out. The old butler had known him since childhood. Michael could remember distinctly when Charles had stopped calling him Master Donahue. He'd been sixteen and visiting the Folley during the summer months. Charles had called him Mr. Donahue and Michael had felt as though he'd just stepped from childhood, over adolescence and into adulthood.

Strange how much of his life had been involved with the Folley and the people who were a part of it. Charles had served him his first whisky—with dignity if not approval on his eighteenth birthday. Years before that, Sweeney had given him his first ear boxing. His parents had never bothered to swat him and his tutors wouldn't have dared. Michael still remembered that after the sting had eased, he'd felt like part of a family.

Pandora had been both bane and fantasy during his adolescence. Apparently that hadn't changed as much as Michael had thought. And Jolley. Jolley had been father, grandfather, friend, son and brother.

Jolley had been Jolley, and Michael had spoken no less than the truth when he'd told Charles he missed the old man. In some part of himself, he always would. Thinking of other things, Michael tore open the message.

Your mother is gravely ill. The doctors are not hopeful.
Make arrangements to fly to Palm Springs immediately.
L. J. KEYSER.

Michael stared at the message for nearly a minute. It wasn't possible; his mother was never ill. She considered it something of a social flaw. He felt a moment's disbelief, a moment's shock. He was reaching for the phone before either had worn off.

When Pandora walked by his room fifteen minutes later, she saw him tossing clothes into a bag. She lifted a brow, leaned against the jamb and cleared her throat. "Going somewhere?"

"Palm Springs." He tossed in his shaving kit.

"Really?" Now she folded her arms. "Looking for a sunnier climate?"

"It's my mother. Her husband sent me a message."

Instantly she dropped her cool, sarcastic pose and came into the room. "Is she ill?"

"The message didn't say much, but it doesn't sound good."

"Oh, Michael, I'm sorry. Can I do anything? Call the airport?"

"I've already done it. I've got a flight in a couple of hours. They're routing me through half a dozen cities, but it was the best I could do."

Feeling helpless, she watched him zip up his bag. "I'll drive you to the airport if you like."

"No, thanks anyway." He dragged a hand through his hair as he turned to face her. The concern was there, though he realized she'd only met his mother once, ten, perhaps fifteen years before. The concern was for him and unexpectedly solid. "Pandora, it's going to take me half the night to get to the coast. And then I don't know—" He broke off, not able to imagine his mother seriously ill. "I might not be able to make it back in time—not in forty-eight hours."

She shook her head. "I don't want you to think about it. I'll call Fitzhugh and explain. Maybe he'll be able to do something. After all, it's an emergency. If he can't, he can't."

He was taking a step that could pull millions of dollars out from under her. Millions of dollars and the home she loved. Torn, Michael went to her and rested his hands on her shoulders. She was so slender. He'd forgotten just how fragile a strong woman could be. "I'm sorry, Pandora. If there was any other way . . ."

"Michael, I told you I didn't want the money. I meant it."

He studied her a moment. Yes, the strength was there, the stubbornness and the basic goodness he often overlooked. "I believe you did," he murmured.

"As for the rest, well, we'll see. Now go ahead before you miss your plane." She waited until he'd grabbed his bag then walked with him to the hall. "Call me if you get the chance and let me know how your mother is."

He nodded, started for the stairs, then stopped. Setting

his bag down, he came back and pulled her against him. The kiss was hard and long, with hints of a fire barely banked. He drew her away just as abruptly. "See you."

"Yeah." Pandora swallowed. "See you."

She stood where she was until she heard the front door slam.

* * *

She had a long time to think about the kiss, through a solitary dinner, during the hours when she tried to read by the cheery fire in the parlor. It seemed to Pandora that there'd been more passion concentrated in that brief contact than she'd experienced in any of her carefully structured relationships. Was it because she'd always been able to restrict passion to her temper, or her work?

It might have been because she'd been sympathetic, and Michael had been distraught. Emotions had a way of feeding emotions. But for the second time she found herself alone in the house, and to her astonishment, lonely. It was foolish because the fire was bright, the book entertaining and the brandy she sipped warming.

But lonely she was. After little more than a month, she'd come to depend on Michael's company. Even to look forward to it, as strange as that may have been. She liked sitting across from him at meals, arguing with him. She especially liked watching the way he fought, exploding when she poked pins in his work. Perverse? she wondered with a sigh. Perhaps she was, but life was so boring without a bit of friction. No one seemed to provide it more satisfactorily than Michael Donahue.

She wondered when she'd see him again. And she wondered if now they'd have to forgo spending the winter together. If the terms of the will were broken, there would be no reason for them to stay on together. In fact, they'd have no right to stay at the Folley at all. They'd both go back to New York where, due to separate lifestyles, they never saw one another. Not until now, when it was a possibility, did Pandora fully realize how much she didn't want it to happen.

She didn't want to lose the Folley. There were so many memories, so many important ones. Wouldn't they begin to fade if she couldn't walk into a room and bring them back? She didn't want to lose Michael. His companionship, she amended quickly. It was more satisfying than she'd imagined to have someone near who could meet you head to head. If she lost that daily challenge, life would be terribly flat. Since it was Michael who was adding that certain spark to the days, it was only natural to want him around. Wasn't it?

With a sigh, Pandora shut the book and decided an early night would be more productive than idle speculation. Just as she reached over to shut out the lamp, it went out on its own. She was left with the glow of the fire.

Odd, she thought and reached for the switch. After turning it back and forth, she rose, blaming a defective bulb. But when she walked into the hall she found it in darkness. The light she'd left burning was out, along with the one always left on at the top of the stairs. Again Pandora reached for a switch and again she found it useless.

Power failure, she decided but found herself hesitating in the dark. There was no storm. Electricity at the Folley went out regularly during snow and thunderstorms, but the back-up generator took over within minutes. Pandora waited, but the house remained dark. It occurred to her as she stood there hoping for the best, that she'd never really considered how dark dark could be. She was already making her way back into the parlor for a candle when the rest occurred to her. The house was heated with electricity, as well. If she didn't see about the power soon, the house was going to be very cold as well as very dark before too long. With two people in their seventies in the house, she couldn't let it go.

Annoyed, she found three candles in a silver holder and lit them. It wasn't any use disturbing Charles's sleep and dragging him down to the basement. It was probably only a faulty fuse or two. Holding the candles ahead of her, Pandora wound her way through the curving halls to the cellar door.

She wasn't bothered about going down into the cellar in the dark. So she told herself as she stood with her hand on the knob. It was, after all, just another room. And one, if memory served, which was full of the remains of several of Uncle Jolley's rejected hobbies. The fuse box was down there. She'd seen it when she'd helped her uncle cart down several boxes of photographic equipment after he'd decided to give up the idea of becoming a portrait photographer. She'd go down, check for faulty fuses and replace them. After the lights and heat were taken care of, she'd have a hot bath and go to bed.

But she drew in a deep breath before she opened the door.

The stairs creaked. It was to be expected. And they were steep and narrow as stairs were in any self-respecting cellar. The light from her candles set the shadows dancing over the crates and boxes her uncle had stored there. She'd have to see if she could talk Michael into helping her sort through them. On some bright afternoon. She was humming nervously to herself before she reached the bottom stair.

Pandora held the candles high and scanned the floor as far as the light circled. She knew mice had an affection for dark, dank cellars and she had no affection for them. When nothing rushed across the floor, she skirted around two six-foot crates and headed for the fuse box. There was the motorized exercise bike that Uncle Jolley had decided took the fun out of staying fit. There was a floor-to-ceiling shelf of old bottles. He'd once been fascinated by a ten-dollar bottle cutter. And there, she saw with a sigh of relief, was the fuse box.

Setting the candles on a stack of boxes, she opened the big metal door and stared inside. There wasn't a single fuse in place.

"What the hell's this?" she muttered. Then as she shifted to look closer, her foot sent something rattling over the concrete floor. Jolting, she stifled a scream and the urge to run. Holding her breath, she waited in the silence. When she thought she could manage it, she picked up the candles again and crouched. Scattered at her feet were a dozen fuses. She picked one up and let it lie in her palm. The cellar might have its quota of mice, but they weren't handy enough to empty a fuse box.

She felt a little shudder, which she ignored as she began to gather up the fuses. Tricks, she told herself. Just silly tricks. Annoying, but not as destructive as the one played in her workshop. It wasn't even a very clever trick, she decided, as it was as simple to put fuses back as it had been to take them out.

Working quickly, and trying not to look over her shoulder, Pandora put the fuses back in place. Whoever had managed to get into the basement and play games had wasted her time, nothing more.

Finished, she went over to the stairs, and though she hated herself, ran up them. But her sigh of relief was premature. The door she'd carefully left open was closed tightly. For a few moments she simply refused to believe it. She twisted the knob, pushed, shoved and twisted again. Then she forgot everything but the fear of being closed in a dark place. Pandora beat on the door, shouted, pleaded, then collapsed half sobbing on the top step. No one would hear her. Charles and Sweeney were on the other side of the house.

For five minutes she gave in to fear and self-pity. She was alone, all alone, locked in a dark cellar where no one would hear her until morning. It was already cold and getting colder. By morning . . . her candles would go out by then, and she'd have no light at all. That was the worst, the very worst, to have no light.

Light, she thought, and called herself an idiot as she wiped away tears. Hadn't she just fixed the lights? Scrambling up, Pandora hit the switch at the top of the stairs. Nothing happened. Holding back a scream, she held the candles up. The socket over the stairs was empty.

So, they'd thought to take out the bulbs. It had been a clever trick after all. She swallowed fresh panic and tried to think. They wanted her to be incoherent, and she refused to give them the satisfaction. When she found out which one of her loving family was playing nasty games . . .

That was for later, Pandora told herself. Now she was going to find a way out. She was shivering, but she told herself it was anger. There were times it paid to lie to yourself. Holding the candles aloft, she forced herself to go down the steps again when cowering at the top seemed so much easier.

The cellar was twice the size of her apartment in New York, open and barnlike without any of the ornate decorating Uncle Jolley had been prone to. It was just dark and slightly damp with concrete floors and stone walls that echoed. She wouldn't think about spiders or things that scurried into corners right now. Slowly, trying to keep calm, she searched for an exit.

There were no doors, but then she was standing several feet underground. Like a tomb. That particular thought didn't soothe her nerves so she concentrated on other things. She'd only been down in the cellar a handful of times and hadn't given a great deal of thought to the setup. Now she had to think about it—and pretend her palms weren't clammy.

She eased by a pile of boxes as high as her shoulders, then let out a scream when she ran into a maze of cobwebs. More disgusted than frightened, she brushed and dragged at them.

It didn't sit well with her to make a fool out of herself, even
if no one was around to see it. Someone was going to pay,
she told herself as she fought her way clear.

Then she saw the window, four feet above her head and tiny.
Though it was hardly the size of a transom, Pandora nearly
collapsed in relief. After setting the candles on a shelf, she began dragging boxes over. Her muscles strained and her back
protested, but she hauled and stacked against the wall. The
first splinter had her swearing. After the third, she stopped
counting. Out of breath, streaming with sweat, she leaned
against her makeshift ladder. Now all she had to do was climb
it. With the candles in one hand, she used the other to haul
herself up. The light shivered and swayed. The boxes groaned
and teetered a bit. The thought passed through her mind that if
she fell, she could lie there on the frigid concrete with broken
bones until morning. She pulled herself high and refused to
think at all.

When she reached the window, she found the little latch
rusted and stubborn. Swearing, praying, she balanced the
candles on the box under her and used both hands. She felt
the latch give, then stick again. If she'd only thought to find
a tool before she'd climbed up. She considered climbing back
down and finding one, then made the mistake of looking behind her. The stack of boxes looked even more rickety from
up there.

Turning back to the window, she tugged with all the
strength she had. The latch gave with a grind of metal against
metal, the boxes swayed from the movement. She saw her
candles start to tip and grabbed for them. Out of reach, they
slid from the box and clattered to the concrete, their tiny
flames extinguished as they hit the ground. She almost followed them, but managed to fight for balance. Pandora found
herself perched nine feet off the floor in pitch-darkness.

She wouldn't fall, she promised herself as she gripped

the little window ledge with both hands. Using her touch to guide her, she pulled the window out and open, then began to ease herself through. The first blast of cold air made her almost giddy. After she'd pushed her shoulders through she gave herself a moment to breathe and adjust to the lesser dark of starlight. From somewhere to the west, she heard a hardy night bird call twice and fall silent. She'd never heard anything more beautiful.

Grabbing the base of a rhododendron, she pulled herself through to the waist. When she heard the crash of boxes behind her, she laid her cheek against the cold grass. Inch by inch, she wiggled her way out, ignoring the occasional rip and scratch. At last, she was flat on her back, looking up at the stars. Cold, bruised and exhausted, she lay there, just breathing. When she was able, Pandora dragged herself up and walked around to the east terrace doors.

She wanted revenge, but first, she wanted a bath.

* * *

After three layovers and two plane changes, Michael arrived in Palm Springs. Nothing, as far as he could see, had changed. He never came to the exclusive little community but that he came reluctantly. Now, thinking of his mother lying ill, he was swamped with guilt.

He rarely saw her. True, she was no more interested in seeing him than he was her. Yet, she was still his mother. They had been on a different wavelength since the day he'd been born, but she'd taken care of him. At least, she'd hired people to take care of him. Affection, Michael realized, didn't have to enter into a child's feelings for his parent. The bond was there whether or not understanding followed it.

With no more than a flight bag, he bypassed the crowd at baggage claim and hailed a cab. After giving his mother's

address, he sat back and checked his watch, subtracting time
zones. Even with the hours he'd gained, it was probably
past visiting hours. He'd get around that, but first he had to
know what hospital his mother was in. If he'd been thinking
straight, he would have called ahead and checked.

If his mother's husband wasn't in, one of the servants
could tell him. It might not be as bad as the message made it
sound. After all, his mother was still young. Then it struck
Michael that he didn't have the vaguest idea how old his
mother was. He doubted his father knew, and certainly not
her current husband. At another time, it might have struck
him as funny.

Impatient, he watched as the cab glided by the gates and
pillars of the elite. His career had caused him to stay in California for extended lengths of time, but he preferred L.A. to
Palm Springs. There, at least, was some action, some movement, some edge. But he liked New York best of all; the pace
matched his own and the streets were tougher.

He thought of Pandora. Both of them lived in New York,
but they never saw each other unless it was miles north of
the city at the Folley. The city could swallow you. Or hide
you. It was another aspect Michael appreciated.

Didn't he often use it to hide—from his stifling upbring-
ing, from his recurring lack of faith in the human race? It was
at the Folley that he felt the easiest, but it was in New York
that he felt the safest. He could be anonymous there if he
chose to be. There were times he wanted nothing more. He
wrote about heroes and justice, sometimes rough but always
human. He wrote, in his own fashion, about basic values and
simple rights.

He'd been raised with the illusions and hypocrisy of wealth
and with values that were just as unstable. He'd broken away
from that, started on his own. New York had helped make it
possible because in the city backgrounds were easily erased.

So easily erased, Michael mused, that he rarely thought of his.

The cab cruised up the long semicircle of macadam, under the swaying palms, toward the towering white house where his mother had chosen to live. Michael remembered there was a lily pond in the back with goldfish the size of groupers. His mother refused to call them carp.

"Wait," he told the driver, then dashed up two levels of stairs to the door. The butler who answered was new. It was his mother's habit to change the staff regularly, before, as she put it, they got too familiar. "I'm Michael Donahue, Mrs. Keyser's son."

The butler glanced over his shoulder at the waiting cab, then back at Michael's disheveled sweater and unshaven face. "Good evening, sir. Are you expected?"

"Where's my mother? I want to go to the hospital directly."

"Your mother isn't in this evening, Mr. Donahue. If you'll wait, I'll see if Mr. Keyser's available."

Intolerant, as always, of cardboard manners, he stepped inside. "I know she's not in. I want to go see her tonight. What's the name of the hospital?"

The butler gave a polite nod. "What hospital, Mr. Donahue?"

"Jackson, where did that cab come from?" Wrapped in a deep-rose smoking jacket, Lawrence Keyser strolled downstairs. He had a thick cigar between the fingers of one hand and a snifter of brandy in the other.

"Well, Lawrence," Michael began over a wave of fury. "You look comfortable. Where's my mother?"

"Well, well, it's—ah, it's Matthew."

"It's Michael."

"Michael, of course. Jackson, pay off Mr. ah, Mr. Donavan's cab."

"No, thanks, Jackson." Michael held up a hand. Another

time, he'd have been amused at his stepfather's groping for his name. "I'll use it to get to the hospital. Wouldn't want to put you out."

"No trouble at all, not at all." Big, round and only partially balding, Keyser gave Michael a friendly grin. "Veronica will be pleased to see you, though we didn't know you were coming. How long are you in town?"

"As long as I'm needed. I left the minute I got the message. You didn't mention the name of the hospital. Since you're home and relaxing," he said with only the slightest trace of venom, "should I assume that my mother's condition's improved?"

"Condition?" Keyser gave a jovial laugh. "Well now, I don't know how she'd take to that term, but you can ask her yourself."

"I intend to. Where is she?"

"Playing bridge at the Bradleys'. She'll be coming along in about an hour. How about a brandy?"

"Playing bridge!" Michael stepped forward and grabbed his surprised stepfather by the lapels. "What the hell do you mean she's playing bridge?"

"Can't stomach the game myself," Keyser began warily. "But Veronica's fond of it."

It came to Michael, clear as a bell. "You didn't send me a message about Mother?"

"A message?" Keyser patted Michael's arm, and hoped Jackson stayed close. "No need to send you a message about a bridge game, boy."

"Mother's not ill?"

"Strong as a horse, though I wouldn't let her hear me say so just that way."

Michael swore and whirled around. "Someone's going to pay," he muttered.

"Where are you going?"

"Back to New York," Michael tossed over his shoulder as he ran down the steps.

Relieved, Keyser opted against the usual protests about his departure. "Is there a message for your mother?"

"Yeah." Michael stopped with a hand on the door of the cab. "Yeah, tell her I'm glad she's well. And I hope she wins—in spades." Michael slammed the door shut behind him.

Keyser waited until the cab shot out of sight. "Odd boy," Keyser grumbled to his butler. "Writes for television."

CHAPTER 6

Pandora, sleeping soundly, was awakened at seven in the morning when Michael dropped on her bed. The mattress bounced. He snuggled his head into the pillow beside her and shut his eyes.

"Sonofabitch," he grumbled.

Pandora sat up, remembered she was naked and grabbed for the sheets. "Michael! You're supposed to be in California. What are you doing in my bed?"

"Getting horizontal for the first time in twenty-four hours."

"Well, do that in your own bed," she ordered, then saw the lines of strain and fatigue. "Your mother." Pandora grabbed for his hand. "Oh, Michael, is your mother—"

"Playing bridge." He rubbed his free hand over his face. Even to him it felt rough and seedy. "I bounced across country, once in a tuna can with propellers, to find out she was sipping sherry and trumping her partner's ace."

"She's better then?"

"She was always better. The message was a hoax." He yawned, stretched and settled. "God, what a night."

"You mean . . ." Pandora tugged on the sheets and glowered. "Well, the rats."

"Yeah. I plotted out several forms of revenge when I

was laid over in Cleveland. Maybe our friend who stomped through your workshop figured it was my turn. Now we each owe them one."

"I owe 'em two." Pandora leaned back against the headboard with the sheets tucked under her arms. Her hair fell luxuriously over her naked shoulders. "Last night while you were off on your wild-goose chase, I was locked in the cellar."

Michael's attention shot away from the thin sheet that barely covered her. "Locked in? How?"

Crossing one ankle over the other, Pandora told him what happened from the time the lights went out.

"Climbed up on boxes? To that little window? It's nearly ten feet."

"Yes, I believe I noticed that at the time."

Michael scowled at her. The anger he'd felt at being treated to a sleepless night doubled. He could picture her groping her way around in the dank cellar all too well. Worse, he could see her very clearly climbing on shaky boxes and crates. "You could've broken your neck."

"I didn't. What I did do was rip my favorite pair of slacks, scratch both knees and bruise my shoulder."

Michael managed to hold back his fury. He'd let it go, he promised himself, when the time was right. "It could've been worse," he said lightly, and thought of what he'd do to whoever had locked her in.

"It was worse," Pandora tossed back, insulted. "While you were sipping Scotch at thirty thousand feet, I was locked in a cold, damp cellar with mice and spiders."

"We might reconsider calling the police."

"And do what with them? We can't prove anything. We don't even know whom we can't prove anything against."

"New rule," Michael decided. "We stick together. Neither of us leaves the house overnight without the other. At least until we find out which of our devoted relations is playing games."

Pandora started to protest, then remembered how frightened she'd been, and before the cellar, before the fear, how lonely. "Agreed. Now . . ." With one hand hanging onto the sheet, she shifted toward him. "I vote for Uncle Carlson on this one. After all, he knows the house better than any of the others. He lived here."

"It's as good a guess as any. But it's only a guess." Michael stared up at the ceiling. "I want to know. Biff stayed here for six weeks one summer when we were kids."

"That's right." Pandora frowned at the ceiling herself. The mirror across the room reflected them lying companionably, hip to hip. "I'd forgotten about that. He hated it."

"He's never had a sense of humor."

"True enough. As I recall he certainly didn't like you."

"Probably because I gave him a black eye."

Pandora's brow lifted. "You would." Then, because the image of Biff with a shiner wasn't so unappealing, she added: "Why did you? You never said."

"Remember the frogs in your dresser?"

Pandora sniffed and smoothed at the sheets. "I certainly do. It was quite immature of you."

"Not me. Biff."

"Biff?" Astonished, she turned toward him again. "You mean that little creep put the frogs in my underwear?" The next thought came, surprisingly pleasing. "And you punched him for it?"

"It wasn't hard."

"Why didn't you deny it when I accused you?"

"It was more satisfying to punch Biff. In any case, he knows the house well enough. And I imagine if we checked up, we'd find most of our happy clan has stayed here, at least for a few days at a time. Finding a fuse box in the cellar doesn't take a lot of cunning. Think it through, Pandora. There are six of them, seven with the charity added on. Split a hundred fifty million seven ways and you end up with plenty of motive. Every one of them has a reason for wanting us to break the terms of the will. None of them, as far as I'm concerned, is above adding a little pressure to help us along."

"Another reason the money never appealed to me," she mused. "They haven't done anything but vandalize and annoy, but, dammit, Michael, I want to pay them back."

"The ultimate payback comes in just under five months." Without thinking about it, Michael put his arm around her shoulders. Without thinking about it, Pandora settled against him. A light fragrance clung to her skin. "Can't you see Carlson's face when the will holds up and he gets nothing but a magic wand and a trick hat?"

His shoulder felt more solid than she'd imagined. "And Biff with three cartons of matchbooks." Comfortable, she chuckled. "Uncle Jolley's still having the last laugh."

"We'll have it with him in a few months."

"It's a date. And you've got your shoes on my sheets."

"Sorry." With two economical movements, he pried them off.

"That's not exactly what I meant. Don't you want to wander off to your own room now?"

"Not particularly. Your bed's nicer than mine. Do you always sleep naked?"

"No."

"My luck must be turning then." He shifted to press his lips to a bruise on her shoulder. "Hurt?"

She shrugged and prayed it came off as negligent. "A little."

"Poor little Pandora. And to think I always thought you were tough-skinned."

"I am—"

"Soft," he interrupted, and skimmed his fingers down her arm. "Very soft. Any more bruises?" He brushed his lips over the curve of her neck. They both felt her quick, involuntary shudder.

"Not so you'd notice."

"I'm very observant." He rolled, smoothly, so that his body pressed more intimately into hers as he looked down on her. He was tired. Yes, he was tired and more than a little punchy with jet lag, but he hadn't forgotten he wanted her. Even if he had, the way her body yielded, the way her face looked rosy and soft with sleep, would've jogged his memory. "Why don't I look for myself?" He ran his fingers down to where the sheet lay, neat, prim and arousing, at her breast.

She sucked in her breath, incredibly moved by his lightest touch. She couldn't let it show . . . could she? She couldn't reach out for something that was only an illusion. He wasn't stable. He wasn't real. He was with her now because she was here and no one else was. Why was it becoming so hard to remember that?

His face was close, filling her vision. She saw the little things she'd tried not to notice over the years. The way a thin ring of gray outlined his irises, the straight, almost aristocratic line of his nose that had remained miraculously unbroken through countless fistfights. The soft, sculpted, somehow poetic shape of his mouth. A mouth, she remembered, that was hot and strong and inventive when pressed against hers.

"Michael . . ." The fact that she hesitated, then fumbled before she reached down to take his hand both pleased and unnerved him. She wasn't as cool and self-contained as she'd always appeared. And because she wasn't, he could slip his way under her skin. But he might not slip out again so easily.

Be practical, she told herself. Be realistic. "Michael, we have almost five months more to get through."

"Good point." He needed the warmth. He needed the

woman. Maybe it was time to risk the consequences. He lowered his head and nibbled at her mouth. "Why waste it?"

She let herself enjoy him. For just a moment, she promised herself. For only a moment. He was warm and his hands
were easy. The night had been long and cold and frighten-
ing. No matter how much she hated to admit it, she'd needed
him. Now, with the sun pouring through the tiny square panes
in the windows, falling bright and hard on the bed, she had
him. Close, secure, comforting.

Her lips opened against his.

He'd had no plan when he'd come into her room. He'd
simply been drawn to her; he'd wanted to lie beside her
and talk to her. Passion hadn't guided him. Desire hadn't
pushed him. There'd only been the basic need to be home,
to be home with her. When she'd snuggled against him, hair
tousled, eyes heavy, it had been so natural that the longing
had snuck up on him. He wanted nothing more than to stay
where he was, wrapped around her, slowly heating.

And for her, passion didn't bubble wildly, but easily, like a
brew that had been left to simmer through the day while spices
were added. One sample, then another, and the taste changed,
enriched, deepened. With Michael, there the flavors were only
hinted at, an aroma to draw in and savor. She could have gone
on, and on, hour after hour, until what they made between
them was perfected. She wanted to give in to the need, the beginnings of greed. If she did, everything would change. It was
a change she couldn't predict, couldn't see clearly, could only
anticipate. So she resisted him and herself and what could
happen between them.

"Michael . . ." But she let her fingers linger in his hair for
just a minute more. "This isn't smart."

He kissed her eyes closed. It was something no one had
done before. "It's the smartest thing either of us has done in
years."

She wanted to agree, felt herself on the edge of agreeing. "Michael, things are complicated enough. If we were lovers and things went wrong, how could we manage to go on here together? We've made a commitment to Uncle Jolley."

"The will doesn't have a damn thing to do with you and me in this bed."

How could she have forgotten just how intense he could look when he was bent on something? How was it she'd never noticed how attractive it made him? She'd have to make a stand now or go under. "The will has everything to do with you and me in this house. If we go to bed together and our relationship changes, then we'll have to deal with all the problems and complications that go with it."

"Name some."

"Don't be amusing, Michael."

"Giving you a laugh wasn't my intention." He liked the way she looked against the pillow—hair spread out like wildfire, cheeks a bit flushed, her mouth on the edge of forming a pout. Strange he'd never pictured her this way before. It didn't take any thought to know he'd picture her like this again and again. "I want you, Pandora. There's nothing amusing about it."

No, that wasn't something she could laugh or shrug off, not when the words brushed over her skin and made her muscles limp. He didn't mean it. He couldn't mean it. But she wanted to believe it. If she couldn't laugh it off, she had to throw up a guard and block it. "Becoming lovers is something that takes a lot of thought. If we're going to discuss it—"

"I don't want to discuss it." He pressed his lips against hers until he felt her body soften. "We're not making a corporate merger, Pandora, we're making love."

"That's just it." She fought back an avalanche of longing. Be practical. It was her cardinal rule. "We're business partners.

Worse, we're family business partners, at least for the next few months. If we change that now it could—"

"If," he interrupted. "It could. Do you always need guarantees?"

Her brows drew together as annoyance competed with desire. "It's a matter of common sense to look at all the angles."

"I suppose you have any prospective lover fill out an application form."

Her voice chilled. It was, in a distorted way, close to the truth. "Don't be crude, Michael."

Pushed to the limit, he glared down at her. "I'd rather be crude than have your brand of common sense."

"You've never had any brand of common sense," she tossed back. "Why else would every busty little blonde you've winked at be public knowledge? You don't even have the decency to be discreet."

"So that's it." Shifting, Michael drew her into a sitting position. There was no soft yielding now. She faced him with fire in her eyes. "Don't forget the brunettes and the redheads."

She hadn't. She promised herself she wouldn't. "I don't want to discuss it."

"You brought it up, and we'll finish it. I've gone to bed with women. So put me in irons. I've even enjoyed it."

She tossed her hair behind her shoulder. "I'm sure you have."

"And I haven't had a debate with every one of them beforehand. Some women prefer romance and mutual enjoyment."

"Romance?" Her brows shot up under her tousled hair. "I've always had another word for it."

"You wouldn't recognize romance if it dropped on your

head. Do you consider it discreet to take lovers and pretend you don't? To pledge undying fidelity to one person while you're looking for another? What you want to call discretion, I call hypocrisy. I'm not ashamed of any of the women I've known, in bed or out."

"I'm not interested in what you are or aren't ashamed of. I'm not going to be your next mutual enjoyment. Keep your passion for your dancers and starlets and chorus girls."

"You're as big a snob as the rest of them."

That hit home and had her shoulders stiffening. "That's not true. I've simply no intention of joining a crowd."

"You flatter me, cousin."

"There's another word for that, too."

"Think about this." He gave her a shake, harder than he'd intended. "I've never made love with a woman I didn't care for and respect." Before he cut loose and did more than shake her, he got up and walked to the door while she sat in the middle of the bed clutching sheets and looking furious.

"It appears you give respect easily."

He turned back to study her. "No," he said slowly. "But I don't make people jump through hoops for it."

* * *

A cold war might not be as stimulating as an active battle, but with the right participants, it could be equally destructive. For days Pandora and Michael circled around each other. If one made a sarcastic comment, the other reached into the stockpile and used equal sarcasm. Neither drew out the red flag for full-scale attack, instead they picked and prodded at each other while the servants rolled their eyes and waited for bloodshed.

"Foolishness," Sweeney declared as she rolled out the crust

for two apple pies. "Plain foolishness." She was a sturdy, red-faced woman, as round as Charles was thin. In her pragmatic, no-nonsense way, she'd married and buried two husbands, then made her way in the world by cooking for others. Her kitchen was always neat and tidy, all the while smelling of the sinfully rich food she prepared. "Spoiled children," she told Charles. "That's what they are. Spoiled children need the back of the hand."

"They've over four months to go." Charles sat gloomily at the kitchen table, hunched over a cup of tea. "They'll never make it."

"Hah!" Sweeney slammed the rolling pin onto a fresh ball of dough. "They'll make it. Too stubborn not to. But it's not enough."

"The master wanted them to have the house. As long as they do, we won't lose it."

"What'll we be doing in this big empty house when both of them go back to the city? How often will either of them be visiting with the master gone?" Sweeney turned the crust into a pan and trimmed it expertly. "The master wanted them to have the house, true enough. And he wanted them to have each other. The house needs a family. It's up to us to see it gets one."

"You didn't hear them over breakfast." Charles sipped his tea and watched Sweeney pour a moist apple mixture into the crust.

"That has nothing to do with it. *I've* seen the way they look at each other when they think the other one's not noticing. All they need's a push."

With quick, economic movements, she filled the second crust. "We're going to give 'em one."

Charles stretched out his legs. "We're too old to push young people."

Sweeney gave a quick grunt as she turned. Her hands were thick, and she set them on her hips. "Being old's the whole trick. You've been feeling poorly lately."

"No, to tell you the truth, I've been feeling much better this week."

"You've been feeling poorly," Sweeney repeated, scowling at him. "Now here's our Pandora coming in for lunch. Just follow my lead. Look a little peaked."

Snow had come during the night, big fat flakes that piled on the ground and hung in the pines. As she walked, Pandora kicked it up, pleased with herself. Her work couldn't have been going better. The earrings she'd finally fashioned had been unique, so unique, she'd designed a necklace to complement them. It was chunky and oversize with geometric shapes of copper and gold. Not every woman could wear it, but the one who could wouldn't go unnoticed.

It was, to Pandora, a statement of the strong, disciplined woman. She was just as pleased with the shoulder-brushing earrings she was making with jet and silver beads. They had been painstakingly strung together and when finished would be elegantly flirtatious. Another aspect of woman. If her pace kept steady, she'd have a solid inventory to ship off to the boutique she supplied. In time for the Christmas rush, she reminded herself smugly.

When she opened the kitchen door, she was ravenously hungry and in the best of moods.

". . . if you're feeling better in a day or two," Sweeney said briskly, then turned as if surprised to see Pandora inside. "Oh, time must've got away from me. Lunch already and I'm just finishing up the pies."

"Apple pies?" Grinning, Pandora moved closer. But Sweeney saw with satisfaction that Pandora was already studying Charles. "Any filling left?" she began, and started to dip her fingers into the bowl. Sweeney smacked them smartly.

"You've been working with those hands. Wash them up in the sink, and you'll have your lunch as soon as I can manage it."

Obediently, Pandora turned on a rush of water. Under the noise, she murmured to Sweeney. "Is Charles not feeling well?"

"Bursitis is acting up. Cold weather's a problem. Just being old's a problem in itself." She pushed a hand at the small of her back as though she had a pain. "Guess we're both slowing down a bit. Aches and pains," Sweeney sighed and cast a sidelong look at Pandora. "Just part of being old."

"Nonsense." Concerned, Pandora scrubbed her hands harder. She told herself she should have been keeping a closer eye on Charles. "You just try to do too much."

"With the holidays coming . . ." Sweeney trailed off and made a business out of arranging a top crust. "Well, decorating the house is a lot of work, but it's its own reward. Charles and I'll deal with the boxes in the attic this afternoon."

"Don't be silly." Pandora shut off the water and reached for a towel. "I'll bring the decorations down."

"No, now, missy, there're too many boxes and most of them are too heavy for a little girl like you. That's for us to see to. Isn't that right, Charles?"

Thinking of climbing the attic stairs a half-dozen times, Charles started to sigh. A look from Sweeney stopped him. "Don't worry, Miss McVie, Sweeney and I will see to it."

"You certainly will not." Pandora hung the towel back on the hook. "Michael and I will bring everything down this afternoon, and that's that. Now I'll go tell him to come to lunch."

Sweeney waited until the door swung shut behind Pandora before she grinned.

Upstairs, Pandora knocked twice on Michael's office door, then walked in. He kept on typing. Putting her pride on hold,

Pandora walked over to his desk and folded her arms. "I need to talk to you."

"Come back later. I'm busy."

Abuse rose up in her throat. Remembering Sweeney's tired voice, she swallowed it. "It's important." She ground her teeth on the word, but said it. "Please."

Surprised, Michael stopped typing in midword. "What? Has one of the family been playing games again?"

"No, it's not that. Michael, we have to decorate the house for Christmas."

He stared at her a moment, swore and turned back to his machine. "I've got a twelve-year-old boy kidnapped and being held for a million-dollar ransom. That's important."

"Michael, will you put away fantasyland for a moment? This is real."

"So's this. Just ask my producer."

"Michael!" Before he could stop her, Pandora grabbed the laptop. He was halfway out of his chair to retaliate. "It's Sweeney and Charles."

It stopped him, though he snatched the computer back from her. "What about them?"

"Charles's bursitis is acting up again, and I'm sure Sweeney's not feeling well. She sounded, well, old."

"She is old." But Michael tossed the paper on the desk. "Think we should call in a doctor?"

"No, they'd be furious." She swung around his desk, trying to pretend she wasn't reading part of his script. "I'd rather just keep an eye on them for a few days and make sure they don't overdo. That's where the Christmas decorations come in."

"I figured you'd get to them. Look, if you want to deck the halls, go ahead. I haven't got time to fool with it today."

"Neither do I." She folded her arms in a manner that amused him. "Sweeney and Charles have it in their heads that it has to be done. Unless we want them dragging up and down the attic stairs, we have to take care of it."

"Christmas is three weeks away."

"I know the date." Frustrated, she strode to the window then back. "They're old and they're set on it. You know Uncle Jolley would've had them up the day after Thanksgiving. It's traditional."

"All right, all right." Trapped, Michael rose. "Let's get started."

"Right after lunch." Satisfied she'd gotten her way, Pandora swept out.

Forty-five minutes later, she and Michael were pushing open the attic door. The attic was, in Jolley's tradition, big enough to house a family of five. "Oh, I'd forgotten what a marvelous place this is." Forgetting herself, Pandora grabbed Michael's hand and pulled him in. "Look at this table, isn't it horrible?"

It was. Old and ornate with curlicues and cupids, it had been shoved into a corner to hold other paraphernalia Jolley had discarded. "And the bird cage out of Popsicle sticks. Uncle Jolley said it took him six months to finish it, then he didn't have the heart to put a bird inside."

"Lucky for the bird," Michael muttered, but found himself, as always, drawn to the dusty charm of the place. "Spats," he said, and lifted a pair from a box. "Can't you see him in them?"

"And this hat." Pandora found a huge circular straw hat with a garden of flowers along the brim. "Aunt Katie's. I've always wished I'd met her. My father said she was just as much fun as Uncle Jolley."

Michael watched Pandora tip the brim over her eyes. "If that was her hat, I believe it. How about this?" He found a black derby and tilted it rakishly.

"It's you," Pandora told him with her first easy laugh

in days. "All you need's a high white collar and a walking stick. Look." She pulled him in front of a tall cheval mirror that needed resilvering. Together, they studied themselves.

"An elegant pair," Michael decided, though his sweater bagged over his hips, and she already had dust on her nose. "All you need is one of those slim little skirts that sweep the floor and a lace blouse with padded shoulders."

"And a cameo on a ribbon," she added as she tried to visualize herself. "No, I probably would've worn bloomers and picketed for women's rights."

"The hat still suits you." He turned to adjust it just a bit. "Especially with your hair long and loose. I've always liked it long, though you looked appealingly lost and big-eyed when you had it all chopped short."

"I was fifteen."

"And you'd just come back from the Canary Islands with the longest, brownest legs I'd ever seen in my life. I nearly ate my saucer when you walked into the parlor."

"You were in college and had some cheerleader hanging on your arm."

Michael grinned. "You had better legs."

Pandora pretended little interest. She remembered the visit perfectly, but was surprised, and pleased, that he did. "I'm surprised you noticed or remembered."

"I told you I was observant."

She acknowledged the thrust with a slight nod. There were times when it was best to pad quietly over dangerous ground. "We'd better start digging out the decorations. Sweeney said the boxes were back along the left and clearly marked." Without waiting for agreement, she turned and began to look. "Oh good grief." She stopped again when she saw the stacks of boxes, twenty, perhaps twenty-five of them. Michael stood at her shoulder and stuck his hands in his pockets.

"Think we can hire some teamsters?"

Pandora blew out a breath. "Roll up your sleeves."

On some trips, they could pile two or three boxes apiece and maneuver downstairs. On others, it took both of them to haul one. Somewhere along the way they'd stopped arguing. It was just too much effort.

Grimy and sweaty, they dropped the last boxes in the parlor. Ignoring the dust on her slacks, Pandora collapsed in the nearest chair. "Won't it be great fun hauling them all up again after New Year's?"

"Couldn't we've settled on a plastic Santa?"

"It'll be worth it." Drumming up the energy, she knelt on the floor and opened the first box. "Let's get started."

Once they did, they went at it with a vengeance. Boxes were opened, garland strewed and bulbs tested. They squabbled good-naturedly about what looked best where and the proper way to drape lights at the windows. When the parlor, the main hall and the staircase were finished, Pandora stood at the front door and took a long look.

The garland was white and silver, twisting and twining down the banister. There were bright red bells, lush green ribbon and tiny lights just waiting for evening.

"It looks good," she decided. "Really good. Of course, Sweeney and Charles will want to decorate the servants' quarters and that entire box goes into the dining room, but it's a wonderful start."

"Start?" Michael sat on the stairs. "We're not entering a contest, cousin."

"These things have to be done right. I wonder if my parents will make it home for Christmas. Well . . ." She brushed that off. They always considered wherever they were home. "I'd say we're ready for the tree. Let's go find one."

"You want to drive into town now?"

"Of course not." Pandora was already pulling coats out

of the hall closet. "We'll go right out in the woods and dig one up."

"We?"

"Certainly. I hate it when people cut trees down and then toss them aside after the new year. The woods are loaded with nice little pines. We'll dig one up, then replant it after the holidays."

"How handy are you with a shovel?"

"Don't be a spoilsport." Pandora tossed his coat to him, then pulled on her own. "Besides, it'll be nice to spend some time outside after being in that stuffy attic. We can have some hot buttered rum when we're finished."

"Heavy on the rum."

They stopped at the toolshed for a shovel. Michael picked two and handed one to Pandora. She took it without a blink, then together they walked through the ankle-high snow to the woods. The air had a bite and the scent of pine was somehow stronger in the snow.

"I love it when it's like this." Pandora balanced the shovel on her shoulder and plowed through the woods. "It's so quiet, so—separated. You know, sometimes I think I'd rather live here and visit the city than the other way around."

He'd had the same thought, but was surprised to hear it from her. "I always thought you liked the bright lights and confusion."

"I do. But I like this, too. How about this one?" She paused in front of a spruce. "No, the trunk's too crooked." She walked on. "Besides, I wonder if it wouldn't be more exciting to go into the city for a week now and again and know you had someplace like this to come back to. I seem to work better here. Here's one."

"Too tall. We're better off digging up a young one. Wouldn't it put a crimp in your social life?"

"What?" She studied the tree in question and was forced

to agree with him. "Oh. My social life isn't a priority, my work is. In any case, I could entertain here."

He had a picture of her spending long, cozy weekends with flamboyant, artsy types who read Keats aloud. "You don't have to come all the way to the Catskills to play house."

Pandora merely lifted a brow. "No, I don't. This one looks good." She stopped again and took a long study of a four-and-a-half-foot spruce. Behind her, Michael worked hard to keep his mouth shut. "It's just the right size for the parlor."

"Fine." Michael stuck his shovel into the ground. "Put your back into it."

As he bent over to dig, Pandora scooped up a shovelful of snow and tossed it into his face. "Oh, sorry." She smiled and batted her eyes. "Looks like my aim's off." Digging with more effort, she began to hum.

He let it go, probably because he appreciated the move and wished he'd thought of it himself. Within fifteen minutes, they had the hole dug.

"There now." Only a little out of breath, Pandora leaned on her shovel. "The satisfaction of a job well done."

"We only have to carry it back to the house, set it up and . . . damn, we need something to wrap the roots and dirt in. There was burlap in the shed."

They eyed each other blandly.

"All right," he said after a moment. "I'll go get it, then you have to sweep up the needles and dirt we trail on the floor."

"Deal."

Content, Pandora turned away to watch a cardinal when a snowball slapped into the back of her head. "Sorry." Michael gave her a companionable smile. "Aim must be off." He whistled as he walked back to the shed.

Pandora waited until he was out of sight, then smiling smugly, knelt down to ball snow. By the time he got back, she calculated, she could have an arsenal at hand. He wouldn't have a chance. She took her time, forming and smoothing each ball into a sophisticated weapon. Secure in her advantage, she nearly fell on her face when she heard a sound behind her. She had the ball in her hand and was already set to throw as she whirled. No one was there. Narrowing her eyes, she waited. Hadn't she seen a movement back in the trees? It would be just like him to skirt around and try to sneak up on her. She saw the cardinal fly up again as if startled and heard the quiet plop of snow hitting snow as it was shaken from branches.

"All right, Michael, don't be a coward." She picked up a ball in her left hand, prepared to bombard.

"Guarding your flank?" Michael asked so that this time when she whirled back around, she slid onto her bottom. He grinned at her and dropped the burlap sack in her lap.

"But weren't you . . ." She trailed off and looked behind her again. How could he be here if he was there? "Did you circle around?"

"No, but from the looks of that mound of balls, I should've. Want to play war?"

"It's just a defense system," she began, then looked over her shoulder again. "I thought I heard you. I would've sworn there was someone just beyond the trees there."

"I went straight to the shed and back." He looked beyond her. "You saw something out there?"

"Michael, if you're playing tricks—"

"No." He cut her off and reached down to pull her to her feet. "No tricks. Let's have a look."

She moved her shoulders but didn't remove her hand from his as they walked deeper into the trees. "Maybe I was a bit jumpy."

"Or expecting me to be sneaky?"

"That, too. It was probably just a rabbit."

"A rabbit with big feet," he murmured as he looked down

at the tracks. They were clear enough in the snow, tracks leading to and away from the spot ten yards behind where they'd dug up the tree. "Rabbits don't wear boots."

"So, we still have company. I was beginning to think they'd given the whole business up." She kept her voice light, but felt the uneasiness of anyone who'd been watched. "Maybe it's time we talked to Fitzhugh, Michael."

"Maybe, in the meantime—" The sound of an engine cut him off. He was off in a sprint with Pandora at his heels. After a five-minute dash, they came, clammy and out of breath, to what was hardly more than a logging trail. Tire tracks had churned up the snow and blackened it. "A Jeep, I'd guess." Swearing, Michael stuck his hands in his pockets. If he'd started out right away, he might have caught someone or at least have caught a glimpse of someone.

Pandora let out an annoyed breath. Racing after someone was one thing, being outmaneuvered another. "Whoever it is is only wasting his time."

"I don't like being spied on." He wanted physical contact. Longed for it. Frustrated, he stared at the tracks that led back to the main road. "I'm not playing cat and mouse for the next four months."

"What are we going to do?"

His smile spread as he looked at the tracks. "We'll spread the word through Fitzhugh that we've been bothered by trespassers. Being as there's any number of valuables on the premises, we've decided to haul out one of Jolley's old .30-.30's."

"Michael! They may be a nuisance, but they're still family." Unsure, she studied him. "You wouldn't really shoot at anyone."

"I'd rather shoot at family than strangers," he countered, then shrugged. "They're also fond of their own skin. I can't think of one of them who wouldn't hesitate to play around if they thought they might be picking buckshot out of embarrassing places."

"I don't like it. Guns, even the threat of guns, are trouble."

"Got a better idea?"

"Let's buy a dog. A really big, mean dog."

"Great, then we can let him loose and have him sink his teeth into one of our favorite relatives. They'd like that a lot better than buckshot."

"He doesn't have to be that mean."

"We'll compromise and do both."

"Michael—"

"Let's call Fitzhugh."

"And take his advice?" Pandora demanded.

"Sure . . . if I like it."

Pandora started to object, then laughed. It was all as silly as a plot of one of his shows. "Sounds reasonable," she decided, then tucked her arm through his. "Let's get the tree inside first."

CHAPTER 7

I know it's Christmas Eve, Darla." Michael picked up his coffee cup, found it empty and lifted the pot from his hot plate. Dregs. He bit off a sigh. The trouble with the Folley was that you had to hike a half a mile to the kitchen whenever the pot ran dry. "I know it'll be a great party, but I can't get away."

That wasn't precisely true, Michael mused as he listened to Darla's rambles about a celebration in Manhattan. *Everyone,* according to her estimate, was going to be there. That meant a loud, elbow-to-elbow party with plenty of booze. He could have taken a day and driven into the city to raise a glass or two with friends. He was well ahead of schedule. So far ahead, he could have taken off a week and not felt the strain. The precise truth was, he didn't want to get away.

"I appreciate that . . . you'll just have to tell everyone Merry Christmas for me. No, I like living in the country, Darla. Weird? Yeah, maybe." He had to laugh. Darla was a top-notch dancer and a barrel of laughs, but she didn't believe life went on outside of the island of Manhattan. "New Year's if I can manage it. Okay, babe. Yeah, yeah, *ciao.*"

More than a little relieved, Michael hung up. Darla was a lot of fun, but he wasn't used to being clung to by a woman, especially one he'd only dated casually. The truth was, she was just as attracted to the influence he had with certain casting agents as she was interested in him. He didn't hold it against her. She had ambition and talent, a combination that could work in the tough-edged business of entertaining if a dash of luck was added. After the holidays he'd make a few calls and see what he could do.

From the doorway, Pandora watched as Michael ran a hand along the back of his neck. Darla, she repeated silently. She imagined the women his taste leaned toward had names like Darla, or Robin and Candy. Sleek, smooth, sophisticated and preferably empty-headed.

"Popularity's such a strain, isn't it, darling?"

Michael turned in his chair to give her a long, narrowed look. "Eavesdropping's so rude, isn't it, darling?"

She shrugged but didn't come in. "If you'd wanted privacy, you should've closed your door."

"Around here you have to nail it shut for privacy."

One brow raised, head slightly inclined, Pandora looked as aloof as royalty. "Your phone conversations have absolutely no interest for me. I only came up as a favor to Charles. You've a package downstairs."

"Thanks." He didn't bother to hide amusement at her tone. If he knew Pandora, and he did, she'd listened to every word. "I thought these were your sacred working hours."

"Some of us schedule our work well enough that we can take some time off during the holidays. No, no, let's not bicker," she decided abruptly before he could retaliate. "It is nearly Christmas after all, and we've had three weeks of peace from our familial practical jokers. Truce," Pandora offered with a smile Michael wasn't sure he should trust. "Or a moratorium if you prefer."

"Why?"

"Let's just say I'm a sucker for holly and ivy. Besides, I'm relieved we didn't have to buy a big drooling dog or a supply of buckshot."

"For now." Not completely satisfied, Michael tipped back in his chair. "Fitzhugh's notion of notifying the local police of trespassers and spreading the rumor of an official investigation might be working temporarily. Or maybe our friends and family are just taking a holiday break themselves. Either way I'm not ready to relax."

"You'd rather break someone's nose than solve things peaceably," Pandora began, then waved a hand. "Never mind. I, for one, am going to enjoy the holidays and not give any of our dear family a thought." She paused a moment, toying with her braided chain of gold and amethyst. "I suppose Darla was disappointed."

Michael watched the way the stones caught the thin winter light and made sparks from it. "She'll pull through."

Pandora twisted the chain one way, twisted it back, then let it go. It was the sort of nervous gesture Michael hadn't expected from her. "Michael, you know you don't have to stay. I really will be fine if you want to run into New York for the holiday."

"Rule number six," he reminded her. "We stick together, and you've turned down a half-dozen invitations for the holidays yourself."

"My choice." She reached for the chain again, then dropped her hands. "I don't want you to feel obligated—"

"My choice," he interrupted. "Or have you suddenly decided I'm chivalrous and unselfish?"

"Certainly not," she tossed back, but smiled. "I prefer thinking you're just too lazy to make the trip."

He shook his head, but his lips curved in response. "I'm sure you would."

She hesitated in the doorway until he lifted a brow in question. "Michael, would you become totally obnoxious if I told you I'm glad you're staying?"

He studied her as she stood, looking slim and neat in the doorway, her hair a riotous contrast to the trim sweater and stovepipe pants. "I might."

"Then I won't tell you." Without another word, she slipped out of the doorway and disappeared.

Contrary woman, Michael thought. He was close to being crazy about her. And crazy was the perfect word. She baited him or, he admitted, he baited her at every possible opportunity. He could imagine no two people less inclined to peaceful coexistence, much less harmony. And yet . . . and yet he was close to being crazy about her. Knowing better than to try to go back to work, he rose and followed her downstairs.

He found her in the parlor, rearranging packages under the tree. "How many have you shaken?"

"All of them," she said easily. But she didn't turn because he might have seen how pleased she was he'd come downstairs with her. "I don't want to show any preference. Thing is," she added, poking at an elegantly wrapped box, "I seem to have missed my present from you."

Michael gave her a bland smile. "Who says I got you anything?"

"You would have been terribly rude and insensitive otherwise."

"Yep. In any case, you seem to've done well enough." He crouched down to study the stacks of boxes under the tree. "Who's Boris?" Idly he picked up a small silver box with flowing white ribbon.

"A Russian cellist who defected. He admires my . . . gold links."

"I bet. And Roger?"

"Roger Madison."

His mouth dropped open, but only for a moment. "The Yankee shortstop who batted .304 last year?"

"That's right. You may've noticed the silver band he wears on his right wrist. I made that for him last March. He seems to think it straightened out his bat or something." She lifted the blue-and-gold box and shook it gently. "He tends to be very generous."

"I see." Michael took a comprehensive study of the boxes. "There don't seem to be a great many packages here for you from women."

"Really?" Pandora took a scan herself. "It appears you make up for that with your pile. Chi-Chi?" she asked as she picked up a box with a big pink bow.

"She's a marine biologist," Michael said with his tongue in his cheek.

"Fascinating. And I imagine Magda's a librarian."

"Corporate attorney," he said blandly.

"Hmm. Well, whoever sent this one's obviously shy." She picked up a magnum of champagne with a glittering red ribbon. The tag read "Happy Holidays, Michael," and nothing more.

Michael scanned the label with approval. "Some people don't want to advertise their generosity."

"How about you?" She tilted her head. "After all, it is a magnum. Are you going to share?"

"With whom?"

"I should've known you'd be greedy." She picked up a box with her name on it. "Just for that I'm eating this entire box of imported chocolates myself."

Michael eyed the box. "How do you know they're chocolates?"

She only smiled. "Henri always gives me chocolate."

"Imported?"

"Swiss."

Michael put out a hand. "Share and share alike."

Pandora accepted it. "I'll chill the wine."

* * *

Hours later when there was starlight on the snow and a fire in the hearth, Pandora lit the tree. Like Michael, she didn't miss any of the crowded, frenzied parties in the city. She was where she wanted to be. It had taken Pandora only a matter of weeks to discover she wasn't as attached to the rush of the city as she'd once thought. The Folley was home. Hadn't it always been? No, she no longer thought of going back to Manhattan in the spring. But what would it be like to live in the Folley alone?

Michael wouldn't stay. True, he'd own half of the Folley in a few months, but his life—including his active social life—was in the city. He wouldn't stay, she thought again, and found herself annoyed with her own sense of regret. Why should he stay? she asked herself as she wandered over to poke at the already crackling fire. How could he stay? They couldn't go on living together indefinitely. Sooner or later she'd have to approach him about her decision to remain there. To do so, she'd have to explain herself. It wouldn't be easy.

Still, she was grateful to Jolley for doing something she'd once resented. Boxing her in. She may have been forced into dealing with Michael on a day-to-day level, but in the few months she'd done so, her life had had more energy and interest than in the many months before. It was that, Pandora told herself, that she hated to give up.

She'd dealt with her attraction to him semisuccessfully. The fact was, he was no more her type than she was his. She jammed hard at a log. From all the many reports, Michael preferred a more flamboyant, exotic sort of woman. Actresses, dancers, models. And he preferred them in droves. She, on the other hand, looked for more intellectual men. The men she spent time with could discuss obscure French novelists and appreciate small, esoteric plays. Most of them wouldn't have known if *Logan's Run* was a television show or a restaurant in SoHo.

The fact that she had a sort of primitive desire for Michael was only a tempest in a teapot. Pandora smiled as she replaced the poker. She couldn't deny she enjoyed a tempest now and again.

When a small one erupted behind her, Pandora turned in disbelief. A little white dog with oversize feet scrambled into the room, slid on the Aubusson carpet and rammed smartly into a table. Barking madly, it rolled over twice, righted itself, then dashed at Pandora to leap halfheartedly and loll its tongue. Entertained, Pandora crouched down and was rewarded when the puppy sprang onto her lap and licked her face.

"Where'd you come from?" Laughing, and defending herself as best she could, Pandora found the card attached to the red bow around the puppy's neck. It read:

My name is Bruno. I'm a mean, ugly dog looking for a lady to defend.

"Bruno, huh?" Laughing again, Pandora stroked his unfortunately long ears. "How mean are you?" she asked as he contented himself with licking her chin.

"He especially likes to attack discontented relatives," Michael announced as he wheeled in a tray carrying an ice bucket and champagne. "He's been trained to go after anyone wearing a Brooks Brothers suit."

"We might add Italian loafers."

"That's next."

Moved, incredibly moved, she concentrated on the puppy.
She hadn't the least idea how to thank Michael without making a fool of herself. "He isn't really ugly," she murmured.

"They promised me he would be."

"They?" She buried her face in the puppy's fur a moment.
"Where did you get him?"

"Pound." Watching her, Michael ripped the foil from the
champagne. "When we went into town for supplies last week
and I deserted you in the supermarket."

"And I thought you'd gone off somewhere to buy porno-
graphic magazines."

"My reputation precedes me," he said half to himself. "In
any case, I went to the pound and walked through the ken-
nels. Bruno bit another dog on the—on a sensitive area in
order to get to the bars first. Then he grinned at me with
absolutely no dignity. I knew he was the one."

The cork came out with a bang and champagne sprayed
up and dripped onto the floor. Bruno scrambled out of Pandora's lap and greedily licked it up. "Perhaps his manners
are lacking a bit," Pandora observed. "But his taste is first
class." She rose, but waited until Michael had poured two
glasses. "It was a lovely thing to do, dammit."

He grinned and handed her a glass. "You're welcome."

"It's easier for me when you're rude and intolerable."

"I do the best I can." He touched his glass to hers.

"When you're sweet, it's harder for me to stop myself from
doing something foolish."

He started to lift his glass, then stopped. "Such as?"

"Such as." Pandora set down her champagne, then took
Michael's and set it on the table as well. Watching him, only
him, she put her arms around his neck. Very slowly—unwise

acts done slowly often take on a wisdom of their own—she touched her mouth to his.

It was, as she'd known it would be, warm and waiting. His hands came to her shoulders, holding her without pressure. Perhaps they'd both come to understand that pressure would never hold her. When she softened, when she gave, she gave through her own volition, not through seduction, not through demand. So it was Pandora who moved closer, Pandora who pressed body to body, offering hints of intimacy with no submission.

It wasn't submission he wanted. It wasn't submission he looked for, though it was often given to him. He didn't look for matching strength, but strength that meshed. In Pandora, where he'd never thought to search for it, he found it. Her scent twisted around him, heightening emotions her taste had just begun to stir. Under his hands, her body was firm with the underlying softness women could exploit or be exploited by. He thought she'd do neither, but would simply be. By being alone, she drew him in.

She didn't resist his touch, not when his hands slipped down to her hips or skimmed up again. It seemed he'd done so before, though only in dreams she'd refused to acknowledge. If this was the time for acceptance, she'd accept. If this was the time for pleasure, she'd take it. If she found both with him, she wouldn't refuse. Even questions could come later. Maybe tonight was a night without questions.

She drew back, but only to smile at him. "You know, I don't think of you as a cousin when I'm kissing you."

"Really?" He nipped at her lips. She had an incredibly alluring mouth—full and pouty. "What do you think of me as?"

She cocked a brow. His arms surrounded her, but didn't imprison. Pandora knew she'd have to analyze the difference later. "I haven't figured that out yet."

"Then maybe we should keep working it out." He started to pull her back, but she resisted.

"Since you've broken tradition to give me my Christmas present a few hours early, I'll do the same." Going to the tree, Pandora reached down and found the square, flat box. "Happy Christmas, Michael."

He sat down on the arm of a chair to open it while Pandora picked up her glass of champagne. She sipped, watching a bit nervously for his reaction. It was only a token after all, she told herself, as she played with the stem of her glass. When he ripped off the paper then said nothing, she shrugged. "It's not as inventive as a guard dog."

Michael stared down at the pencil sketch of their uncle without any idea what to say. The frame she'd made herself, he knew. It was silver and busily ornate in a style Jolley would have appreciated. But it was the sketch that held him silent. She'd drawn Jolley as Michael remembered him best, standing, a bit bent forward from the waist as though he were ready to pop off on a new tangent. What thin hair he'd had left was mussed. His cheeks were stretched out in a big, wide-open grin. It had been drawn with love, talent and humor, three qualities Jolley had possessed and admired. When Michael looked up, Pandora was still twisting the stem of the glass in her hands.

Why, she's nervous, he realized. He'd never expected her to be anything but arrogantly confident about her work. About herself. The secrets he was uncovering were just as unnerving to him as they were to her. A man tended to get pulled into a woman who had soft spots in unexpected places. If he was pulled in, how would he work his way out again? But she was waiting, twisting the stem of her glass in her hand.

"Pandora. No one's ever given me anything that's meant more."

The line between her brows smoothed out as her smile bloomed. The ridiculous sense of pleasure was difficult to mask. "Really?"

He held a hand out to her. "Really." He glanced down at the sketch again and smiled. "It looks just like him."

"It looks like I remember him." She let her fingers link with Michael's. Pandora could tell herself it was Jolley who drew them together, and nothing else. She could nearly believe it. "I thought you might remember him that way, too. The frame's a bit gaudy."

"And suitable." He studied it with more care. The silver shone dully, set off with the deep curls and lines she'd etched. It could, he realized, be put in an antique shop and pass for an heirloom. "I didn't know you did this sort of thing."

"Now and again. The boutique carries a few of them."

"Doesn't fit in the same category as bangles and beads," he mused.

"Doesn't it?" Her chin tilted. "I thought about making you a big gold collar with rhinestones just to annoy you."

"It would have."

"Maybe next year then. Or perhaps I'll make one for Bruno." She glanced around. "Where'd he go?"

"He's probably behind the tree gnawing on presents. During his brief stay in the garage, he ate a pair of golf shoes."

"We'll put a stop to that," Pandora declared, and went to find him.

"You know, Pandora, I'd no idea you could draw like this." Michael settled against the back of the chair to study the sketch again. "Why aren't you painting?"

"Why aren't you writing the Great American Novel?"

"Because I enjoy what I'm doing."

"Exactly." Finding no sign of the puppy around the tree, Pandora began to search under the furniture. "Though certainly a number of painters have toyed with jewelry design successfully enough—Dali for one—I feel . . . Michael!"

He set his untouched champagne back down and hurried over to where she knelt by a divan. "What is it?" he demanded, then saw for himself. Eyes closed, breathing fast and heavy, the puppy lay half under the divan. Even as Pandora reached for him, Bruno whimpered and struggled to stand.

"Oh, Michael, he's sick. We should get him to a vet."

"It'll be midnight before we get to town. We won't find a vet at midnight on Christmas Eve." Gently Michael laid a hand on Bruno's belly and heard him moan. "Maybe I can get someone on the phone."

"Do you think it's something he ate?"

"Sweeney's been supervising his feeding like a new mother." On cue Bruno struggled and shuddered and relieved himself of what offended his stomach. Exhausted from the effort, he lay back and dozed fitfully. "Something he drank," Michael murmured.

Pampering and soothing, Pandora stroked the dog. "That little bit of champagne shouldn't have made him ill." Because the dog was already resting easier, she relaxed a bit. "Charles isn't going to be pleased Bruno cast up his accounts on the carpet. Maybe I should—" She broke off as Michael grabbed her arm.

"How much champagne did you drink?"

"Only a sip. Why—" She broke off again to stare. "The champagne. You think something's wrong with it?"

"I think I'm an idiot for not suspecting an anonymous present." He grabbed her by the chin. "Only a sip. You're sure? How do you feel?"

Her skin had gone cold, but she answered calmly enough. "I'm fine. Look at my glass, it's still full." She turned her head to look at it herself. "You—you think it was poisoned?"

"We'll find out."

Logic seeped through, making her shake her head. "But, Michael, the wine was corked. How could it have been tampered with?"

"The first season on *Logan* I used a device like this." He thought back, remembering how he'd tested the theory by adding food coloring to a bottle of Dom Perignon. "The killer poisoned champagne by shooting cyanide through the cork with a hypodermic."

"Fiction," Pandora claimed, and fought a shiver. "That's just fiction."

"Until we find out differently, we're going to treat it as fact. The rest of the bottle's going into New York to Sanfield Labs for testing."

Shaky, Pandora swallowed. "For testing," she said on an unsteady breath. "All right, I suppose we'll both be easier when we're sure. Do you know someone who works there?"

"We own Sanfield." He looked down at the sleeping puppy. "Or we will own it in a matter of months. That's just one of the reasons someone might've sent us some doctored champagne."

"Michael, if it was poisoned . . ." She tried to imagine it and found it nearly impossible. "If it was poisoned," she repeated, "this wouldn't just be a game anymore."

He thought of what might have happened if they hadn't been distracted from the wine. "No, it wouldn't be a game."

"It doesn't make any sense." Uneasy and fighting to calm herself, Pandora rose. "Vandalism I can see, petty annoyances I can understand, but I just can't attribute something like this to one of the family. We're probably overreacting. Bruno's had too much excitement. He could very well have picked up something in the pound."

"I had him sent to the vet for his shots before he was delivered here yesterday." Michael's voice was calm, but his eyes were hot. "He was healthy, Pandora, until he lapped up some spilled champagne."

One look at him told her rationalizing was useless. "All right. The wine should be tested in any case so we can stop speculating. We can't do anything about it until day after tomorrow. In the meantime, I don't want to dwell on it."

"Pulling the blinds down, Pandora?"

"No." She picked up Bruno, who whimpered and burrowed into her breast. "But until it's proven, I don't want to consider that a member of my family tried to kill me. I'll fix him something warm to drink, then I'm going to take him upstairs. I'll keep an eye on him tonight."

"All right." Fighting a combination of frustration and fury, Michael stood by the fire.

* * *

Long after midnight when he couldn't sleep, couldn't work, Michael looked in on her. She'd left a light burning low across the room so that the white spreads and covers took on a rosy hue. Outside snow was falling again in big, festive flakes. Michael could see her, curled in the wide bed, the blankets up to her chin. The fire was nearly out. On the rug in front of it, the puppy snored. She'd put a mohair throw over him and had set a shallow bowl filled with what looked like tea nearby. Michael crouched beside the dog.

"Poor fella," he murmured. As he stroked, Bruno stirred, whimpered, then settled again.

"I think he's better."

Glancing over, Michael saw the light reflected in Pandora's eyes. Her hair was tousled, her skin pale and soft. Her shoulders, gently sloped, rose just above the covers pooled around her. She looked beautiful, desirable, arousing. He told

himself he was mad. Pandora didn't fit into his carefully de-
tailed notion of beauty. Michael looked back at the dog.

"Just needs to sleep it off. You could use another log on
this fire." Needing to keep busy, Michael dug in the wood-
box, then added a log to the coals.

"Thanks. Can't sleep?"

"No."

"Me, either." They sat in silence a moment, Pandora in
the big bed, Michael on the hearth rug. The fire crackled
greedily at the fresh log and flickered light and shadow. At
length, she drew her knees up to her chest. "Michael, I'm
frightened."

It wasn't an easy admission. He knew it cost her to tell
him. He stirred at the fire a moment, then spoke lightly as he
replaced the screen. "We can leave. We can drive into New
York tomorrow and stay there. Forget this whole business
and enjoy the holidays."

She didn't speak for a minute, but she watched him carefully. His face was turned away toward the fire so that she
had to judge his feelings by the way he held himself. "Is that
what you want to do?"

He thought of Jolley, then he thought of Pandora. Every
muscle in his body tightened. "Sure." He tossed it off like
a shrug. "I've got to think about myself." He said it as if to
remind himself it had once been true.

"For someone who earns his living by making up stories,
you're a lousy liar." She waited until he turned to face her.
"You don't want to go back. What you want is to gather all
our relatives together and beat them up."

"Can you see me pounding Aunt Patience?"

"With a few exceptions," Pandora temporized. "But the
last thing you want is to give up."

"All right, that's me." He rose and, hands in pockets,

paced back and forth in front of the fire. He could smell the
woodsmoke mixed with some light scent from one of the
bottles on Pandora's dresser. "What about you? You didn't
want to hassle with this whole business from the beginning.
I talked you into it. I feel responsible."

For the first time in hours she felt her humor return. "I
hate to dent your ego, Michael, but you didn't talk me into
anything. No one does. And I'm completely responsible
for myself. I don't want to quit," she added before he could
speak. "I said I didn't want the money, and that was true. I
also said I didn't need it, and that's not precisely true. Over
and above that, there's pride. I'm frightened, yes, but I don't
want to quit. Oh, stop pacing around and come sit down."
The order was cross and impatient, nearly making him smile.
He came over and sat on the bed.

"Better?"

She gave him a long, steady look that had the hint of a
smile fading. "Yes. Michael, I've been lying here for hours
thinking this thing through. I've realized a few things. You
called me a snob once, and perhaps you were right in a way.
I've never thought much about money. Never allowed myself
to. When Uncle Jolley cut everyone out, I thought of it as a
cross between a joke and a slap on the wrist. I figured they'd
grumble and complain certainly, but that was all." She lifted
her hand palm up. "It was only money, and every one of them
has their own."

"Ever heard of greed or the lust for power?"

"That's just it, I didn't think. How much do I know about
any of those people? They bore or annoy me from time to
time, but I've never thought about them as individuals." Now
she ran the hand through her hair so that the blankets fell to
her waist. "Ginger must be about the same age as I am, and
I can't think of two things we have in common. I'd probably
pass Biff's wife on the street without recognizing her."

"I have a hard time remembering her name," Michael put in, and earned a sigh from Pandora.

"That's my point. We don't really know them. The family, in a group, is a kind of parlor joke. Separately, who are they and what are they capable of? I've just begun to consider it. It's not a joke, Michael."

"No, it's not."

"I want to fight back, but I don't know how."

"The surest way is by staying. And maybe," he added, and took her hand. It was cool and soft. "Add a little psychological warfare."

"Such as?"

"What if we sent each one of our relatives a nice bottle of champagne?"

Her smile came slowly. "A magnum."

"Naturally. It'd be interesting to see what sort of reaction we get."

"It would be a nasty gesture, wouldn't it?"

"Uh-hmm."

"Maybe I haven't given your creative brain enough credit." She fell silent as he wound her hair around his finger. "I suppose we should get some sleep."

"I suppose." But his fingers skimmed down her shoulders. "I'm not very tired."

"We could play canasta."

"We could." But she made no move to stop him when he nudged the thin straps of her chemise from her shoulders. "There's always cribbage."

"That, too."

"Or . . ." It was her decision, they both understood that. "We might finish playing out the hand we started downstairs earlier."

He lifted her hand and pressed his lips to the palm. "Always best to finish what you start before going on. As

I recall, we were . . . here." He lowered his mouth to hers. Slowly, on a sigh, she wound her arms around his neck.

"That seems about right."

Holding fast, they sunk into the bed together.

Perhaps it was because they knew each other well. Perhaps it was because they'd already waited a lifetime, but each moved slowly. Desire, for the moment, was comfortable, easy to satisfy with a touch, a taste. Passion curled inside him then unwound with a sigh. There was inch after inch of her to explore with his fingertips, with his lips. He'd waited too long, wanted too long, to miss any part of what they could give to each other.

She was more generous than he'd imagined, less inhibited, more open. She didn't ask to be coaxed, she didn't pretend to need persuasion. She ran her hands over him with equal curiosity. Her mouth took from him and gave again. When his lips parted from hers, her eyes were on him, clouded with desire, dark with amusement of a shared joke. They were together, Michael thought as he buried his face in her hair. About to become lovers. The joke was on both of them.

Her hands were steady when she pulled his sweatshirt over his head, steady still as she ran them over his chest. Her pulse wasn't. She'd avoided this, refused this. Now she was accepting it though she knew there would be consequences she couldn't anticipate.

The fire crackled steadily. The soft light glowed. Consequences were for more practical times.

Her skin slid over his with each movement. Each movement enticed. With his heartbeat beginning to hammer in his head, he journeyed lower. With openmouthed kisses he learned her body in a way he'd only been able to imagine. Her scent was everywhere, subtle at the curve of her waist, stronger at the gentle underside of her breasts. He drew it in and let it swim in his head.

He felt the instant her lazy enjoyment darkened with power. When her breath caught on a moan, he took her deeper. They reached a point where he no longer knew what they did to each other, only that strength met need and need became desperation.

His skin was damp. She tasted the moistness of it and craved more. So this was passion. This was the trembling, churning hunger men and women longed for. She'd never wanted it. That's what she told herself as her body shuddered. Pleasure and pain mixed, needs and fears tangled. Her mind was as swamped with sensations as her flesh—heat and light, ecstasy and terror. The vulnerability overwhelmed her though her body arched taut and her hands clung. No one had ever brushed back her defenses so effortlessly and taken. Taken and taken.

Breathless and desperate, she dragged his mouth back to hers. They rolled over the bed, rough, racing. Neither had had enough. While she tugged and pulled at his jeans, Michael drove her higher. He'd wanted the madness, for himself and for her. Now he felt the wild strength pouring out of her. No thought here, no logic. He rolled on top of her again, reveling in her frantic breathing.

She curled around him, legs and arms. When he plunged into her, they watched the astonishment on each other's faces. Not like this—it had never been like this. They'd come home. But home, each discovered, wasn't always a peaceful place.

* * *

There was silence, stunned, awkward silence. They lay tangled in the covers as the log Michael had set to fire broke apart and showered sparks against the screen. They knew each other well, too well to speak of what had happened just yet. So they lay in silence as their skin cooled and their pulses leveled. Michael shifted to pull the spread up over them both.

"Merry Christmas," he murmured.

With a sound that was both sigh and laugh, Pandora settled beside him.

CHAPTER 8

They left the Folley in the hard morning light the day after Christmas. Sun glared off snow, melting it at the edges and forming icicles down branches and eaves. It was a postcard with biting wind.

After a short tussle they'd agreed that Pandora would drive into the city and Michael would drive back. He pushed his seat back to the limit and managed to stretch out his legs. She maneuvered carefully down the slushy mountain road that led from the Folley. They didn't speak until she'd reached clear highway.

"What if they don't let us in?"

"Why shouldn't they?" Preferring driving to sitting, Michael shifted in his seat. For the first time he was impatient with the miles of road between the Folley and New York.

"Isn't that like counting your chickens?" Pandora turned the heat down a notch and loosened the buttons of her coat. "We don't own the place yet."

"Just a technicality."

"Always cocky."

"You always look at the negative angles."

"Someone has to."

"Look . . ." He started to toss back something critical, then noticed how tightly she gripped the wheel. All nerves, he mused. Though the scenery was a print by Currier and Ives, it wasn't entirely possible to pretend they were off on a holiday jaunt. He was running on nerves himself, and they didn't all have to do with doctored champagne. How would he have guessed he'd wake up beside her in the cool light of dawn and feel so involved? So responsible. So hungry.

He took a deep breath and watched the scenery for another moment. "Look," he began again in a lighter tone. "We may not own the lab or anything else at the moment, but we're still Jolley's family. Why should a lab technician refuse to do a little analysis?"

"I suppose we'll find out when we get there." She drove another ten miles in silence. "Michael, what difference is an analysis going to make?"

"I have this odd sort of curiosity. I like to know if someone's tried to poison me."

"So we'll know if, and we'll know why. We still won't know who."

"That's the next step." He glanced over. "We can invite them all to the Folley for New Year's and take turns grilling them."

"Now you're making fun of me."

"No, actually, I'd thought of it. I just figure the time's not quite right." He waited a few minutes. In thin leather gloves, her fingers curled and uncurled on the wheel. "Pandora, why don't you tell me what's really bothering you?"

"Nothing is." Everything was. She hadn't been able to think straight for twenty-four hours.

"Nothing?"

"Nothing other than wondering if someone wants to kill me." She tossed it off arrogantly. "Isn't that enough?"

He heard the edge under the sarcasm. "Is that why you hid in your room all day yesterday?"

"I wasn't hiding." She had enough pride to sound brittle. "I was tending to Bruno. And I was tired."

"You hardly ate any of that enormous goose Sweeney slaved over."

"I'm not terribly fond of goose."

"I've had Christmas dinner with you before," he corrected. "You eat like a horse."

"How gallant of you to point it out." For no particular reason, she switched lanes, pumped the gas and passed another car. "Let's just say I wasn't in the mood."

"How did you manage to talk yourself into disliking what happened between us so quickly?" It hurt. He felt the hurt, but it didn't mean he had to let it show. His voice, as hers had been, was cool and hard.

"I haven't. That's absurd." Dislike? She hadn't been able to think of anything else, feel anything else. It scared her to death. "We slept together." She managed to toss it off with a shrug. "I suppose we both knew we would sooner or later."

He'd told himself precisely the same thing. He'd lost count of the number of times. He'd yet to figure out when he'd stopped believing. For himself. "And that's it?"

The question was deadly calm, but she was too preoccupied with her own nerves to notice. "What else?" She had to stop dwelling on a moment of impulse. Didn't she? She couldn't go on letting her common sense be overrun by an attraction that would lead nowhere. Could she? "Michael, there's no use blowing what happened out of proportion."

"Just what is that proportion?"

The car felt stuffy and close. Pandora switched off the heat and concentrated on the road. "We're two adults," she began, but had to swallow twice.

"And?"

"Dammit, Michael, I don't have to spell it out."

"Yes, you do."

"We're two adults," she said again, but with temper replacing nerves. "We have normal adult needs. We slept together and satisfied them."

"How practical."

"I am practical." Abruptly, and very badly, she wanted to weep. "Much too practical to weave fantasies about a man who likes his women in six packs. Too practical," she went on, voice rising, "to picture myself emotionally involved with a man I spent one night with. And too practical to romanticize what was no more than an exchange of normal and basic lust."

"Pull over."

"I will not."

"Pull over to the shoulder, Pandora, or I'll do it for you."

She gritted her teeth and debated calling his bluff. There was just enough traffic on the road to force her hand. With only a slight squeal of tires, Pandora pulled off to the side of the road. Michael turned off the key then grabbed her by the lapels and pulled her half into his seat. Before she could struggle away, he closed his mouth over hers.

Heat, anger, passion. They seemed to twist together into one emotion. He held her there as cars whizzed by, shaking the windows. She infuriated him, she aroused him, she hurt him. In Michael's opinion, it was too much for one man to take from one woman. As abruptly as he'd grabbed her, he released her.

"Make something practical out of that," he challenged.

Breathless, Pandora struggled back into her own seat. In

a furious gesture, she turned the key, gunning the motor.
"Idiot."

"Yeah." He sat back as she pulled back onto the highway.
"We finally agree on something."

* * *

It was a long ride into the city. Longer still when you sat in
a car in tense silence. Once they entered Manhattan, Pandora was forced to follow Michael's directions to the lab.

"How do you know where it is?" she demanded after they
left the car in a parking garage. The sidewalk was mobbed
with people hurrying to exchange what had been brightly
boxed and wrapped the day before. As they walked, Pandora
held her coat closed against the wind.

"I looked the address up in Jolley's files yesterday."
Michael walked the half block hatless, his coat flapping
open, clutching the box with the champagne under one arm.
He wasn't immune to the cold but found it a relief after the
hot tension of the drive. With a brisk gesture to Pandora, he
pushed through revolving doors and entered the lobby of a
steel-and-glass building. "He owned the whole place."

Pandora looked across the marble floor. It sloped upward
and widened into a crowded, bustling area with men and
women carrying briefcases. "This whole place?"

"All seventy-two floors."

It hit her again just how complicated the estate was. How
many companies operated in the building? How many people
worked there? How could she possibly crowd her life with
this kind of responsibility? If she could get her hands on
Uncle Jolley—Pandora broke off, almost amused. How he
must be enjoying this, she thought.

"What am I supposed to do with seventy-two floors in
midtown?"

"There are plenty of people to do it for you." Michael gave their names to the guard at the elevators. With no delay, they were riding to the fortieth floor.

"So there are people to do it for us. Who keeps track of them?"

"Accountants, lawyers, managers. It's a matter of hiring people to look after people you hire."

"That certainly clears that up."

"If you're worried, think about Jolley. Having a fortune didn't seem to keep him from enjoying himself. For the most part, he looked at the whole business as a kind of hobby."

Pandora watched the numbers above the door. "A hobby."

"Everyone should have a hobby."

"Tennis is a hobby," she muttered.

"The trick is to keep the ball moving. Jolley tossed it in our court, Pandora."

She folded her arms. "I'm not ready to be grateful for that."

"Look at it this way then." He put a hand on her shoulder and squeezed lightly. "You don't have to know how to build a car to own one. You just have to drive steady and follow the signs. If Jolley didn't think we could follow the signs, he wouldn't have given us the keys."

It helped to look at it that way. Still it was odd to consider she was riding on an elevator she would own when the six months were up. "Do we know whom to go to?" Pandora glanced at the box Michael held, which contained the bottle of champagne.

"A man named Silas Lockworth seems to be in charge."

"You did your homework."

"Let's hope it pays off."

When the elevator stopped, they walked into the reception area for Sanfield Laboratories. The carpet was pale rose, the walls lacquered in cream. Two huge split-leaf philodendrons flanked the wide glass doors that slid open at their approach. A woman behind a gleaming desk folded her hands and smiled.

"Good morning. May I help you?"

Michael glanced at the computer terminal resting on an extension of her desk. Top of the line. "We'd like to see Mr. Lockworth."

"Mr. Lockworth's in a meeting. If I could have your names, perhaps his assistant can help you."

"I'm Michael Donahue. This is Pandora McVie."

"McVie?"

Pandora saw the receptionist's eyebrows rise. "Yes, Maximillian McVie was our uncle."

Already polite and efficient, the receptionist became gracious. "I'm sure Mr. Lockworth would have greeted you himself if we'd known you were coming. Please have a seat. I'll ring through."

It took under five minutes.

The man who strode out into reception didn't look like Pandora's conception of a technician or scientist. He was six-three, lean as a gymnast with blond hair brushed back from a tanned, lantern-jawed face. He looked, Pandora thought, more like a man who'd be at home on the range than in a lab with test tubes.

"Ms. McVie." He walked with an easy rolling gait, hand outstretched. "Mr. Donahue. I'm Silas Lockworth. Your uncle was a good friend."

"Thank you." Michael accepted the handshake. "I apologize for dropping in unannounced."

"No need for that." Lockworth's smile seemed to mean it. "We never knew when Jolley was going to drop in on us. Let's go back to my office."

He led them down the corridor. Lockworth's office was

the next surprise. It was plush enough, with curvy chairs and clever lithographs, to make you think of a corporate executive. The desk was piled high with enough files and papers to make you think of a harried clerk. It carried the scent from the dozens of leather-bound books on a floor-to-ceiling shelf. Built into one wall was a round aquarium teeming with exotic fish.

"Would you like coffee? I can guarantee it's hot and strong."

"No." Pandora was already twisting her gloves in her hands. "Thank you. We don't want to take too much of your time."

"It's my pleasure," Lockworth assured her. "Jolley certainly spoke often of both of you," Lockworth went on as he gestured to chairs. "There was never a doubt you were his favorites."

"And he was ours," Pandora returned.

"Still you didn't come to pass the time." Lockworth leaned back on his desk. "What can I do for you?"

"We have something we'd like analyzed," Michael began. "Quickly and quietly."

"I see." Silas stopped there, brow raised. Lockworth was a man who picked up impressions of people right away. In Pandora he saw nerves under a sheen of politeness. In Michael he saw violence, not so much buried as thinly coated. He thought he detected a bond between them though they hadn't so much as looked at each other since entering the room.

Lockworth could have refused. His staff was slimmed down during the holidays, and work was backlogged. He was under no obligation to either of them yet. But he never forgot his obligation to Jolley McVie. "We'll try to accommodate you."

In silence, Michael opened the box and drew out the

bottle of champagne. "We need a report on the contents of this bottle. A confidential report. Today."

Lockworth took it and examined the label. His lips curved slightly. "Seventy-two. A good year. Were you thinking of starting a vineyard?"

"We need to know what's in there other than champagne."

Rather than showing surprise, Lockworth leaned back on the desk again. "You've reason to think there is?"

Michael met the look. "We wouldn't be here otherwise."

Lockworth only inclined his head. "All right. I'll run it through the lab myself."

With a quick scowl for Michael's manners, Pandora rose and offered her hand. "We appreciate the trouble, Mr. Lockworth. I'm sure you have a great many other things to do, but the results are important to Michael and me."

"No problem." He decided he'd find out why it was important after he'd analyzed the wine. "There's a coffee shop for the staff. I'll show you where it is. You can wait for me there."

* * *

There was absolutely no reason to be rude." Pandora settled herself at a table and looked at a surprisingly varied menu.

"I wasn't rude."

"Of course you were. Mr. Lockworth was going out of his way to be friendly, and you had a chip on your shoulder. I think I'm going to have the shrimp salad."

"I don't have a chip on my shoulder. I was being cautious. Or maybe you think we should spill everything to a total stranger."

Pandora folded her hands and smiled at the waitress. "I'd like the shrimp salad and coffee."

"Two coffees," Michael muttered. "And the turkey platter."

"I've no intention of spilling, as you put it, everything to a total stranger." Pandora picked up her napkin. "However, if we weren't going to trust Lockworth, we'd have been better off to buy a chemistry set and try to handle it ourselves."

"Drink your coffee," Michael muttered, and picked up his own the moment the waitress served it.

Pandora frowned as she added cream. "How long do you think it'll take?"

"I don't know. I'm not a scientist."

"He didn't look like one, either, did he?"

"Bronc rider." Michael sipped his black coffee and found it as strong as Lockworth had promised.

"What?"

"Looks like a bronc rider. I wonder if Carlson or any of the others have any interest in this building."

Pandora set her coffee down before she tasted it. "I hadn't thought of that."

"As I remember, Jolley turned over Tristar Corporation to Monroe about twenty-five years ago. I remember my parents talking about it."

"Tristar. Which one is that?"

"Plastics. I know he gave little pieces of the pie out here and there. He told me once he wanted to give all his relatives a chance before he crossed them off the list."

After a moment's thought, she shrugged and picked up her coffee again. "Well, if he did give a few shares of Sanfield to one of them, what difference does it make?"

"I don't know how much we should trust Lockworth."

"You'd have felt better if he'd been bald and short with Coke-bottle glasses and a faint German accent."

"Maybe."

"See?" Pandora smiled. "You're just jealous because he

has great shoulders." She fluttered her lashes. "Here's your turkey."

They ate slowly, drank more coffee, then passed more time with pie. After an hour and a half, both of them were restless and edgy. When Lockworth came in, Pandora forgot to be nervous about the results.

"Thank God, here he comes."

After maneuvering around chairs and employees on lunch break, Lockworth set a computer printout on the table and handed the box back to Michael. "I thought you'd want a copy." He took a seat and signaled for coffee. "Though it's technical."

Pandora frowned down at the long chemical terms printed out on the paper. It meant little more than nothing to her, but she doubted trichloroethanol or any of the other multisyllabic words belonged in French champagne. "What does it mean?"

"I wondered that myself." Lockworth reached in his pocket and drew out a pack of cigarettes. Michael looked at it for a moment with longing. "I wondered why anyone would put rose dust in vintage champagne."

"Rose dust?" Michael repeated. "Pesticide. So it was poisoned."

"Technically, yes. Though there wasn't enough in the wine to do any more than make you miserably ill for a day or two. I take it neither one of you had any?"

"No." Pandora looked up from the report. "My puppy did," she explained. "When we opened the bottle, some spilled and he lapped it up. Before we'd gotten around to drinking it, he was ill."

"Luckily for you, though I find it curious that you'd jumped to the conclusion that the champagne had been poisoned because a puppy was sick."

"Luckily for us, we did." Michael folded the report and slipped it into his pocket.

"You'll have to pardon my cousin," Pandora said. "He has no manners. We appreciate you taking time out to do this for us, Mr. Lockworth. I'm afraid it isn't possible to fully explain ourselves at this point, but I can tell you that we had good reason to suspect the wine."

Lockworth nodded. As a scientist he knew how to theorize. "If you find you need a more comprehensive report, let me know. Jolley was an important person in my life. We'll call it a favor to him."

As he rose, Michael stood with him. "I'll apologize for myself this time." He held out a hand.

"I'd be a bit edgy myself if someone gave me pesticide disguised as Moët et Chandon. Let me know if I can do anything else."

"Well," Pandora began when they were alone. "What next?"

"A little trip to the liquor store. We've some presents to buy."

They sent, first-class, a bottle of the same to each of Jolley's erstwhile heirs. Michael signed the cards simply, "One good turn deserves another." After it was done and they walked outside in the frigid wind, Pandora huffed and pulled on her gloves.

"An expensive gesture."

"Look at it as an investment," Michael suggested.

It wasn't the money, she thought, but the sudden futility she felt. "What good will it do really?"

"Several bottles'll be wondered over, then appreciated. But one," Michael said with relish. "One makes a statement, even a threat."

"An empty threat," Pandora returned. "It's not as if we'll be there when everyone gets one to gauge reactions."

"You're thinking like an amateur."

Michael was halfway across the street when Pandora grabbed his arm. "Just what does that mean?"

"When an amateur plays a practical joke, he thinks he has to be in on the kill."

Ignoring the people who brushed by them, Pandora held her ground. "Since when is pesticide poisoning a practical joke?"

"Revenge follows the same principle."

"Oh, I see. And you're an expert."

The light changed. Cars started for them, horns blaring. Gritting his teeth, Michael grabbed her arm and pulled her to the curb. "Maybe I am. It's enough for me to know someone's going to look at the bottle and be very nervous. Someone's going to look at it and know we intend to give as good as we get. Your trouble is you don't like to let your emotions loose long enough to appreciate revenge."

"Leave my emotions alone."

"That's the plan," he said evenly, and started walking again.

In three strides she'd caught up with him. Her face was pink from the wind, the anger in her voice came out in thin wisps. "You're not annoyed with Lockworth or about the champagne or over differing views on revenge. You're mad because I defined our relationship in practical terms."

He stared at her as her phrasing worked on both his temper and his humor. "Okay," he declared, turning to walk on. Patience straining, he turned back when Pandora grabbed his arm. "You want to hash this out right here?"

"I won't let you make me feel inadequate just because I broke things off before you had a chance to."

"Before I had a chance to?" He took her by the coat. With the added height from the heels on her boots, she looked straight into his eyes. Another time, another place, he might have considered her magnificent. "I barely had the chance to recover from what happened before you were shoving me out. I wanted you. Dammit, I still want you. God knows why."

"Well, I want you, too, and I don't like it, either."

"Looks like that puts us in the same fix, doesn't it?"

"So what're we going to do about it?"

He looked at her and saw the anger. But he looked closely enough to see confusion, as well. One of them had to make the first move. He decided it was going to be him. Taking her hand, he dragged her across the street.

"Where are we going?"

"The Plaza."

"The Plaza Hotel? Why?"

"We're going to get a room, put the chain on the door and make love for the next twenty-four hours. After that, we'll decide how we want to handle it."

There were times, Pandora decided, when it was best to go along for the ride. "We don't have any luggage."

"Yeah. My reputation's about to be shattered."

She made a sound that might have been a laugh. When they walked into the elegant lobby, the heat warmed her skin and stirred up her nerves. It was all impulse, she told herself. She knew better than to make any important decision on impulse. He could change everything. That was something she hadn't wanted to admit but had known for years. When she started to draw away, his hand locked on her arm.

"Coward," he murmured. He couldn't have said anything more perfectly designed to make her march forward.

"Good afternoon." Michael smiled at the desk clerk. Pandora wondered briefly if the smile would have been so charming if the clerk had been a man. "Checking in."

"You have a reservation?"

"Donahue. Michael Donahue."

The clerk punched some buttons and stared at her computer screen. "I'm afraid I don't show anything under Donahue for the twenty-sixth."

"Katie," Michael said on a breath of impatience. He sent Pandora a long suffering look. "I should never have trusted her to handle this."

Catching the drift, Pandora patted his hand. "You're going to have to let her go, Michael. I know she's worked for your family for forty years, but when a person gets into their seventies . . ." She trailed off and let Michael take the ball.

"We'll decide when we get home." He turned back to the desk clerk. "Apparently there's been a mix-up between my secretary and the hotel. We'll only be in town overnight. Is anything available?"

The clerk went back to her buttons. Most people in her experience raised the roof when there was a mix-up in reservations. Michael's quiet request touched her sympathies. "You understand there's a problem because of the holiday." She punched more buttons, wanting to help. "We do have a suite available."

"Fine." Michael took the registration form and filled it out. With the key in his hand, he sent the clerk another smile. "I appreciate the trouble." Noting the bellhop hovering at his elbow, he handed him a bill. "We'll handle it, thanks."

The clerk looked at the twenty in his palm and the lack of luggage. "Yes, sir!"

"He thinks we're having an illicit affair," Pandora murmured as they stepped onto the elevator.

"We are." Before the doors had closed again, Michael grabbed her to him and locked her in a kiss that lasted twelve floors. "We don't know each other," he told her as they stepped into the hallway. "We've just met. We don't have mutual childhood memories or share the same family." He put the key in the lock. "We don't give a damn what the other does for a living nor do we have any long-standing opinions about each other."

"Is that supposed to simplify things?"

Michael drew her inside. "Let's find out."

He didn't give her a chance to wonder, a chance to debate. The moment the door was shut behind them, he had her in his arms. He took questions away. He took choice away. For once, she wanted him to. In a fury of passions, of hungers, of cravings, they came together. Each fought to draw more, still more out of the other, to touch faster, to possess more quickly. They forgot what they knew, what they thought and reveled in what they felt.

Coats, still chill from the wind, were pushed to the floor. Sweaters and shirts followed. Hardly more than a foot inside the door, they slid to the carpet.

"Damn winter," Michael muttered as he fought with her boots.

Laughing, Pandora struggled with his, then moaned when he pressed his lips to her breast.

It was a race, part warring, part loving. Neither gave the other respite. When their clothes were shed, they sprinted ahead, hands reaching, lips arousing. There was none of the dreamy déjà vu they'd experienced the first time. This was new. The fingers tracing her skin had never been felt before. The lips, hot and searing, had never been tasted. Fresh, erotically fresh, their mouths met and clung.

Her heart had never beat so fast. She was sure of it. Her body had never ached and pulsed so desperately. She'd never wanted it to. Now she wanted more, everything. Him. She rolled so that she could press quick, hungry kisses over his face, his neck, his chest. Everywhere.

His mind was teeming with her, with every part of her

that he could touch or taste or smell. She was wild in a way he'd never imagined. She was demanding in a way any man would desire. His body seemed to fascinate her, every curve, every angle. She exploited it until he was half mad, then he groped for her.

She'd never known a man could give so much. Racked with sensations, she arched under him. Hot and ready, she offered. But he was far from through. The taste of her thighs was subtle, luring him toward the heat. He found her, drove her and kept her helplessly trapped in passion. Helplessly. The sensation shivered over her. She'd never known what it had meant to be truly vulnerable to another. He could have taken anything from her then, asked anything and she couldn't have refused. But he didn't ask, he gave.

She crested wave after wave. Between heights and depths she pinwheeled, delighting in the spin. On the rug with the afternoon light streaming through the windows, she was locked in blinding darkness without any wish to see. *Make me feel,* her mind seemed to shout. More. Again. Still.

And he was inside her, joined, melded. She found there was more. Impossibly more.

* * *

They stayed where they were, sprawled on scattered clothes. Gradually Pandora found her mind swimming back to reality. She could see the pastel walls, the sunlight. She could smell the body heat that was a mix of hers and his. She could feel Michael's hair brushing over her cheek, the beat of his heart, still fast, against her breast.

It happened so fast, she thought. Or had it taken hours? All she was certain of was that she'd never experienced anything like it. Never permitted herself to, she amended.

Strange things could happen to a woman who lifted the lid from her passion. Other things could sneak in before the top closed again. Things like affection, understanding. Even love.

She caught herself stroking Michael's hair and let her hand fall to the carpet. She couldn't let love in, not even briefly. Love took as well as gave. That she'd always known. And it didn't always give and take in equal shares. Michael wasn't a man a woman could love practically, and certainly not wisely. That she understood. He wouldn't follow the rules.

She'd be his lover, but she wouldn't love him. Though there would be no pretending they could live with each other for the next three months platonically, she wouldn't risk her heart. For an instant Pandora thought she felt it break, just a little. Foolishness, she told herself. Her heart was strong and unimpaired. What she and Michael had together was a very basic, very uncomplicated arrangement. Arrangement, she thought, sounded so much more practical than romance.

But her sigh was quiet, and a little wistful.

"Figure it all out?" He shifted a little as he spoke, just enough so that he could brush his lips down her throat.

"What do you mean?"

"Have you figured out the guidelines for our relationship?" Lifting his head, he looked down at her. He wasn't smiling, but Pandora thought he was amused.

"I don't know what you're talking about."

"I can almost hear the wheels turning. Pandora, I can see just what's going on in your head."

Annoyed that he probably could, she lifted a brow. "I thought we'd just met."

"I'm psychic. You're thinking. . . ." He trailed off to nibble at her lips. "That there should be a way to keep our . . . relationship on a practical level. You're wondering how you'll keep an emotional distance when we're sleeping together. You've decided that there'll be absolutely no romantic overtones to any arrangement between us."

"All right." He made her feel foolish. Then he ran a hand over her hip and made her tremble. "Since you're so smart, you'll see that I've only been using common sense."

"I like it better when your skin gets hot, and you haven't any sense at all. But—" he kissed her before she could answer "—we can't stay in bed all the time. I don't believe in practical affairs, Pandora. I don't believe in emotional distance between lovers."

"You've had a great deal of experience there."

"That's right." He sat up, drawing her with him. "And I'll tell you this. You can wall up your emotions all you want. You can call whatever we have here by any practical term you can dream up. You can turn up your nose at candlelight dinners and quiet music. It's not going to make any difference." He gathered her hair in his hand and pulled her head back. "I'm going to get to you, cousin. I'm going to get to you until you can't think of anything, anyone but me. If you wake up in the middle of the night and I'm not there, you'll wish I were. And when I touch you, any time I touch you, you're going to want me."

She had to fight the shudder. She knew, as well as she'd ever known anything, that he was right. And she knew, perhaps they both did, that she'd fight it right down to the end. "You're arrogant, egocentric and simpleminded."

"True enough. And you're stubborn, willful and perverse. The only thing we can be sure of at this point is that one of us is going to win."

Sitting on the pile of discarded clothes, they studied each other. "Another game?" Pandora murmured.

"Maybe. Maybe it's the only game." With that, he stood and lifted her into his arms.

"Michael, I don't need to be carried."

"Yes, you do."

He walked across the suite toward the bedroom. Pandora started to struggle, then subsided. Maybe just this once, she decided, and relaxed in his arms.

CHAPTER 9

January was a month of freezing wind, pelting snow and gray skies. Each day was as bitterly cold as the last, with tomorrow waiting frigidly in the wings. It was a month of frozen pipes, burst pipes, overworked furnaces and stalled engines. Pandora loved it. The frost built up on the windows of her shop, and the inside temperature always remained cool even with the heaters turned up. She worked until her fingers were numb and enjoyed every moment.

Throughout the month, the road to the Folley was often inaccessible. Pandora didn't mind not being able to get out. It meant no one could get in. The pantry and freezer were stocked, and there was over a cord of wood stacked beside the kitchen door. The way she looked at it, they had everything they needed. The days were short and productive, the nights long and relaxing. Since the incident of the champagne, it had been a quiet, uneventful winter.

Uneventful, Pandora mused, wasn't precisely the right term. With quick, careful strokes, she filed the edges of a thick copper bracelet. It certainly wasn't as though nothing had happened. There'd been no trouble from outside sources, but . . . Trouble, as she'd always known, was definitely one of Michael Donahue's greatest talents.

Just what was he trying to pull by leaving a bunch of violets on her pillow? She was certain a magic wand would have been needed to produce the little purple flowers in January. When she'd questioned him about them, he'd simply smiled and told her violets didn't have thorns. What kind of an answer was that? Pandora wondered, and examined the clasp of the bracelet through a magnifying glass. She was satisfied with the way she'd designed it to blend with the design.

Then, there'd been the time she'd come out of the bath to find the bedroom lit with a dozen candles. When she'd asked if there'd been a power failure, Michael had just laughed and pulled her into bed.

He did things like reaching for her hand at dinner and whispering in her ear just before dawn. Once he'd joined her in the shower uninvited and silenced her protests by washing every inch of her body himself. She'd been right. Michael Donahue didn't follow the rules. He'd been right. He was getting to her.

Pandora removed the bracelet from the vise, then absently began to polish it. She'd made a half a dozen others in the last two weeks. Big chunky bracelets, some had gaudy stones, some had ornate engraving. They suited her mood—daring, opinionated and a bit silly. She'd learned to trust her instincts, and her instincts told her they'd sell faster than she could possibly make them—and be copied just as quickly.

She didn't mind the imitations. After all, there was only one of each type that was truly a Pandora McVie. Copies would be recognized as copies because they lacked that something special, that individuality of the genuine.

Pleased, she turned the bracelet over in her hand. No one would mistake any of her work for an imitation. She might often use glass instead of precious or semiprecious stones because glass expressed her mood at the time. But each piece she created carried her mark, her opinion and her honesty. She never gave a thought to the price of a piece when she crafted it or its market value. She created what she needed to create first, then after it was done, her practical side calculated the profit margin. Her art varied from piece to piece, but it never lied.

Looking down at the bracelet, Pandora sighed. No, her art never lied, but did she? Could she be certain her emotions were as genuine as the jewelry she made? A feeling could be imitated. An emotion could be fraudulent. How many times in the past few weeks had she pretended? Not pretended to feel, Pandora thought, but pretended not to feel. She was a woman who'd always prided herself on her honesty. Truth and independence went hand in hand with Pandora's set of values. But she'd lied—over and over again—to herself, the worst form of deception.

It was time to stop, Pandora told herself. Time to face the truth of her feelings if only in the privacy of her own heart and mind.

How long had she been in love with Michael? She had to stand and move around the shop as the question formed in her mind. Weeks? Months? Years? It wasn't something she could answer because she would never be sure. But she was certain of the emotion. She loved. Pandora understood it because she loved only a few people, and when she did, she loved boundlessly. Perhaps that was the biggest problem. Wasn't it a sort of suicide to love Michael boundlessly?

Better to face it, she told herself. No problem resolved itself without being faced first and examined second. However much a fool it made her, she loved Michael. Pandora rubbed at the steam on the windows and looked out at the snow. Strange, she'd really believed once she accepted it she'd feel better. She didn't.

What options did she have? She could tell him. And have him gloat, Pandora thought with a scowl. He would, too, before he trotted off to his next conquest. *She* certainly wasn't fool enough to think he'd be interested in a long-term relationship. Of course, she wasn't interested in one either, Pandora told herself as she began to noisily pack her tools.

Another option was to cut and run. What the relatives hadn't been able to accomplish with their malice and mischief, her own heart would succeed in doing. She could get in the car, drive to the airport and fly to anywhere. Escape was the honest word. Then, she'd not only be a coward, she'd be a traitor. No, she wouldn't let Uncle Jolley down; she wouldn't run. That left her, as Pandora saw it, with one option.

She'd go on as she was. She'd stay with Michael, sleep with Michael, share with Michael—share with him everything but what was in her heart. She'd take the two months they had left together and prepare herself to walk away with no regrets.

He'd gotten to her, Pandora admitted. Gotten to her in places no other man had touched. She loved him for it. She hated him for it. With her mood as turbulent as her thoughts, she locked the shop and stomped across the lawn.

"Here she comes now." With a new plan ready to spring, Sweeney turned away from the kitchen window and signaled to Charles.

"It's never going to work."

"Of course it is. We're going to push those children together for their own good. Any two people who spat as much as they do should be married."

"We're interfering where it's not our place."

"What malarkey!" Sweeney took her seat at the kitchen table. "Whose place is it to interfere if not ours, I'd like to know? Who'll be knocking around this big empty house if they go back to the city if not us? Now pick up that cloth and fan me. Stoop over a bit and look feeble."

"I am feeble," Charles muttered, but picked up the cloth.

When Pandora walked into the kitchen, she saw Sweeney sprawled back in a chair, eyes closed, with Charles standing over her waving a dishcloth at her face.

"God, what's wrong? Charles, did she faint?" Before he could answer, Pandora had dashed across the room. "Call Michael," she ordered. "Call Michael quickly." She brushed Charles away and crouched. "Sweeney, it's Pandora. Are you in pain?"

Barely suppressing a sigh of satisfaction, Sweeney let her eyes flutter open and hoped she looked pale. "Oh, missy, don't you worry now. Just one of my spells is all. Now and then my heart starts to flutter so that I feel it's coming right out of my head."

"I'm going to call the doctor." Pandora had taken only one step when her hand was caught in a surprisingly strong grip.

"No need for that." Sweeney made her voice thin and weary. "Saw him just a few months past and he told me I'd have to expect one of these now and again."

"I don't believe that," Pandora said fiercely. "You're just plain working too hard, and it's going to stop."

A little trickle of guilt worked its way in as Sweeney saw the concern. "Now, now, don't fret."

"What is it?" Michael swung through the kitchen door. "Sweeney?" He knelt down beside her and took her other hand.

"Now look at all this commotion." Mentally she leaped up and kicked her heels. "It's nothing but one of my little spells. The doctor said I'd have to watch for them. Just a nuisance, that's all." She looked hard at Charles when he came in. Eventually she looked hard enough so that he remembered his cue.

"And you know what he said."

"Now, Charles—"

"You're to have two or three days of bed rest."

Pleased that he'd remembered his lines, Sweeney pretended to huff. "Pack of nonsense. I'll be right as rain in a few minutes. I've dinner to cook."

"You won't be cooking anything." In a way Sweeney considered properly masterful, Michael picked her up. "Into bed with you."

"Just who'll take care of things?" Sweeney demanded. "I'll not have Charles spreading his germs around my kitchen."

Michael was nearly out of the room with Sweeney before Charles remembered the next step. He coughed into his hand, looked apologetic and coughed again.

"Listen to that!" Pleased, Sweeney let her head rest against Michael's shoulder. "I won't go to bed and let him infect my kitchen."

"How long have you had that cough?" Pandora demanded. When Charles began to mutter, she stood up. "That's enough. Both of you into bed. Michael and I will take care of everything." Taking Charles's arm, she began to lead him into the servants' wing. "Into bed and no nonsense. I'll make both of you some tea. Michael, see that Charles gets settled, I'll look after Sweeney."

Within a half hour, Sweeney had them both where she wanted them. Together.

"Well, they're all settled in and there's no fever." Satisfied, Pandora poured herself a cup of tea. "I suppose all they need is a few days' rest and some pampering. Tea?"

He made a face at the idea and switched on the coffee. "Since the days of house calls are over, I'd think they'd be better off here in bed than being dragged into town. We can take turns keeping an eye on them."

"Mmm-hmm." Pandora opened the refrigerator and studied. "What about meals? Can you cook?"

"Sure." Michael rattled cups in the cupboard. "Badly, but I can cook. Meat loaf's my specialty." When this was met with no enthusiasm, he turned his head. "Do you?"

"Cook?" Pandora lifted a plastic lid hopefully. "I can broil a steak and scramble eggs. Anything else is chancy."

"Life's nothing without a risk." Michael joined her in her rummage through the refrigerator. "Here's almost half an apple cobbler."

"That's hardly a meal."

"It'll do for me." He took it out and went for a spoon. Pandora watched as he sat down at the table and dug in. "Want some?"

She started to refuse on principle, then decided not to cut off her nose. Going to the cupboard, she found a bowl. "What about the bedridden?" she asked as she scooped out cobbler.

"Soup," Michael said between bites. "Nothing better than hot soup. Though I'd let them rest awhile first."

With a nod of agreement, she sat across from him. "Michael . . ." She trailed off as she played with her cobbler. The steam from her tea rose up between them. She'd been thinking about how to broach the subject for days. It seemed the time had come. "I've been thinking. In two months, the will should be final. When Fitzhugh wrote us last week, he said Uncle Carlson's lawyers were advising him to drop the probate."

"So?"

"The house, along with everything else, will be half yours, half mine."

"That's right."

She took a bite of cobbler, then set down her spoon. "What're you smiling at?"

"You're nice to look at. I find it relaxing to sit here alone in the kitchen, in the quiet, and look at you."

It was that sort of thing, just that sort of thing, that left her light-headed and foolish. She stared at him a moment, then dropped her gaze to her bowl. "I wish you wouldn't say things like that."

"No, you don't. So you've been thinking," he prompted.

"Yes." She gave herself a moment, carefully spooning out another bite of cobbler. "We'll have the house between us, but we won't be living here together any longer. Sweeney and Charles will be here alone. I've worried about that for a while. Now, after this, I'm more concerned than ever. They can't stay here alone."

"No, I think you're right. Ideas?"

"I mentioned before that I was considering moving here on a semipermanent basis." She found she had no appetite after all and switched back to her tea. "I think I'm going to make it permanent all around."

He heard a trace of nervousness in her voice. "Because of Charles and Sweeney?"

"Only partly." She drank more tea, set the cup down and toyed with her cobbler again. She wasn't accustomed to discussing her decisions with anyone. Though she found it difficult, Pandora had already resolved that she had an obligation to do so. More, she'd realized she needed to talk to him, to be, as she couldn't be on other levels, honest. "I always felt the Folley was home, but I didn't realize just how much of a home. I need it, for myself. You see, I never had one." She lifted her gaze and met his. "Only here."

To say her words surprised him was to say too little. All his life he'd seen her as the pampered pet, the golden girl with every advantage. "But your parents—"

"Are wonderful," Pandora said quickly. "I adore them. There's nothing about them I'd change. But . . ." How could she explain? How could she not? "We never had a kitchen like this—a place you could come back to day after day and know it'd be the same. Even if you changed the wallpaper and the paint, it would be the same. It sounds silly." She shifted restlessly. "You wouldn't understand."

"Maybe I would." He caught her hand before she could rise. "Maybe I'd like to."

"I want a home," she said simply. "The Folley's been that to me. I want to stay here after the term's up."

He kept her hand in his, palm to palm. "Why are you telling me this, Pandora?"

Reasons. Too many reasons. She chose the only one she could give him safely. "In two months, the house belongs to you as much as to me. According to the terms of the will—"

He swore and released her hand. Rising, he stuck his hands in his back pockets and strode to the window. He'd thought for a moment, just for a moment, she'd been ready to give him more. By God, he'd waited long enough for only a few drops more. There'd been something in her voice, something soft and giving. Perhaps he'd just imagined it because he'd wanted to hear it. Terms of the will, he thought. It was so like her to see nothing else.

"What do you want, my permission?"

Disturbed, Pandora stayed at the table. "I suppose I wanted you to understand and agree."

"Fine."

"You needn't be so curt about it. After all, you haven't any plans to use the house on a regular basis."

"I haven't made any plans," he murmured. "Perhaps it's time I did."

"I didn't mean to annoy you."

He turned slowly, then just as slowly smiled. "No, I'm sure you didn't. There's never any doubt when you annoy me intentionally."

There was something wrong here, something she couldn't quite pinpoint. So she groped. "Would you mind so much if I were to live here?"

It surprised him when she rose to come to him, offering a hand. She didn't make such gestures often or casually. "No, why should it?"

"It would be half yours."

"We could draw a line down the middle."

"That might be awkward. I could buy you out."

"No."

He said it so fiercely, her brows shot up. "It was only an offer."

"Forget it." He turned to look for soup.

Pandora stood back a moment, watching his back, the tension in the muscles. "Michael . . ." With a sigh, she wrapped her arms around his waist. She felt him stiffen, but didn't realize it was from surprise. "I seem to be saying all the wrong things. Maybe I have an easier time when we snap at each other than when I try to be considerate."

"Maybe we both do." He turned to frame her face with his hands. For a moment they looked like friends, like lovers. "Pandora. . . ." Could he tell her he found it impossible to think about leaving her or her leaving him? Would she understand if he told her he wanted to go on living with her, being with her? How could she possibly take in the fact that he'd been in love with her for years when he was just becoming able to accept it himself? Instead he kissed her forehead. "Let's make soup."

*   *   *

They couldn't work together without friction, but they discovered over the next few days that they could work together. They cooked meals, washed up, dusted furniture while the servants stayed in bed or sat, bundled up, on sofas drinking tea. True, there were times when Sweeney itched to get up and be about her business, or when Charles suffered pangs of conscience, but they were convinced they were doing their duty. Both servants felt justified when they heard laughter drift through the house.

Michael wasn't sure there had been another time in his life when he'd been so content. He was, in essence, playing house, something he'd never had the time or inclination for. He would write for hours, closed off in his office, wrapped up in plots and characters and what-ifs. Then he could break away and reality was the scent of cooking or furniture polish. He had a home, a woman, and was determined to keep them.

Late in the afternoon, he always laid a fire in the parlor. After dinner they had coffee there, sometimes quietly, sometimes during a hard-fought game of rummy. It seemed ordinary, Michael admitted. It was ordinary, unless you added Pandora. He was just setting fire to the kindling when Bruno raced into the room and upset a table. Knickknacks went flying.

"We're going to have to send you to charm school," Michael declared as he rose to deal with the rubble. Though it had been just over a month, Bruno had nearly doubled in size already. He was, without a doubt, going to grow into his paws. After righting the table, he saw the dog wiggling its way under a sofa. "What've you got there?"

Besides being large, Bruno had already earned a reputation as a clever thief. Just the day before, they'd lost a slab of pork chops. "All right, you devil, if that's tonight's chicken, you're going into solitary confinement in the garage." Getting down on all fours, Michael looked under the couch. It wasn't chicken the dog was gnawing noisily on, but Michael's shoe.

"Damn!" Michael made a grab but the dog backed out of reach and kept on chewing. "That shoe's worth five times what you are, you overgrown mutt. Give it here." Flattening, Michael scooted halfway under the sofa. Bruno merely dragged the shoe away again, enjoying the game.

"Oh, how sweet." Pandora walked into the parlor and eyed Michael from the waist down. He did, she decided, indeed have some redeeming qualities. "Are you playing with the dog, Michael, or dusting under the sofa?"

"I'm going to make a rug out of him."

"Dear, dear, we sound a little cross this evening. Bruno, here, baby." Carrying the shoe like a trophy, Bruno squirmed out from under the couch and pranced over to her. "Is this what you were after?" Pandora held up the shoe while petting Bruno with her other hand. "How clever of you to teach Bruno to fetch."

Michael pulled himself up, then yanked the shoe out of her hand. It was unfortunately wet and covered with teeth marks. "That's the second shoe he's ruined. And he didn't even have the courtesy to take both from one pair."

She looked down at what had been creamy Italian leather. "You never wear anything but tennis shoes or boots anyway."

Michael slapped the shoe against his palm. Bruno, tongue lolling, grinned up at him. "Obedience school."

"Oh, Michael, we can't send our child away." She patted his cheek. "It's just a phase."

"This phase has cost me two pairs of shoes, my dinner and we never did find that sweater he dragged off."

"You shouldn't drop your clothes on the floor," Pandora said easily. "And that sweater was already ratty. I'm sure Bruno thought it was a rag."

"He never chews up anything of yours."

Pandora smiled. "No, he doesn't, does he?"

Michael gave her a long look. "Just what're you so happy about?"

"I had a phone call this afternoon."

Michael saw the excitement in her eyes and decided the issue of the shoe could wait. "And?"

"From Jacob Morison."

"The producer?"

"*The* producer," Pandora repeated. She'd promised herself she wouldn't overreact, but the excitement threatened to burst inside her. "He's going to be filming a new movie. Jessica Wainwright's starring."

Jessica Wainwright, Michael mused. Grande dame of the theater and the screen. Eccentric and brilliant, her career had spanned two generations. "She's retired. Wainwright hasn't made a film in five years."

"She's making this one. Billy Mitchell's directing."

Michael tilted his head in consideration as he studied Pandora's face. It made him think of the cat and the canary. "Sounds like they're pulling out all the stops."

"She plays a half-mad reclusive countess who's dragged back to reality by a visit from her granddaughter. Cass Barkley's on the point of signing for the part of the granddaughter."

"Oscar material. Now, are you going to tell me why Morison called you?"

"Wainwright's an admirer of my work. She wants me to design all her jewelry for the movie. All!" After an attempt to sound businesslike, Pandora laughed and did a quick spin. "Morison said the only way he could talk her out of retirement was to promise her the best. She wants me."

Michael grabbed her close and spun her around. Bruno

raced around the room barking and shaking tables. "We'll celebrate," he decided. "Champagne with our fried chicken."

Pandora held on tight. "I feel like an idiot."

"Why?"

"I've always thought I was, well, beyond star adoration. I'm a professional." Bubbling with excitement, she clung to Michael. "While I was talking to Morison I told myself it was a great career opportunity, a wonderful chance to express myself in a large way. Then I hung up and all I could think was Jessica Wainwright! A Morison production! I felt as silly as any bubble-headed fan."

"Proves you're not half the snob you think you are." Michael cut off her retort with a kiss. "I'm proud of you," he murmured.

That threw her off. All of her pleasure in the assignment was dwarfed by that one sentence. No one but Jolley had ever been proud of her. Her parents loved her, patted her head and told her to do what she wanted. Pride was a valued addition to affection. "Really?"

Surprised, Michael drew her back and kissed her again. "Of course I am."

"But you've never thought much of my work."

"No, that's not true. I've never understood why people feel the need to deck themselves out in bangles, or why you seemed content to design on such a small scale. But as far as your work goes I'm not blind, Pandora. Some of it's beautiful, some of it's extraordinary and some of it's incomprehensible. But it's all imaginative and expertly crafted."

"Well." She let out a long breath. "This is a red-letter day. I always thought you felt I was playing with beads because I didn't want to face a real job. You even said so once."

He grinned. "Only because it made you furious. You're spectacular to look at when you're furious."

She thought about it a moment, then let out a sigh. "I suppose this is the best time to tell you."

He tensed, but forced his voice to come calmly. "To tell me what?"

"I watch the Emmy Awards every time you're nominated."

Tension flowed out in a laugh. There'd been guilt in every syllable. "What?"

"Every time," Pandora repeated, amazed that her cheeks were warm. "It made me feel good to watch you win. And . . ." She paused to clear her throat. "I've watched a few episodes of *Logan's Run*."

Michael wondered if she realized she sounded as though she was confessing a major social flaw. "Why?"

"Uncle Jolley was always going on about it; I'd even hear it discussed at parties. So I thought I'd see for myself. Naturally, it was just a matter of intellectual curiosity."

"Naturally. And?"

She moved her shoulders. "Of its kind—"

He stopped that line of response by twisting her ear. "Some people only tell the truth under duress."

"All right." Half laughing, she reached to free herself. "It's good!" she shouted when he held on. "I liked it."

"Why?"

"Michael, that hurts!"

"We have ways of making you talk."

"I liked it because the characters are genuine, the plots are intelligent. And—" she had to swallow hard on this one "—it has style."

When he let go of her ear to kiss her soundly, she gave him a halfhearted shove. "If you repeat that to anyone, I'll deny it."

"It'll be our little secret." He kissed her again, not so playfully.

Pandora was almost becoming used to the sensation of having her muscles loosen and feeling as if her bones were dissolving. She moved closer, delighting in the feeling of having her body mold against his. When his heart thudded, she felt the pulse inside herself. When his tiny moan escaped, she tasted it on her tongue. When the need leaped forward, she saw it in his eyes.

She pressed her mouth to his again and let her own hunger rule. There would be consequences. Hadn't she already accepted it? There would be pain. She was already braced for it. She couldn't stop what would happen in the weeks ahead, but she could direct what would happen tonight and perhaps tomorrow. It had to be enough. Everything she felt, wanted, feared, went into the kiss.

It left him reeling. She was often passionate, wildly so. She was often demanding, erotically so. But he'd never felt such pure emotion from her. There was a softness under the strength, a request under the urgency. He drew her closer, more gently than was his habit, and let her take what she wanted.

Her head tilted back, inviting, luring. His grip tightened. His fingers wound into her hair and were lost in the richness of it. He felt the need catapult through his body so that he was tense against her sudden, unexpected yielding. She never submitted, and until that moment he hadn't known how stirring it could be to have her do so. Without a thought to time and place, they lowered to the sofa.

Because she was pliant, he was tender. Because he was gentle, she was patient. In a way they'd never experienced, they made love without rush, without fire, without the whirlwind. Thoroughly, they gave to each other. A touch, a taste, a murmured request, a whispered answer. The fire sizzled gently behind them as night fell outside the windows. Fingers brushed, lips skimmed so that they learned the power of quiet arousal. Though they'd been lovers for weeks, they brought love to passion for the first time.

The room was quiet, the light dim. If she'd never looked for romance, it found her there, wrapped easily in Michael's arms. Closer they came, but comfortably. Deeper they dived, but lazily. As they came together, Pandora felt her firm line of independence crack to let him in. But the weakness she'd expected didn't follow. Only contentment.

It was contentment that followed her into that quick and final burst of pleasure.

They were still wrapped together, half dozing, when the phone rang. With a murmur of complaint, Michael reached over his head to the table and lifted the receiver.

"Hello."

"Michael Donahue, please."

"Yeah, this is Michael."

"Michael, it's Penny."

He rubbed a hand over his eyes as he tried to put a face with the name. Penny—the little blonde in the apartment next to his. Wanted to be a model. He remembered vaguely leaving her the number of the Folley in case something important was delivered to his apartment. "Hi." He watched Pandora's eyes flutter open.

"Michael, I hate to do this, but I had to call. I've already phoned the police. They're on their way."

"Police?" He struggled into a half-sitting position. "What's going on?"

"You've been robbed."

"What?" He sat bolt upright, nearly dumping Pandora on the floor. "When?"

"I'm not sure. I got home a few minutes ago and noticed your door wasn't closed all the way. I thought maybe you'd come back so I knocked. Anyway, I pushed the door open a bit. The place was turned upside down. I came right over here and called the cops. They asked me to contact you and told me not to go back over."

"Thanks." Dozens of questions ran through his mind but there was no one to answer them. "Look, I'll try to come in tonight."

"Okay. Hey, Michael, I'm really sorry."

"Yeah. I'll see you."

"Michael?" Pandora grabbed his hand as soon as he hung up the receiver.

"Somebody broke into my apartment."

"Oh no." She'd known the peace couldn't last. "Do you think it was—"

"I don't know." He dragged a hand through his hair. "Maybe. Or maybe it was someone who noticed no one had been home for a while."

She felt the anger in him but knew she couldn't soothe it. "You've got to go."

Nodding, he took her hand. "Come with me."

"Michael, one of us has to be here with Sweeney and Charles."

"I'm not leaving you alone."

"You have to go," she repeated. "If it was one of the family, maybe you can find something to prove it. In any case, you have to see to this. I'll be fine."

"Just like the last time I was away."

Pandora lifted a brow. "I'm not incompetent, Michael."

"But you'll be alone."

"I have Bruno. Don't give me that look," she ordered. "He may not be ferocious, but he certainly knows how to bark. I'll lock every door and window."

He shook his head. "Not good enough."

"All right, we'll call the local police. They have Fitzhugh's report about trespassers. We'll explain that I'm going to be alone for the night and ask them to keep an eye on the place."

"Better." But he rose to pace. "If this is a setup . . ."

"Then we're prepared for it this time."

Michael hesitated, thought it through, then nodded. "I'll call the police."

CHAPTER 10

The moment Michael left, Pandora turned the heavy bolt on the main door. Though it had taken them the better part of an hour, she was grateful he'd insisted on checking all the doors and windows with her. The house, with Pandora safely in it, was locked up tight.

It was entirely too quiet.

In defense, Pandora went to the kitchen and began rattling pots and pans. She had to be alone, but she didn't have to be idle. She wanted to be with Michael, to stand by him when he faced the break-in of his apartment. Was it as frustrating for him to go on alone, she wondered, as it was for her to stay behind? It couldn't be helped. There were two old people in the house who couldn't be left. And they needed to eat.

The chicken was to have been a joint effort and a respite from the haphazard meals they'd managed to date. Michael had claimed to know at least the basics of deep frying. While he'd volunteered to deal with the chicken, she'd been assigned to try her hand at mashing potatoes. She'd thought competition if nothing else would have improved the end result.

Pandora resigned herself to a solo and decided the effort

of cooking would keep her mind off fresh trouble. Needing company, she switched on the tuner on the kitchen wall unit and fiddled with the dial until she found a country-music station. Dolly Parton bubbled out brightly. Satisfied, she pulled one of Sweeney's cookbooks from the shelf and began to search the index. Fried chicken went on picnics, she mused. How much trouble could it be?

She had two counters crowded and splattered, and flour up to her wrists when the phone rang. Using a dishcloth, Pandora plucked the receiver from the kitchen extension. Her foot was tapping to a catchy rendition of "On the Road Again."

"Hello."

"Pandora McVie?"

Her mind on more immediate matters, Pandora stretched the cord to the counter and picked up a drumstick. "Yes."

"Listen carefully."

"Can you speak up?" Tongue caught between her teeth, Pandora dipped the drumstick in her flour mixture. "I can't hear you very well."

"I have to warn you and there's not much time. You're in danger. You're not safe in that house, not alone."

The cookbook slid to the floor and landed on her foot. "What? Who is this?"

"Just listen. You're alone because it was arranged. Someone's going to try to break in tonight."

"Someone?" She shifted the phone and listened hard. It wasn't malice she detected, but nervousness. Whoever was on the other end was as shaky as she was. She was certain—almost certain—it was a man's voice. "If you're trying to frighten me—"

"I'm trying to warn you. When I found out . . ." Already low and indistinct, the voice became hesitant. "You shouldn't have sent the champagne. I don't like what's going on, but it won't stop. No one was going to be hurt, do you understand? But I'm afraid of what might happen next."

Pandora felt fear curl in her stomach. Outside the kitchen windows it was dark, pitch-dark. She was alone in the house with two old, sick servants. "If you're afraid, tell me who you are. Help me stop what's going on."

"I'm already risking everything by warning you. You don't understand. Get out, just get out of the house."

It was a ploy, she told herself. A ploy to make her leave. Pandora straightened her shoulders, but her gaze shifted from blank window to blank window. "I'm not going anywhere. If you want to help, tell me who I should be afraid of."

"Just get out," the voice repeated before the line went dead.

Pandora stood holding the silent receiver. The oil in the fryer had begun to sizzle, competing with the radio. Watching the windows, listening, she hung up the phone. It was a trick, she told herself. It was only a trick to get her out of the house in hopes she'd be frightened enough to stay out. She wouldn't be shooed away by a quivering voice on the telephone.

Besides, Michael had already called the police. They knew she was alone in the house. At the first sign of trouble, she only had to pick up the phone.

Her hands weren't completely steady, but she went back to cooking with a vengeance. She slipped coated chicken into the fryer, tested the potatoes she had cooking, then decided a little glass of wine while she worked was an excellent idea. She was pouring it when Bruno raced into the room to run around her feet.

"Bruno." Pandora crouched and gathered the dog close. He felt warm, solid. "I'm glad you're here," she murmured. But for a moment, she allowed herself to wish desperately for Michael.

Bruno licked her face, made a couple of clumsy leaps

toward the counter, then dashed to the door. Jumping up against it, he began to bark.

"Now?" Pandora demanded. "I don't suppose you could wait until morning."

Bruno raced back to Pandora, circled her then raced back to the door. When he'd gone through the routine three times, she relented. The phone call had been no more than a trick, a clumsy one at that. Besides, she told herself as she turned the lock, it wouldn't hurt to open the door and take a good look outside.

The moment she opened it, Bruno jumped out and tumbled into the snow. He began to sniff busily while Pandora stood shivering in the opening and straining her eyes against the dark. Music and the smells of cooking poured out behind her.

There was nothing. She hugged herself against the cold and decided she hadn't expected to see anything. The snow was settled, the stars bright and the woods quiet. It was as it should have been; a very ordinary evening in the country. She took a deep breath of winter air and started to call the dog back. They saw the movement at the edge of the woods at the same time.

Just a shadow, it seemed to separate slowly from a tree and take on its own shape. A human shape. Before Pandora could react, Bruno began to bark and plow through the snow.

"No, Bruno! Come back." Without giving herself a chance to think, Pandora grabbed the old pea coat that hung beside the door and threw it on. As an afterthought, she reached for a cast-iron skillet before bolting through the door after her dog. "Bruno!"

He was already at the edge of the woods and hot on the trail. Picking up confidence as she went, Pandora raced in pursuit. Whoever had been watching the house had run at the sight of the clumsy, overgrown puppy. She'd found she was susceptible to fear, but she refused to be frightened by a coward. With as much enthusiasm as Bruno, Pandora sprinted into the woods. Out of breath and feeling indestructible, she paused long enough to look around and listen. For a moment there was nothing, then off to the right, she heard barking and thrashing.

"Get 'em, Bruno!" she shouted, and headed toward the chaos. Excited by the chase, she called encouragement to the dog, changing direction when she heard his answering bark. As she ran, snow dropped from the branches to slide cold and wet down the back of her neck. The barking grew wilder, and in her rush, Pandora fell headlong over a downed tree. Spitting out snow and swearing, she struggled to her knees. Bruno bounded out of the woods and sent her sprawling again.

"Not me." Flat on her back, Pandora shoved at the dog. "Dammit, Bruno, if you don't—" She broke off when the dog stiffened and began to growl. Sprawled on the snow, Pandora looked up and saw the shadow move through the trees. She forgot she was too proud to fear a coward.

Though her hands were numb from cold, she gripped the handle of the skillet and, standing, inched her way along toward the nearest tree. Struggling to keep her breathing quiet, she braced herself for attack and defense. Relative or stranger, she'd hold her own. But her knees were shaking. Bruno tensed and hurled himself forward. The moment he did, Pandora lifted the skillet high and prepared to swing.

"What the hell's going on?"

"Michael!" The skillet landed in the snow with a plop as she followed Bruno's lead and hurled herself forward. Giddy with relief, she plastered kisses over Michael's face. "Oh, Michael, I'm so glad it's you."

"Yeah. You sure looked pleased when you were hefting that skillet. Run out of hair spray?"

"It was handy." Abruptly she drew back and glared at him. "Dammit, Michael, you scared me to death. You're supposed to be halfway to New York, not skulking around the woods."

"And you're supposed to be locked in the house."

"I would've been if you hadn't been skulking in the woods. Why?"

In an offhanded gesture, he brushed snow from her face. "I got ten miles away, and I couldn't get rid of this bad feeling. It was too pat. I decided to stop at a gas station and phone my neighbor."

"But your apartment."

"I talked to the police, gave them a list of my valuables. We'll both run into New York in a day or two." Snow was scattered through her hair and matted to her coat. He thought of what might have happened and resisted the urge to shake her. "I couldn't leave you alone."

"I'm going to start believing you're chivalrous after all." She kissed him. "That explains why you're not in New York, but what were you doing in the woods?"

"Just a hunch." He bent to retrieve the frying pan. A good whack with that, he discovered, and he'd have been down for the count.

"The next time you have a hunch, don't stand at the edge of the woods and stare at the house."

"I wasn't." Michael took her arm and headed back toward the house. He wanted her inside again, behind locked doors.

"I saw you."

"I don't know who you saw." Disgusted, Michael looked back at the dog. "But if you hadn't let the dog out, we'd both know. I decided to check around outside before coming in, and I saw footprints. I followed them around, then cut into the woods." He glanced over his shoulder, still tight with tension. "I was just coming up behind whoever made them when Bruno tried his attack. I started chasing." He swore and slapped a palm against the skillet. "I was gaining when this hound ran between my legs and sent me face first into the snow. About that time, you started yelling at the dog. Whoever I was chasing had enough time to disappear."

Pandora swore and kicked at the snow. "If you'd let me know what was going on, we could've worked together."

"I didn't know what was going on until it was already happening. In any case, the deal was you'd stay inside with the doors locked."

"The dog had to go out," Pandora muttered. "And I had this phone call." She looked back over her shoulder and sighed. "Someone called to warn me."

"Who?"

"I don't know. I thought it was a man's voice, but—I'm just not sure."

Michael's hand tightened on her arm. "Did he threaten you?"

"No, no it wasn't like a threat. Whoever it was certainly seemed to know what's been going on and isn't happy about it. That much was clear. He—she said someone was going to try to break into the Folley, and I should get out."

"And, of course, you handled that by running into the woods with a skillet. Pandora." This time he did shake her. "Why didn't you call the police?"

"Because I thought it was another trick and it made me mad." She sent Michael a stubborn look. "Yes, it frightened me at first, then it just plain made me mad. I don't like intimidation. When I looked out and saw someone near the woods, I only wanted to fight back."

"Admirable," he said but took her shoulders. "Stupid."

"You were doing the same thing."

"It's not the same thing. You've got brains, you've got style. I'll even give you guts. But, cousin, you're not a heavyweight.

What if you'd caught up with whoever was out there and they wanted to play rough?"

"I can play rough, too," Pandora muttered.

"Fine." With a quick move, he hooked a foot behind hers and sent her bottom first into the snow. She didn't have the opportunity to complain before he was standing over her, gesturing with the skillet. Bruno decided it was a game and leaped on top of her. "I might've come back tomorrow and found you half-buried in the snow." Before she could speak, he hauled her to her feet again. "I'm not risking that."

"You caught me off balance," she began.

"Shut up." He had her by the shoulders again, and this time his grip wasn't gentle. "You're too important, Pandora, I'm through taking chances. We're going inside and calling the cops. We're going to tell them everything."

"What can they do?"

"We'll find out."

She let out a long breath, then leaned against him. The chase might have been exciting, but her knees had yet to stop shaking. "Okay, maybe you're right. We're no farther along now than when we started."

"Calling the police isn't giving up, it's just changing the odds. I might not have come back here tonight, Pandora. The dog may not have frightened anyone off. You'd have been alone." He took both her hands, pressing them to his lips and warming them. "I'm not going to let anything happen to you."

Confused by the sense of pleasure his words gave her, she tried to draw her hands away. "I can take care of myself, Michael."

He smiled but didn't let go. "Maybe. But you're not going to have the chance to find out. Let's go home. I'm hungry."

"Typical," she began, needing to lighten the mood. "You'd think of your stomach—oh my God, the chicken!" Breaking away, Pandora loped toward the house.

"I'm not that hungry." Michael sprinted after her. The relief came again when he scooped her up into his arms. When he'd heard her shout in the woods, had realized she was outside and vulnerable, his blood had simply stopped flowing. "In fact," he said as he scooped her up, "I can think of more pressing matters than eating."

"Michael." She struggled, but laughed. "If you don't put me down, there won't be a kitchen to eat in."

"We'll eat somewhere else."

"I left the pan on. There's probably nothing left of the chicken but charred bones."

"There's always soup." With that, he pushed open the kitchen door.

Rather than a smoky, splattered mess, they found a platter piled high with crisp, brown chicken. Sweeney had wiped up the spills, and had the pans soaking in the sink.

"Sweeney." From her perch in Michael's arms, Pandora surveyed the room. "What are you doing out of bed?"

"My job," she said briskly, but gave them a quick sidelong look. As far as she was concerned, her plans were working perfectly. She imagined Pandora and Michael had decided to take a little air while dinner was cooking, and, as young people would, had forgotten the time.

"You're supposed to be in bed," Pandora reminded her.

"Posh. I've been in bed long enough." And the days of little or no activity had nearly bored her to tears. It was worth it, however, to see Pandora snug in Michael's arms. "Feeling fit as a fiddle now, I promise you. Wash up for dinner."

Michael and Pandora each took separate and careful studies. Sweeney's cheeks were pink and round, her eyes bright. She bustled from counter to counter in her old businesslike fashion. "We still want you to take it easy," Michael decided. "No heavy work."

"That's right. Michael and I'll take care of the washing up." She saw him scowl, just a little, and patted his shoulder. "We like to do it."

At Michael and Pandora's insistence, all four ate in the kitchen. Charles, sitting next to Sweeney, was left uncertain how much he should cough and settled on a middle road, clearing his throat every so often. In an unspoken agreement, Pandora and Michael decided to keep the matter of trespassers to themselves. Both of them felt the announcement that someone was watching the house would be too upsetting for the two old people while they were recuperating.

On the surface, dinner was an easy meal, but Pandora kept wondering how soon they could nudge the servants along to bed and contact the police. More than once, Pandora caught Sweeney looking from her to Michael with a smug smile. Sweet old lady, Pandora mused, innocently believing the cook to be pleased to have her kitchen back. It made Pandora only more determined to protect her and Charles from any unpleasantness. She concentrated on cleaning up and packing them off to bed, and it was nearly nine before she was able to meet Michael in the parlor.

"Settled?"

She heard the familiar restlessness in his voice and merely nodded, pouring a brandy. "It's a bit like cajoling children, but I managed to find a Cary Grant movie that interested them." She sipped the brandy, waiting for her muscles to relax with it. "I'd rather be watching it myself."

"Another time." Michael took a sip from her snifter. "I've called the police. They'll be here shortly."

She took the glass back. "It still bothers me to take the business to outsiders. After all, anything beyond simple trespass is speculation."

"We'll let the police speculate."

She managed to smile. "Your Logan always handles things on his own."

"Someone told me once that that was just fiction." He poured himself a brandy and toasted her. "I discovered I don't like having you in the middle of a story line."

The brandy and firelight gave the evening an illusion of normalcy. Pandora took his statement with a shrug. "You seem to have developed a protect-the-woman syndrome, Michael. It's not like you."

"Maybe not." He tossed back a gulp. "It's different when it's my woman."

She turned, brow lifted. It was ridiculous to feel pleasure at such a foolish and possessive term. "Yours?"

"Mine." He cupped the back of her neck with his hand. "Got a problem with that?"

Her heart beat steadily in her throat until she managed to swallow. Maybe he meant it—now. In a few months when he was back moving in his own world, with his own people, she'd be no more than his somewhat annoying cousin. But for now, just for now, maybe he meant it. "I'm not sure."

"Give it some thought," he advised before he lowered his mouth to hers. "We'll come back to it."

He left her flustered and went to answer the door.

When he returned, Pandora was sitting calmly enough in a high-backed chair near the fire. "Lieutenant Randall, Pandora McVie."

"How d'you do?" The lieutenant pulled off a wool muffler and stuck it in his coat pocket. He looked, Pandora thought, like someone's grandfather. Comfy, round and balding. "Miserable night," he announced, and situated himself near the fire.

"Would you like some coffee, Lieutenant?"

Randall gave Pandora a grateful look. "Love it."

"Please, have a seat. I'll be back in a minute."

She took her time heating coffee and arranging cups and saucers on a tray. Not putting off, Pandora insisted, just preparing. She'd never had occasion to talk to a policeman on any subject more complex than a parking ticket. She'd come out on the short end on that one. Now, she was about to discuss her family and her relationship with Michael.

Her relationship with Michael, she thought again as she fussed with the sugar bowl. That's what really had her hiding in the kitchen. She hadn't yet been able to dull the feeling that had raced through her when he'd called her his woman. Adolescent, Pandora told herself. It was absolutely absurd to feel giddy and self-satisfied and unnerved because a man had looked at her with passion in his eyes.

But they'd been Michael's eyes.

She found linen napkins and folded them into triangles. She didn't want to be anyone's woman but her own. It had been the strain and excitement of the evening that had made her react like a sixteen-year-old being offered a school ring. She was an adult; she was self-sustaining. She was in love. Talk yourself out of that one, Pandora challenged herself. Taking a long breath, she hefted the tray and went back to the parlor.

"Gentlemen." Pandora set the tray on a low table and stuck on a smile. "Cream and sugar, Lieutenant?"

"Thanks. A healthy dose of both." He set a dog-eared notepad on his knee when Pandora handed him a cup. "Mr. Donahue's been filling me in. Seems you've had a few annoyances."

She smiled at the term. Like his looks, his voice was comfortable. "A few."

"I'm not going to lecture." But he gave them both a stern look. "Still, you should've notified the police after the first incident. Vandalism's a crime."

"We'd hoped by ignoring it, it would discourage repetition." Pandora lifted her cup. "We were wrong."

"I'll need to take the champagne with me." Again, he sent them a look of disapproval. "Even though you've had it analyzed, we'll want to run it through our own lab."

"I'll get it for you." Michael rose and left them alone.

"Miss McVie, from what your cousin tells me, the terms of Mr. McVie's will were a bit unconventional."

"A bit."

"He also tells me he talked you into agreeing to them."

"That's Michael's fantasy, Lieutenant." She sipped her coffee. "I'm doing exactly what I chose to do."

Randall nodded and noted. "You agree with Mr. Donahue's idea that these incidents are connected and one of your relatives is responsible."

"I can't think of any reason to disagree."

"Do you have any reason to suspect one more than another?"

Pandora thought it through as she'd thought it through before. "No. You see, we're not at all a close family. The truth is I don't know any of them very well."

"Except Mr. Donahue."

"That's right. Michael and I often visited our uncle, and we ran into each other here at the Folley." Whether we wanted to or not, she added to herself in her own private joke. "None of the others came by very often."

"The champagne, Lieutenant." Michael brought in the box. "And the report from Sanfield Laboratories."

Randall skimmed the printout, then tucked the sheet into the box. "Your uncle's attorney . . ." He referred quickly to his notes. "Fitzhugh reported trespassing several weeks ago. We've had a squad car cruise the area, but at this point you might agree to having a man patrol the grounds once a day."

"I'd prefer it," Michael told him.

"I'll contact Fitzhugh." Seeing his cup was empty, Pandora took it and filled it again. "I'll also need a list of the relatives named in the will."

Pandora frowned over her rim. Between her and Michael, they tried to fill in the lieutenant, as best as they could. When they had finished, Pandora sent Randall an apologetic look. "I told you we aren't close."

"I'll get the lawyer to fill in the details." Randall rose and tried not to think about the cold drive back to town. "We'll keep the inquiries as quiet as possible. If anything else happens, call me. One of my men will be around to look things over."

"Thank you, Lieutenant." Michael helped the pudgy man on with his coat.

Randall took another look around the room. "Ever think of installing a security system?"

"No."

"Think again," he advised, and made his way out.

"We've just been scolded," Pandora murmured.

Michael wondered if *Logan's Run* had room for a cranky, well-padded cop. "Seems that way."

"You know, Michael, I have two schools of thought on bringing in the police."

"Which are?"

"It's either going to calm things down or stir things up."

"You pay your money and take your choice."

She gave him a knowing look. "You're counting on the second."

"I came close tonight." He bypassed the coffee and poured another brandy. "I nearly had my hands on something. Someone." When he looked at her, the faint amusement in his eyes had faded. The recklessness was back. "I like my fights in the open, face-to-face."

"It's better if we look at it as a chess game rather than a boxing match." She came close to wrap her arms around him and press her cheek to his shoulder. It was the kind of gesture he didn't think he'd ever get used to from her. As he rested his head on her hair, he realized that the fact that he wouldn't only added to the sweetness of the feeling. When had he stopped remembering that she didn't fit into his long-established picture of the ideal woman? Her hair was too red, her body too thin, her tongue too sharp. Michael nuzzled against her and found they fit very well.

"I've never had the patience for chess."

"Then we'll just leave it to the police." She held him tighter. The need to protect rose as sharply as the desire to be protected. "I've been thinking about what might have happened out there tonight. I don't want you hurt, Michael."

With two fingers under her chin, he lifted it. "Why not?"

"Because . . ." She looked into his eyes and felt her heart melt. But she wouldn't be a fool; she wouldn't risk her pride. "Because then I'd have to do the dishes by myself."

He smiled. No, he didn't have a great deal of patience, but he could call on it when circumstances warranted. He brushed a kiss on either side of her mouth. Sooner or later, he'd have more out of her. Then he'd just have to decide what to do with it. "Any other reason?"

Absorbing the sensations, Pandora searched her mind for another easy answer. "If you were hurt, you couldn't work. I'd have to live with your foul temper."

"I thought you were already living with it."

"I've seen it fouler."

He kissed her eyes closed in his slow, sensuous way. "Try one more time."

"I care." She opened her eyes, and her look was tense and defiant. "Got a problem with that?"

"No." His kiss wasn't gentle this time, it wasn't patient.

He had her caught close and reeling within moments. If there was tension in her still, he couldn't feel it. "The only problem's been dragging it out of you."

"You're family after all—"

With a laugh, he nipped the lobe of her ear. "Don't try to back out."

Indignant, she stiffened. "I never back out."

"Unless you can rationalize it. Just remember this." He had her molded against him again. "The family connection's distant." Their lips met, urgently, then parted. "This connection isn't."

"I don't know what you want from me," she whispered.

"You're usually so quick."

"Don't joke, Michael."

"It's no joke." He drew her away, holding her by the shoulders. Briefly, firmly, he ran his hands down to her elbows, then back. "No, I'm not going to spell it out for you, Pandora. I'm not going to make it easy on you. You have to be willing to admit we both want the same thing. And you will."

"Arrogant," she warned.

"Confident," he corrected. He had to be, or he'd be on his knees begging. There'd come a time, he'd promised himself, when she'd drop the last of her restrictions. "I want you."

A tremor skipped up her spine. "I know."

"Yeah." He linked his fingers with hers. "I think you do."

CHAPTER 11

Winter raged its way through February. There came a point when Pandora had to shovel her way from the house to her workshop. She found herself grateful for the physical labor. Winter was a long quiet time that provided too many hours to think.

In using this time, Pandora came to several uncomfortable realizations. Her life, as she'd known it, as she'd guided it, would never be the same. As far as her art was concerned, she felt the months of concentrated effort with dashes of excitement had only improved her crafting. In truth, she often used her jewelry to take her mind off what was happening to and around her. When that didn't work, she used what was happening to and around her in her work.

The sudden blunt understanding that her health, even her life, had been endangered made her take a step away from her usual practical outlook. It caused her to appreciate little things she'd always taken for granted. Waking up in a warm bed, watching snow fall while a fire crackled beside her. She'd learned that every second in life was vital.

Already she was considering taking a day to drive back to New York and pack what was important to her. More than packing, it would be a time of decision making. What she kept, what she didn't, would in some ways reflect the changes she'd accepted in herself.

Both the lease on her apartment and the lease on the shop over the boutique were coming up for renewal. She'd let them lapse. Rather than living alone, she'd have the company and the responsibility of her uncle's old servants. Though she'd once been determined to be responsible only to herself and her art, Pandora made the choice without a qualm. Though she had lived in the city, in the rush, in the crowds, she'd isolated herself. No more.

Through it all wove Michael.

In a few short weeks, what they had now would be over. The long winter they'd shared would be something to think of during other winters. As she prepared for a new and different life, Pandora promised herself she'd have no regrets. But she couldn't stop herself from having wishes. Things were already changing.

The police had come, and with their arrival had been more questions. Everything in her shop had to be locked up tightly after dark, and there were no more solitary walks in the woods after a snowfall. It had become a nightly ritual to go through the Folley and check doors and windows that had once been casually ignored. Often when she walked back to the house from her shop, she'd see Michael watching from the window of his room. It should have given her a warm, comfortable feeling, but she knew he was waiting for something else to happen. She knew, as she knew him, that he wanted it. Inactivity was sitting uneasily on him.

Since they'd driven into New York to deal with the break-in at his apartment, he'd been distant, with a restlessness roiling underneath. Though they both understood the wisdom of having the grounds patrolled, she thought they felt intruded upon.

They had no sense of satisfaction from the police investigation. Each one of their relatives had alibis for one or more of the incidents. So far the investigation seemed to have twin results. Since the police had been called in, nothing else had happened. There'd been no anonymous phone calls, no shadows in the woods, no bogus messages. It had, as Pandora had also predicted, stirred things up. She'd dealt with an irate phone call from Carlson who insisted they were using the investigation in an attempt to undermine his case against the will.

On the heels of that had come a disjointed letter from Ginger who'd had the idea that the Folley was haunted. Michael had had a two-minute phone conversation with Morgan who'd muttered about private family business, overreacting and hogwash. Biff, in his usual style, had sent a short message:

Cops and robbers? Looks like you two are playing games with each other.

From Hank they heard nothing.

The police lab had confirmed the private analysis of the champagne; Randall was plodding through the investigation in his precise, quiet way. Michael and Pandora were exactly where they'd been weeks before: waiting.

He didn't know how she could stand it. As Michael made his way down the narrow path Pandora had shoveled, he wondered how she could remain so calm when he was ready to chew glass. It had only taken him a few days of hanging in limbo to realize it was worse when nothing happened. Waiting for someone else to make the next move was the most racking kind of torture. Until he was sure Pandora was safe, he couldn't relax. Until he had his hands around someone's throat, he wouldn't be satisfied. He was caught in a trap of inactivity that was slowly driving him mad. Pausing just outside her shop, he glanced around.

The house looked big and foolish with icicles hanging and dripping from eaves, gutters and shutters. It belonged in a book, he thought, some moody, misty gothic. A fairy tale— the grim sort. Perhaps one day he'd weave a story around it himself, but for now, it was just home.

With his hands in his pockets he watched smoke puff out of chimneys. Foolish it might be, but he'd always loved it. The longer he lived in it, the surer he was that he was meant to. He was far from certain how Pandora would take his decision to remain after the term was over.

His last script for the season was done. It was the only episode to be filmed before the show wrapped until fall. He could, as he often did, take a few weeks in the early spring and find a hot, noisy beach. He could fish, relax and enjoy watching women in undersize bikinis. Michael knew he wasn't going anywhere.

For the past few days, he'd been toying with a screenplay for a feature film. He'd given it some thought before, but somehow something had always interfered. He could write it here, he knew. He could perfect it here with Pandora wielding her art nearby, criticizing his work so that he was only more determined to make it better. But he was waiting. Waiting for something else to happen, waiting to find who it was who'd used fear and intimidation to try to drive them out. And most of all, he was waiting for Pandora. Until she gave him her complete trust, willingly, until she gave him her heart unrestrictedly, he had to go on waiting.

His hands curled into fists and released. He wanted action.

He tried the door and satisfied himself that she'd kept her word and locked it from the inside. "Pandora?" He knocked with the side of his fist. She opened the door with a drill in her hand. After giving her flushed face and tousled hair a quick look, Michael lifted his hands, palms out. "I'm un-armed."

"And I'm busy." But her lips curved. There was a light of pleasure in her eyes. He found it easy to notice such small things.

"I know, I've invaded scheduled working hours, but I have a valid excuse."

"You're letting in the cold," she complained. Once, she might have shut the door in his face without a second thought. This time she shut it behind him.

"Not a hell of a lot warmer in here."

"It's fine when I'm working. Which I am."

"Blame Sweeney. She's sending me in for supplies, and she insisted I take you." He sent Pandora a bland look. "'That girl holes herself up in that shed too much. Needs some sun.'"

"I get plenty of sun," Pandora countered. Still, the idea of a drive into town appealed. It wouldn't hurt to talk to the jeweler in the little shopping center. She was beginning to think her work should spread out a bit, beyond the big cities. "I suppose we should humor her, but I want to finish up here first."

"I'm in no hurry."

"Good. Half an hour then." She went to exchange the drill for a jeweler's torch. Because she didn't hear the door open or shut, she turned and saw Michael examining her rolling mill. "Michael," she said with more than a trace of exasperation.

"Go ahead, take your time."

"Don't you have anything to do?"

"Not a thing," he said cheerfully.

"Not one car chase to write?"

"No. Besides, I've never seen you work."

"Audiences make me cranky."

"Broaden your horizons, love. Pretend I'm an apprentice."

"I'm not sure they can get that broad."

Undaunted, he pointed to her worktable. "What is that thing?"

"This thing," she began tightly, "is a pendant. A waterfall effect made with brass wire and some scraps of silver I had left over from a bracelet."

"No waste," he murmured. "Practical as ever. So what's the next step?"

With a long breath, she decided it would be simpler to play along than to throw him out. "I've just finished adjusting the curves of the wires. I've used different thicknesses and lengths to give it a free-flowing effect. The silver scraps I've cut and filed into elongated tear-drops. Now I solder them onto the ends of the wires."

She applied the flux, shifting a bit so that he could watch. After she'd put a square of solder beside each wire, she used the torch to apply heat until the solder melted. Patient, competent, she repeated the procedure until all twelve teardrops were attached.

"Looks easy enough," he mused.

"A child of five could do it."

He heard the sarcasm and laughed as he took her hands. "You want flattery? A few minutes ago I saw a pile of metal. Now I see an intriguing ornament. Ornate and exotic."

"It's supposed to be exotic," Pandora replied. "Jessica Wainwright will wear it in the film. It's to have been a gift from an old lover. The countess claims he was a Turkish prince."

Michael studied the necklace again. "Very appropriate."

"It'll droop down from brass and silver wires twisted together. The lowest teardrop should hang nearly to her waist." Pleased, but knowing better than to touch the metal before the solder cooled, Pandora held up her sketch.

"Ms. Wainwright was very specific. She wants nothing ordinary, nothing even classic. Everything she wears should add to the character's mystique."

She set the sketch down and tidied her tools. She'd solder on the hoop and fashion the neck wire when they returned from town. Then if there was time, she'd begin the next project. The gold-plated peacock pin with its three-inch filigree tail would take her the better part of two weeks.

"This thing has potential as a murder weapon," Michael mused, picking up a burnisher to examine the curved, steel tip.

"I beg your pardon?"

He liked the way she said it, so that even with her back turned she was looking down her nose. "For a story line."

"Leave my tools out of your stories." Pandora took the burnisher from him and packed it away. "Going to buy me lunch in town?" She stripped off her apron then grabbed her coat.

"I was going to ask you the same thing."

"I asked first." She locked the shop and welcomed the cold. "The snow's beginning to melt."

"In a few weeks, the five dozen bulbs Jolley planted during his gardening stage will be starting to bloom."

"Daffodils," she murmured. It didn't seem possible when you felt the air, saw the mounds of snow, but spring was closing in. "The winter hasn't seemed so long."

"No, it hasn't." He slipped an arm around her shoulders. "I never expected six months to go so quickly. I figured one of us would've attempted murder by this time."

With a laugh, Pandora matched her step to his. "We've still got a month to go."

"Now we have to behave ourselves," he reminded her. "Lieutenant Randall has his eye on us."

"I guess we blew our chance." She turned to wind her arms

around his neck. "There have been times I've wanted to hit you with a blunt instrument."

"Feeling's mutual," he told her as he lowered his mouth. Her lips were cool and curved.

At the side window, Sweeney drew back the drape. "Look at this!" Cackling, she gestured to Charles. "I told you it would work. In a few more weeks, I'll be putting bells on a wedding cake."

As Charles joined Sweeney at the window, Pandora scooped a hand into the snow and tossed it in Michael's face. "Don't count your chickens," he muttered.

In a desperate move to avoid retaliation, Pandora raced to the garage. She ducked seconds before snow splattered against the door. "Your aim's still off, cousin." Hefting the door, she sprinted inside and jumped into his car. Smug, she settled into the seat. He wouldn't, she was sure, mar his spotless interior with a snowball. Michael opened the door, slid in beside her and dumped snow over her head. She was still squealing when he turned the key.

"I'm better at close range."

Pandora sputtered as she wiped at the snow. Because she'd appreciated the move, it was difficult to sound indignant. "One would have thought that a man who drives an ostentatious car would be more particular with it."

"It's only ostentatious if you buy it for status purposes."

"And, of course, you didn't."

"I bought it because it gets terrific gas mileage." When she snorted, he turned to grin at her. "And because it looks great wrapped around redheads."

"And blondes and brunettes."

"Redheads," he corrected, twining her hair around his finger. "I've developed a preference."

It shouldn't have made her smile, but it did. She was still

smiling when they started down the long, curvy road. "We can't complain about the road crews," she said idly. "Except for those two weeks last month, the roads've been fairly clear." She glanced toward the mounds of snow the plows had pushed to the side of the road.

"Too bad they won't do the driveway."

"You know you loved riding that little tractor. Uncle Jolley always said it made him feel tough and macho."

"So much so he'd race it like a madman over the yard."

As they came to a curve, Michael eased on the brake and downshifted. Pandora leaned forward and fiddled with the stereo. "Most people have equipment like this in their den."

"I don't have a den."

"You don't have a stereo to put in one, either," she remembered. "Or a television."

He shrugged, but mentally listed what he'd lost from his apartment. "Insurance'll cover it."

"The police are handling that as though it were a normal break-in." She switched channels. "It might've been."

"Or it might've been a smoke screen. I wish we—" He broke off as they approached another curve. He'd pressed the brake again, but this time, the pedal had gone uselessly to the floor.

"Michael, if you're trying to impress me with your skill as a driver, it's not working." Instinctively Pandora grabbed the door handle as the car careered down the curve.

Whipping the steering wheel with one hand, Michael yanked on the emergency brake. The car continued to barrel down. He gripped the wheel in both hands and fought the next curve. "No brakes." As he told her, Michael glanced down to see the speedometer hover at seventy.

Pandora's knuckles turned white on the handle. "We won't make it to the bottom without them."

He never considered lying. "No." Tires squealed as he rounded the next curve. Gravel spit under the wheels as the car went wide. There was the scrape and scream of metal as the fender kissed the guardrail.

She looked at the winding road spinning in front of her. Her vision blurred then cleared. The sign before the S-turn cautioned for a safe speed of thirty. Michael took it at seventy-five. Pandora shut her eyes. When she opened them and saw the snowbank dead ahead, she screamed. With seconds to spare, Michael yanked the car around. Snow flew skyward as the car skidded along the bank.

Eyes intense, Michael stared at the road ahead and struggled to anticipate each curve. Sweat beaded on his forehead. He knew the road, that's what terrified him. In less than three miles, the already sharp incline steepened. At high speed, the car would ram straight through the guardrail and crash on the cliffs below. The game Jolley had begun would end violently.

Michael tasted his own fear, then swallowed it. "There's only one chance; we've got to turn off on the lane leading into the old inn. It's coming up after that curve." He couldn't take his eyes from the road to look at her. His fingers dug into the wheel. "Hang on."

She was going to die. Her mind was numb from the thought of it. She heard the tires scream as Michael dragged at the wheel. The car tilted, nearly going over. She saw trees rush by as the car slid on the slippery edge of the lane. Almost, for an instant, the rubber seemed to grip the gravel beneath. But the turn was too sharp, the speed too fast. Out of control, the car spiraled toward the trees.

"I love you," she whispered, and grabbed for him before the world went black.

He came to slowly. He hurt, and for a time didn't understand why. There was noise. Eventually he turned his head toward it. When he opened his eyes, Michael saw a boy with wide eyes and black hair gawking through the window.

"Mister, hey, mister. You okay?"

Dazed, Michael pushed open the door. "Get help," he managed, fighting against blacking out again. He took deep gulps of air to clear his head as the boy dashed off through the woods. "Pandora." Fear broke through the fog. In seconds, he was leaning over her.

His fingers shook as he reached for the pulse of her neck, but he found it. Blood from a cut on her forehead ran down her face and onto his hands. With his fingers pressed against the wound, he fumbled in the glove compartment for the first-aid kit. He'd stopped the bleeding and was checking her for broken bones when she moaned. He had to stop himself from dragging her against him and holding on.

"Take it easy," he murmured when she began to stir. "Don't move around." When she opened her eyes, he saw they were glazed and unfocused. "You're all right." Gently he cupped her face in his hands and continued to reassure her. Her eyes focused gradually. As they did, she reached for his hand.

"The brakes. . . . ."

"Yeah." He rested his cheek against hers a moment. "It was a hell of a trip, but it looks like we made it."

Confused, she looked around. The car was stopped, leaning drunkenly against a tree. It had been the deep, slushy snow that had slowed them down enough to prevent the crash from being fatal. "We—you're all right?" The tears started when she reached out and took his face in her hands as he had with hers. "You're all right."

"Terrific." His wrist throbbed like a jackhammer and his head ached unbelievably, but he was alive. When she started to move, he held her still. "No, don't move around. I don't know how badly you're hurt. There was a kid. He's gone for help."

"It's just my head." She started to take his hand, and saw the blood. "Oh God, you're bleeding. Where?" Before she could begin her frantic search, he gripped her hands together.

"It's not me. It's you. Your head's cut. You probably have a concussion."

Shaky, she lifted her hand and touched the bandage. The wound beneath it hurt, but she drew on that. If she hurt, she was alive. "I thought I was dead." She closed her eyes but tears slipped through the lashes. "I thought we were both dead."

"We're both fine." They heard the siren wail up the mountain road. He was silent until she opened her eyes again. "You know what happened?"

Her head ached badly, but it was clear. "Attempted murder."

He nodded, not turning when the ambulance pulled into the slushy lane. "I'm through waiting, Pandora. I'm through waiting all around."

* * *

Lieutenant Randall found Michael in the emergency-room lounge. He unwrapped his muffler, unbuttoned his coat and sat down on the hard wooden bench. "Looks like you've had some trouble."

"Big time."

Randall nodded toward the Ace bandage on Michael's wrist. "Bad?"

"Just a sprain. Few cuts and bruises and a hell of a headache. Last time I saw it, my car looked something like an accordion."

"We're taking it in. Anything we should look for?"

"Brake lines. It seemed I didn't have any when I started the trip down the mountain."

"When's the last time you used your car?" Randall had his notepad in hand.

"Ten days, two weeks." Wearily, Michael rubbed a temple. "I drove into New York to talk to police about the robbery in my apartment."

"Where do you keep your car?"

"In the garage."

"Locked?"

"The garage?" Michael kept his eye on the hallway where Pandora had been wheeled away. "No. My uncle had installed one of those remote control devices a few years back. Never worked unless you turned on the television. Anyway, he took it out again and never replaced the lock. Pandora's car's in there," he remembered suddenly. "If—"

"We'll check it out," Randall said easily. "Miss McVie was with you?"

"Yeah, she's with a doctor." For the first time in weeks, Michael found himself craving a cigarette. "Her head was cut." He looked down at his hands and remembered her blood on them. "I'm going to find out who did this, Lieutenant, and then I'm going to—"

"Don't say anything to me I might have to use later," Randall warned. There were some people who threatened as a means to let off steam or relieve tension. Randall didn't think Michael Donahue was one of them. "Let me do my job, Mr. Donahue."

Michael gave him a long, steady look. "Someone's been playing games, deadly ones, with someone very important to me. If you were in my place, would you twiddle your thumbs and wait?"

Randall smiled, just a little. "You know, Donahue, I never miss your show. Great entertainment. Some of this business sounds just like one of your shows."

"Like one of my shows," Michael repeated slowly.

"Problem is, things don't work the same way out here in the world as they do on television. But it sure is a pleasure to watch. Here comes your lady."

Michael sprang up and headed for her.

"I'm fine," she told him before he could ask.

"Not entirely." Behind her a young, white-coated doctor stood impatiently. "Miss McVie has a concussion."

"He put a few stitches in my head and wants to hold me prisoner." She gave the doctor a sweet smile and linked arms with Michael. "Let's go home."

"Just a minute." Keeping her beside him, Michael turned to the doctor. "You want her in the hospital?"

"Michael—"

"Shut up."

"Anyone suffering from a concussion should be routinely checked. Miss McVie would be wise to remain overnight with professional care."

"I'm not staying in the hospital because I have a bump on the head. Good afternoon, Lieutenant."

"Miss McVie."

Lifting her chin, she looked back at the doctor. "Now, Doctor . . ."

"Barnhouse."

"Dr. Barnhouse," she began. "I will take your advice to a point. I'll rest, avoid stress. At the first sign of nausea or dizziness, I'll be on your doorstep. I can assure you, now that you've convinced Michael I'm an invalid, I'll be properly smothered and hovered over. You'll have to be satisfied with that."

Far from satisfied, the doctor directed himself to Michael. "I can't force her to stay, of course."

Michael lifted a brow. "If you think I can, you've got a lot to learn about women."

Resigned, Barnhouse turned back to Pandora. "I want to

see you in a week, sooner if any of the symptoms we discussed show up. You're to rest for twenty-four hours. That
means horizontally."

"Yes, Doctor." She offered a hand, which he took grudgingly. "You were very gentle. Thank you."

His lips twitched. "A week," he repeated and strode back
down the hall.

"If I didn't know better," Michael mused, "I'd say he
wanted to keep you here just to look at you."

"Of course. I look stunning with blood running down my
face and a hole in my head."

"I thought so." He kissed her cheek, but used the gesture
to get a closer look at her wound. The stitches were small
and neat, disappearing into her hairline. After counting six
of them, his determination iced. "Come on, we'll go home
so I can start pampering you."

"I'll take you myself." Randall gestured toward the door.
"I might as well look around a bit while I'm there."

* * *

Sweeney clucked like a mother hen and had Pandora bundled into bed five minutes after she'd walked in the door.
If she'd had the strength, Pandora would have argued for
form's sake. Instead she let herself be tucked under a com-
forter, fed soup and sweet tea, and fussed over. Though
the doctor had assured her it was perfectly safe to sleep,
she thought of the old wives' tale and struggled to stay
awake. Armed with a sketch pad and pencil, she whiled
away the time designing. But when she began to tire of
that, she began to think.

Murder. It would have been nothing less than murder.
Murder for gain, she mused, an impossible thing for her
to understand. She'd told herself before that her life was

threatened, but somehow it had seemed remote. She had only to touch her own forehead now to prove just how direct it had become.

An uncle, a cousin, an aunt? Which one wanted Jolley's fortune so badly to murder for it? Not for the first time, Pandora wished she knew them better, understood them better. She realized she'd simply followed Jolley's lead and dismissed them as boring.

And that was true enough, Pandora assured herself. She'd been to a party or two with all of them. Monroe would huff, Biff would preen, Ginger would prattle, and so on. But boring or not, one of them had slipped over the line of civilized behavior. And they were willing to step over her to do it. Slowly, from memory, she began to sketch each of her relatives. Perhaps that way, she'd see something that was buried in her subconscious.

When Michael came in, she had sketches lined in rows over her spread. "Quite a rogues' gallery."

He'd come straight from the garage, where he and Randall had found the still-wet brake fluid on the concrete. Not all of it, Michael mused. Whoever had tampered with the brakes had left enough fluid in so that the car would react normally for the first few miles. And then, nothing. Michael had already concluded that the police would find a hole in the lines. Just as they'd find one in the lines of Pandora's, to match the dark puddle beneath her car. It had been every bit as lethal as his.

He wasn't ready to tell Pandora that whoever had tried to kill them had been as close as the garage a day, perhaps two, before. Instead he looked at her sketches.

"What do you see?" she demanded.

"That you have tremendous talent and should give serious thought to painting."

"I mean in their faces." Impatient with herself, she drew

her legs up cross-legged. "There's just nothing there. No spark, no streak of anything that tells me this one's capable of killing."

"Anyone's capable of killing. Oh yes," Michael added when she opened her mouth to disagree. "Anyone. It's simply that the motive has to fit the personality, the circumstances, the need. When a person's threatened, he kills. For some it's only when their lives or the lives of someone they love are threatened."

"That's entirely different."

"No." He sat on the bed. "It's a matter of different degrees. Some people kill because their home is threatened, their possessions. Some kill because a desire is threatened. Wealth, power, those are very strong desires.

"So a very ordinary, even conventional person might kill to achieve that desire."

He gestured to her sketches. "One of them tried. Aunt Patience with her round little face and myopic eyes."

"You can't seriously believe—"

"She's devoted to Morgan, obsessively so. She's never married. Why? Because she's always taken care of him."

He picked up the next sketch. "Or there's Morgan himself, stout, blunt, hard-nosed. He thought Jolley was mad and a nuisance."

"They all did."

"Exactly. Carlson, straitlaced, humorless, and Jolley's only surviving son."

"He tried contesting the will."

"Going the conventional route. Still, he knew his father was shrewd, perhaps better than anyone. Who's to say he wouldn't cover his bases in a more direct way? Biff . . ." He had a laugh as he looked at the sketch. Pandora had drawn him precisely as he was. Self-absorbed.

"I can't see him getting his hands dirty."

"For a slice of a hundred fifty million? I can. Pretty little Ginger. One wonders if she can possibly be as sweet and spacey as she appears. And Hank." Pandora had drawn him with his arm muscle flexed. "Would he settle for a couple of thousand when he could have millions?"

"I don't know—that's just the point." Pandora shuffled the sketches. "Even when I have them all lined up in front of me, I don't know."

"Lined up," Michael murmured. "Maybe that is the answer. I think it's time we had a nice family party."

"Party? You don't mean actually invite them all here."

"It's perfect."

"They won't come."

"Oh yes, they will." He was already thinking ahead. "You can bank on it. A little hint that things aren't going well around here, and they'll jump at the chance to give us an extra push. You see the doctor in a week. If he gives you a clean bill of health, we're going to start a little game of our own."

"What game?"

"In a week," he repeated, and took her face in his hands. It was narrow, dominated by the mop of hair and sharp eyes. Not beautiful, but special. It had taken him a long time to admit it. "A bit pale."

"I'm always pale with a concussion. Are you going to pamper me?"

"At least." But his smile faded as he gathered her close. "Oh God, I thought I'd lost you."

The trace of desperation in his voice urged her to soothe. "We'd both have been lost if you hadn't handled the car so well." She snuggled into his shoulder. It was real and solid, like the one she'd sometimes imagined leaning on. It wouldn't hurt, just this once, to pretend it would always be there. "I never thought we'd walk away from that one."

"But we did." He drew back to look at her. She looked tired

and drawn, but he knew her will was as strong as ever. "And now we're going to talk about what you said to me right before we crashed."

"Wasn't I screaming?"

"No."

"If I criticized your driving, I apologize."

He tightened his grip on her chin. "You told me you loved me." He watched her mouth fall open in genuine surprise. Some men might have been insulted. Michael could bless his sense of humor. "It could technically be called a deathbed confession."

Had she? She could only remember reaching for him in those last seconds, knowing they were about to die together. "I was hysterical," she began, and tried to draw back.

"It didn't sound like raving to me."

"Michael, you heard Dr. Barnhouse. I'm not supposed to have any stress. If you want to be helpful, see about some more tea."

"I've something better for relaxing the muscles and soothing the nerves." He laid her back against the pillows, sliding down with her. Sweetly, tenderly, he ran his lips down the lines of her cheekbones. "I want to hear you tell me again, here."

"Michael—"

"No, lie back." And his hands, gentle and calm, stilled her. "I need to touch you, just touch you. There's plenty of time for the rest."

He was so kind, so patient. More than once she'd wondered how such a restive, volatile man could have such comforting hands. Taking off only his shoes, he slipped into bed with her. He held her in the crook of his arm and stroked until he felt her sigh of relief. "I'm going to take care of you," he murmured. "When you're well, we'll take care of each other."

"I'll be fine tomorrow." But her voice was thick and sleepy.

"Sure you will." He'd keep her in bed another twenty-four hours if he had to chain her. "You haven't told me again. Are you in love with me, Pandora?"

She was so tired, so drained. It seemed she'd reached a point where she could fight nothing. "What if I am?" She managed to tilt her head back to stare at him. His fingers rubbed gently at her temple, easing even the dull echo of pain. "People fall in and out of love all the time."

"People." He lowered his head so that he could just skim her lips with his. "Not Pandora. It infuriates you, doesn't it?"

She wanted to glare but closed her eyes instead. "Yes. I'm doing my best to reverse the situation."

He snuggled down beside her, content for now. She loved him. He still had time to make her like the idea. "Let me know how it works out," he said, and lulled her to sleep.

CHAPTER 12

Michael studied the dark stains on the garage floor with a kind of grim fascination. Draining the brake fluid from an intended victim's car was a hackneyed device, one expected from time to time on any self-respecting action-adventure show. Viewers and readers alike developed a certain fondness for old, reliable angles in the same way they appreciated the new and different. Though it took on a different picture when it became personal, the car careering out of control down a steep mountain road was as old as the Model T.

He'd used it himself, just as he'd used the anonymous gift of champagne. And the bogus-message routine, he mused as an idea began to stir. Just last season one of *Logan's* heroines of the week had been locked in a cellar—left in the dark after going to investigate a window slamming in the wind. It too was a classic. Each and every one of the ploys used against himself and Pandora could have been lifted from one of his own plots. Randall had pointed it out, though he'd been joking. It didn't seem very funny.

Michael cursed himself, knowing he should have seen the pattern before. Perhaps he hadn't simply because it had been a pattern, a trite one by Hollywood standards. Whether it was accidental or planned, Michael decided he wasn't about to be outplotted. He'd make his next move taking a page from the classic mystery novels. Going into the house, Michael went to the phone and began to structure his scene.

He was just completing his last call when Pandora came down the hall toward him. "Michael, you've got to do something about Sweeney."

Michael leaned back against the newel post and studied her. She looked wonderful—rested, healthy and annoyed. "Isn't it time for your afternoon nap?"

"That's just what I'm talking about." The annoyance deepened between her brows and pleased him. "I don't need an afternoon nap. It's been over a week since the accident." She pulled a leather thong out of her hair and began to run it through her fingers. "I've seen the doctor, and he said I was fine."

"I thought it was more something along the lines of you having a head like a rock."

She narrowed her eyes. "He was annoyed because I healed perfectly without him. The point is, I am healed, but if Sweeney keeps nagging and hovering, I'll have a relapse." It came out as a declaration as she stood straight in front of him, chin lifted, looking as though she'd never been ill a day in her life.

"What would you like me to do?"

"She'll listen to you. For some reason she has the idea that you're infallible. Mr. Donahue this, Mr. Donahue that." She slapped the leather against her palm. "For the past week all I've heard is how charming, handsome and strong you are. It's a wonder I recovered at all."

His lips twitched, but he understood Sweeney's flattery could undo any progress he'd made. "The woman's perceptive.

However . . ." He stopped Pandora's retort by holding up a hand. "Because I'd never refuse you anything—" when she snorted he ignored it "—and because she's been driving me crazy fussing over my wrist, I'm going to take care of it."

Pandora tilted her head. "How?"

"Sweeney's going to be too busy over the next few days to fuss over us. She'll have the dinner party to fuss over."

"What dinner party?"

"The dinner party we're going to give next week for all our relatives."

She glanced at the phone, remembering he'd been using it when she'd come down the hall. "What have you been up to?"

"Just setting the scene, cousin." He rocked back on his heels, already imagining. "I think we'll have Sweeney dig out the best china, though I doubt we'll have time to use it."

"Michael." She didn't want to seem a coward, but the accident had taught her something about caution and self-preservation. "We won't just be inviting relatives. One of them tried to kill us."

"And failed." He took her chin in his hand. "Don't you think he'll try again, Pandora, and again? The police can't patrol the grounds indefinitely. And," he added with his fingers tightening, "I'm not willing to let bygones be bygones." His gaze skimmed up to where her hair just covered the scar on her forehead. The doctor had said it would fade, but Michael's memory of it never would. "We're going to settle this, my way."

"I don't like it."

"Pandora." He gave her a charming smile and pinched her cheek. "Trust me."

The fact that she did only made her more nervous. With

a sigh, she took his hand. "Let's tell Sweeney to kill the fatted calf."

*   *   *

Right down to the moment the first car arrived, Pandora was certain no one would come. She'd sat through a discussion of Michael's plan, argued, disagreed, admired and ultimately she'd given up. Theatrics, she'd decided. But there was enough Jolley in her to look forward to the show, especially when she was one of the leads. And she had, as they said in the business, her part cold.

She'd dressed for the role in a slim, strapless black dress. For flair, she'd added a sterling silver necklace she'd fashioned in an exaggerated star burst. Matching earrings dripped nearly to her chin. If Michael wanted drama, who was she to argue? As the night of the dinner party had grown closer, her nerves had steeled into determination.

When he saw her at the top of the stairs, he was speechless. Had he really convinced himself all these years she had no real beauty? At the moment, poised, defiant and enjoying herself, she made every other woman he'd known look like a shadow. And if he told her so, she wouldn't believe it for a moment. Instead he merely nodded and rocked back on his heels.

"Perfect," he told her as she walked down the main stairs. Standing at the base in a dark suit, Michael looked invincible, and ruthless. "The sophisticated heroine." He took her hand. "Cool and sexy. Hitchcock would've made you a star."

"Don't forget what happened to Janet Leigh."

He laughed and sent one of her earrings spinning. "Nervous?"

"Not as much as I'd thought I'd be. If this doesn't work—"

"Then we're no worse off than we are now. You know what to do."

"We've rehearsed it a half-dozen times. I still have the bruises."

He leaned closer to kiss both bare shoulders. "I always thought you'd be a natural. When this is over, we have a scene of our own to finish. No, don't pull back," he warned as she attempted to. "It's too late to pull back." They stood close, nearly mouth to mouth. "It's been too late all along."

Nerves she'd managed to quell came racing back, but they had nothing to do with plots or plans. "You're being dramatic."

With a nod, he tangled his fingers in her hair. "My sense of drama, your streak of practicality. An interesting combination."

"An uneasy one."

"If life's too easy, you sleep through it," Michael decided. "It sounds like the first of our guests are arriving," he murmured as they heard the sound of a car. He kissed her briefly. "Break a leg."

She wrinkled her nose at his back. "That's what I'm afraid of."

Within a half hour, everyone who had been at the reading of the will, except Fitzhugh, was again in the library. No one seemed any more relaxed than they'd been almost six months before. Jolley beamed down on them from the oil painting. From time to time Pandora glanced up at it almost expecting him to wink. To give everyone what they'd come for, Pandora and Michael kept arguing about whatever came to mind. Time for the game to begin, she decided.

Carlson stood with his wife near a bookshelf. He looked cross and impatient and glowered when Pandora approached.

"Uncle Carlson, I'm so glad you could make it. We don't see nearly enough of each other."

"Don't soft-soap me." He swirled his scotch but didn't drink. "If you've got the idea you can talk me out of contesting this absurd will, you're mistaken."

"I wouldn't dream of it. Fitzhugh tells me you don't have a chance." She smiled beautifully. "But I have to agree the will's absurd, especially after being forced to live in the same house with Michael all these months." She ran a finger down one of the long, flattened prongs of her necklace. "I'll tell you, Uncle Carlson, there have been times I've seriously considered throwing in the towel. He's done everything possible to make the six months unbearable. Once he pretended his mother was ill, and he had to go to California. Next thing I knew I was locked in the basement. Childish games," she muttered, sending Michael a look of utter dislike. Out of the corner of her eye, she saw Carlson take a quick, nervous drink. "Well, the sentence is nearly up." She turned back with a fresh smile. "I'm so glad we could have this little celebration. Michael's finally going to open a bottle of champagne he's been hoarding since Christmas."

Pandora watched Carlson's wife drop her glass on the Turkish carpet. "Dear me," Pandora said softly. "We'll have to get something to mop that up. Freshen your drink?"

"No, she's fine." Carlson took his wife by the elbow. "Excuse me."

As they moved away, Pandora felt a quick thrill of excitement. So, it had been Carlson.

"I quit smoking about six months ago," Michael told Hank and his wife, earning healthy approval.

"You'll never regret it," Hank stated in his slow, deliberate way. "You're responsible for your own body."

"I've been giving that a lot of thought lately," Michael said dryly. "But living with Pandora the past few months hasn't made it easy. She's made this past winter miserable. She had someone send me a fake message so I'd go flying off to

California thinking my mother was ill." He glanced over his shoulder and scowled at Pandora's back.

"If you've gotten through six months without smoking . . ." Meg began, guiding the conversation back to Michael's health.

"It's a miracle I have living with that woman. But it's almost over." He grinned at Hank. "We're having champagne instead of carrot juice for dinner. I've been saving this bottle since Christmas for just the right occasion."

He saw Hank's fingers whiten around his glass of Perrier and Meg's color drain. "We don't—" Hank looked helplessly at Meg. "We don't drink."

"Champagne isn't drinking," Michael said jovially. "It's celebrating. Excuse me." He moved to the bar as if to freshen his drink and waited for Pandora to join him. "It's Hank."

"No." She added a splash of vermouth to her glass. "It's Carlson." Following the script, she glared at him. "You're an insufferable bore, Michael. Putting up with you isn't worth any amount of money."

"Intellectual snob." He toasted her. "I'm counting the days."

With a sweep of her skirts, Pandora walked over to Ginger. "I don't know how I manage to hold my temper with that man."

Ginger checked her face in a pretty silver compact. "I've always thought he was kind of cute."

"You haven't had to live with him. We were hardly together a week when he broke into my workshop and vandalized it. Then he tried to pass the whole thing off as the work of a vagrant."

Ginger frowned and touched a bit of powder to her nose. "It didn't seem like something he'd do to me. I told—" She caught herself and looked back at Pandora with a vague smile. "Those are pretty earrings."

Michael steeled himself to listen to Morgan's terse opinion on the stock market. The moment he found an opening, he broke in. "Once everything's settled, I'll have to come to you for advice. I've been thinking about getting more actively involved with one of Jolley's chemical firms. There's a lot of money in fertilizer—and pesticides." He watched Patience flutter her hands and subside at a glare from Morgan.

"Software," Morgan said briefly.

Michael only smiled. "I'll look into it."

Pandora tried unsuccessfully to pump Ginger. The five-minute conversation left her suspicious, confused and with the beginnings of a headache. She decided to try her luck on Biff.

"You're looking well." She smiled at him and nodded at his wife.

"You're looking a bit pale, cousin."

"The past six months haven't been a picnic." She cast a look at Michael. "Of course, you've always detested him."

"Of course," Biff said amiably.

"I've yet to discover why Uncle Jolley was fond of him. Besides being a bore, Michael has an affection for odd practical jokes. He got a tremendous kick out of locking me in the cellar."

Biff smiled into his glass. "He's never quite been in our class."

Pandora bit her tongue, then agreed. "Do you know, he even called me one night, disguising his voice. He tried to frighten me by saying someone was trying to kill me."

Biff's brows drew together as he stared into Pandora's eyes. "Odd."

"Well, things are almost settled. By the way, did you enjoy the champagne I sent you?"

Biff's fingers froze on his glass. "Champagne?"

"Right after Christmas."

"Oh yes." He lifted his glass again, studying her as he drank. "So it was you."

"I got the idea when someone sent Michael a bottle at Christmastime. He promises to finally open it tonight. Excuse me, I want to check on dinner."

Her eyes met Michael's briefly as she slipped from the room. They'd set his scene, she thought. Now she had to move the action along. In the kitchen she found Sweeney finishing up the final preparation for the meal.

"If they're hungry," Sweeney began, "they'll just have to wait ten minutes."

"Sweeney, it's time to turn off the main power switch."

"I know, I know. I was just finishing this ham."

Sweeney had been instructed to, at Pandora's signal, go down to the cellar, turn off the power, then wait exactly one minute and turn it on again. She had been skeptical about the whole of Michael and Pandora's plan but had finally agreed to participate in it. Wiping her hands on her apron, the cook went to the cellar door. Pandora took a deep breath and walked back to the library.

Michael had positioned himself near the desk. He gave Pandora the slightest of nods when she entered. "Dinner in ten minutes," she announced brightly as she swept across the room.

"That gives us just enough time." Michael took the stage and couldn't resist starting with a tried and true line. He didn't have to see Pandora to know she was taking her position. "You all must be wondering why we brought you here tonight." He lifted his glass and looked from one face to the next. "One of you is a murderer."

On cue, the lights went out and pandemonium struck. Glasses shattered, women screamed, a table was overturned. When the lights blinked on, everyone froze. Lying half under the desk, facedown, was Pandora. Beside her was a letter opener with a curved, ornate hilt and blood on the blade. In an instant Michael was beside her, lifting her into his arms before anyone had a chance to react. Silently, he carried her from the room. Several minutes passed before he returned, alone. He gazed, hot and hard, at every face in the room.

"A murderer," he repeated. "She's dead."

"What do you mean she's dead?" Carlson pushed his way forward. "What kind of game is this? Let's have a look at her."

"No one's touching her." Michael effectively blocked his way. "No one's touching anything or leaving this room until the police get here."

"Police?" Pale and shaken, Carlson glanced around. "We don't want that. We'll have to handle this ourselves. She's just fainted."

"Her blood's all over this," Michael commented gesturing to the bloodstained letter opener.

"No!" Meg pushed forward until she'd broken through the crowd around the desk. "No one was supposed to be hurt. Only frightened. It wasn't supposed to be like this. Hank." She reached out, then buried her face against his chest.

"We were only going to play some tricks," he murmured.

"First-degree murder isn't a trick."

"We never—" He looked at Michael in shock. "Not murder," he managed, holding Meg as tightly as she was holding him.

"You didn't want to drink the champagne, either, did you, Hank?"

"That's when I wanted to stop." Still sobbing, Meg turned in her husband's arms. "I even called and tried to warn her. I thought it was wrong all along, just a mean trick, but we needed money. The gym's drained everything we have. We thought if we could make the two of you angry enough with each other, you'd break the terms of the will. But that's all. Hank and I stayed in the cabin and waited. Then he went into Pandora's shop and turned things upside down. If she thought you did it—"

"I never thought she would," Ginger piped up. Two tears rolled down her cheeks. "Really, it all seemed silly and— exciting."

Michael looked at his pretty, weeping cousin. "So you were part of it."

"Well, I didn't really do anything. But when Aunt Patience explained it to me . . ."

"Patience?" There were patterns and patterns. A new one emerged.

"Morgan deserved his share." The old woman wrung her hands and looked everywhere but at the bloodstained letter opener. She'd thought she'd done the right thing. It all sounded so simple. "We thought we could make one of you leave, then it would all be the way it should be."

"Message," Morgan said, puffing wide-eyed on his cigar. "Not murder." He turned to Carlson. "Your idea."

"It's preposterous." Carlson mopped his brow with a white silk handkerchief. "The lawyers were incompetent. They haven't been able to do a thing. I was merely protecting my rights."

"With murder."

"Don't be ridiculous." He nearly sounded staid and stuffy again. "The plan was to get you out of the house. I did nothing more than lock her in the cellar. When I heard about the champagne, I had a doubt or two, but after all, it wasn't fatal."

"Heard about the champagne." It was what Michael had waited for. "From whom?"

"It was Biff," Meg told him. "Biff set it all up, promised nothing would go wrong."

"Just an organizer." Biff gauged the odds, then shrugged. "All's fair, cousin. Everyone in this room had their hand in." He held his up, examining it. "There's no blood on mine. I'd vote for you." He gave Michael a cool smile. "After all, it's no secret you couldn't abide each other."

"You set it up." Michael took a step closer. "There's also a matter of tampering with my car."

Biff moved his shoulders again, but Michael saw the sweat bead above his lips. "Everyone in this room had a part in it. Any of you willing to turn yourselves in?" His breath came faster as he backed away. "One of them panicked and did this. You won't find my fingerprints on that letter opener."

"When someone's attempted murder once," Michael said calmly, "it's easier to prove he tried again."

"You won't prove anything. Any of us might have drained the brake lines in your car. You can't prove I did."

"I don't need to." In a quick move, Michael caught him cleanly on the jaw and sent him reeling. Before he could fall, Michael had him by the collar. "I never said anything about draining the lines."

Feeling the trap close, Biff struck out blindly. Fists swinging, they tumbled to the floor. A Tiffany lamp shattered in a pile of color. They rolled, locked together, into a Belker table that shook from the impact. Shocked and ineffective, the rest stepped back and gave them room.

"Michael, that's quite enough." Pandora entered the room, her hair mussed and her clothes disheveled. "We have company."

Panting, he dragged Biff to his feet. His wrist sang a bit, but he considered it a pleasure. Charles, looking dignified in his best suit, opened the library doors. "Dinner is served."

* * *

Two hours later, Pandora and Michael shared a small feast in the library. "I never thought it would work," Pandora said over a mouthful of ham. "It shouldn't have."

"The more predictable the moves, the more predictable the end."

"Lieutenant Randall didn't seem too pleased."

"He wanted to do it his way." Michael moved his shoulders. "Since he'd already discovered Biff had been visiting other members of the family and making calls to them, he was bound to find out something eventually."

"The easy way." She rubbed the back of her neck. "Do you know how uncomfortable it is to play dead?"

"You were great." He leaned over to kiss her. "A star."

"The letter opener with the stage blood was a nice touch. Still, if they'd all stuck together . . ."

"We already knew someone was weakening because of the warning call. Turned out that Meg had had enough."

"I've been thinking about investing in their gym."

"It wouldn't hurt."

"What do you think's going to happen?"

"Oh, Carlson'll get off more or less along with the rest of them, excluding Biff. I don't think we have to worry about going to court over the will. As for our dear cousin—" Michael lifted a glass of champagne "—he's going to be facing tougher charges than malicious mischief or burglary. I may never get my television back, but he isn't going to be wearing any Brooks Brothers suits for a while. Only prison blues."

"You gave him another black eye," Pandora mused.

"Yeah." With a grin, Michael drank the wine. "Now you and I only have to cruise through the next two weeks."

"Then it's over."

"No." He took her hand before she could rise. "Then it begins." He slipped the glass from her other hand and pressed her back against the cushions. "How long?"

Pandora struggled to keep the tension from showing. "How long what?"

"Have you been in love with me?"

She jerked, then was frustrated when he held her back. "I'm not sitting here feeding your ego."

"All right, we'll start with me." He leaned back companionably and boxed her in. "I think I fell in love with you when you came back from the Canary Islands and walked into the parlor. You had legs all the way to your waist and you looked down your nose at me. I've never been the same."

"I've had enough games, Michael," she said stiffly.

"So've I." He traced a finger down her cheek. "You said you loved me, Pandora."

"Under duress."

"Then I'll just have to keep you under duress because I'm not giving you up now. Why don't we get married right here?"

She'd started to give him a hefty shove and stopped with her hands pressed against his chest. "What?"

"Right here in the library." He glanced around, ignoring the overturned tables and broken china. "It'd be a nice touch."

"I don't know what you're talking about."

"It's very simple. Here's the plot. You love me, I love you."

"That's not simple," she managed. "I've just been accessible. Once you get back to your blond dancers and busty starlets, you'll—"

"What blond dancers? I can't stand blond dancers."

"Michael, this isn't anything I can joke about."

"Just wait. You buy a nice white dress, maybe a veil. A veil would suit you. We get a minister, lots of flowers and have a very traditional marriage ceremony. After that, we settle into the Folley, each pursuing our respective careers. In a year, two at the most, we give Charles and Sweeney a baby to fuss over. See?" He kissed her ear.

"People's lives aren't screenplays," she began.

"I'm crazy about you, Pandora. Look at me." He took her chin and held it so that their faces were close. "As an artist, you're supposed to be able to see below the surface. That should be easy since you've always told me I'm shallow."

"I was wrong." She wanted to believe. Her heart already did. "Michael, if you're playing games with me, I'll kill you myself."

"Games are over. I love you, it's that simple."

"Simple," she murmured, surprised she could speak at all. "You want to get married?"

"Living together's too easy."

She was more surprised that she could laugh. "Easy?"

"That's right." He shifted her until she was lying flat on the sofa, his body pressed into hers. When his mouth came down, it wasn't patient, wasn't gentle, and everything he thought, everything he felt, communicated itself through that one contact. As she did rarely, as he asked rarely, she went limp and pliant. Her arms went around him. Perhaps it was easy after all.

"I love you, Michael."

"We're getting married."

"It looks that way."

His eyes were intense when he lifted his head. "I'm going to make life tough on you, Pandora. That's just to pay you back for the fact that you'll be the most exasperating wife on record. Do we understand each other?"

Her smile bloomed slowly. "I suppose we always have."

Michael pressed a kiss to her forehead, to the tip of her nose, then to her lips. "He understood both of us."

She followed his gaze to Jolley's portrait. "Crazy old goat has us right where he wants us. I imagine he's having a good laugh." She rubbed her cheek against Michael's. "I just wish he could be here to see us married."

Michael lifted a brow. "Who says he won't be?" He pulled her up and picked up both glasses. "To Maximillian Jolley McVie."

"To Uncle Jolley." Pandora clinked her glass to Michael's. "To us."

Home for Christmas

CHAPTER 1

So much can change in ten years. He was prepared for it. All during the flight from London and the long, winding drive north from Boston to Quiet Valley, New Hampshire, population 326—or it had been ten years before when Jason Law had last been there—he'd thought of how different things would be. A decade, even for a forgotten little town in New England was bound to bring changes. There would have been deaths and births. Houses and shops would have changed hands. Some of them might not be there at all.

Not for the first time since Jason had decided to visit his hometown did he feel foolish. After all, it was very likely he wouldn't even be recognized. He'd left a thin, defiant twenty-year-old in a scruffy pair of jeans. He was coming back a man who'd learned how to replace defiance with arrogance and succeed. His frame was still lean, but it fitted nicely into clothes tailored on Savile Row and Seventh Avenue. Ten years had changed him from a desperate boy determined to make his mark to an outwardly complacent man who had. What ten years hadn't changed, was what was inside. He was still looking for roots, for his place. That was why he was heading back to Quiet Valley.

The road still twisted and turned through the woods, up

the mountains and down again, as it had when he'd headed in the opposite direction on a Greyhound. Snow covered the ground, smooth here, bumpy there where it was heaped over rocks. In the sunlight trees shimmered with it. Had he missed it? He'd spent one winter in snow up to his waist in the Andes. He'd spent another sweltering in Africa. The years ran together, but oddly enough, Jason could remember every place he'd spent Christmas over the last ten years, though he'd never celebrated the holiday. The road narrowed and swept into a wide curve. He could see the mountains, covered with pines and dusted with white. Yes, he'd missed it.

Sun bounced off the mounds of snow. He adjusted his dark glasses and slowed down, then on impulse, stopped. When he stepped from the car, his breath came in streams of smoke. His skin tingled with the cold but he didn't button his coat or reach in his pockets for his gloves. He needed to feel it. Breathing in the thin, icy air was like breathing in thousands of tiny needles. Jason walked the few feet to the top of the ridge and looked down on Quiet Valley.

He'd been born there, raised there. He'd learned of grief there—and he'd fallen in love. Even from the distance he could see her house—her parents' house, Jason reminded himself and felt the old, familiar surge of fury. She'd be living somewhere else now, with her husband, with her children.

When he discovered that his hands were balled into fists, he carefully relaxed them. Channeling emotion was a skill he'd turned into an art over the past decade. If he could do it in his work, reporting on famine, war, and suffering, he could do it for himself. His feelings for Faith had been a boy's feelings. He was a man now, and she, like Quiet Valley, was only part of his childhood. He'd traveled more than five thousand miles just to prove it. Turning away, he got back in the car and started down the mountain.

From the distance, Quiet Valley had looked like a Currier and Ives painting, all white and snug between mountain and forest. As he drew closer, it became less idyllic and more approachable. The tired paint showed here and there on some of the outlying houses. Fences bowed under snow. He saw a few new houses in what had once been open fields. Change. He reminded himself he'd expected it.

Smoke puffed out of chimneys. Dogs and children raced in the snow. A check of his watch showed him it was half past three. School was out, and he'd been traveling for fifteen hours. The smart thing to do was to see if the Valley Inn was still in operation and get a room. A smile played around his mouth as he wondered if old Mr. Beantree still ran the place. He couldn't count the times Beantree had told him he'd never amount to anything but trouble. He had a Pulitzer and an Overseas Press Award to prove differently.

Houses were grouped closer together now, and he recognized them. The Bedford place, Tim Hawkin's house, the Widow Marchant's. He slowed again as he passed the widow's tidy blue clapboard. She hadn't changed the color, he noticed and felt foolishly pleased. And the old spruce in the front yard was already covered with bright-red ribbons. She'd been kind to him. Jason hadn't forgotten how she had fixed hot chocolate and listened to him for hours when he'd told her of the travels he wanted to make, the places he dreamed of seeing. She'd been in her seventies when he'd left, but of tough New England stock. He thought he might still find her in her kitchen patiently fueling the wood stove and listening to her Rachmaninoff.

The streets of the town were clear and tidy. New Englanders were a practical lot, and Jason thought, as sturdy as the bedrock they'd planted themselves on. The town had not changed as he'd anticipated. Railings Hardware still sat on the corner off Main and the post office still occupied a brick building no bigger than a garage. The same red garland was strung from lamppost to lamppost as it had been all through his youth during each holiday season. Children were building a snowman in front of the Litner place. But whose children? Jason wondered. He scanned the red mufflers and bright boots knowing any of them might be Faith's. The fury came back and he looked away.

The sign on the Valley Inn had been repainted, but nothing else about the three-story square stone building was different. The walkway had been scraped clean and smoke billowed out of both chimneys. He found himself driving beyond it. There was something else to do first, something he'd already known he would have to do. He could have turned at the corner, driven a block and seen the house where he grew up. But he didn't.

Near the end of Main would be a tidy white house, bigger than most of the others with two big bay windows and a wide front porch. Tom Monroe had brought his bride there. A reporter of Jason's caliber knew how to ferret out such information. Perhaps Faith had put up the lace curtains she'd always wanted at the windows. Tom would have bought her the pretty china tea sets she'd longed for. He'd have given her exactly what she'd wanted. Jason would have given her a suitcase and a motel room in countless cities. She'd made her choice.

After ten years he discovered it was no easier to accept. Still, he forced himself to be calm as he pulled up to the curb. He and Faith had been friends once, lovers briefly. He'd had other lovers since, and she had a husband. But he could still remember her as she'd looked at eighteen, lovely, soft, eager. She had wanted to go with him, but he wouldn't let her. She had promised to wait, but she hadn't. He took a deep breath as he climbed from the car.

The house was lovely. In the big bay window that faced the street was a Christmas tree, cluttered and green in the daylight. At night it would glitter like magic. He could be sure of it because Faith had always believed so strongly in magic.

Standing on the sidewalk he found himself dealing with fear. He'd covered wars and interviewed terrorists but he'd never felt the stomach-churning fear that he did now, standing on a narrow snow-brushed sidewalk facing a pristine white house with holly bushes by the door. He could turn around, he reminded himself. Drive back to the inn or simply out of town again. There was no need to see her again. She was out of his life. Then he saw the lace curtains at the window and the old resentment stirred, every bit as strong as fear.

As he started down the walk a girl raced around the side of the house just ahead of a well-aimed snowball. She dived, rolled and evaded. In an instant, she was up again and hurling one of her own.

"Bull's-eye, Jimmy Harding!" With a whoop, she turned to run and barreled into Jason. "Sorry." With snow covering her from head to foot, she looked up and grinned. Jason felt the world spin backward.

She was the image of her mother. The sable hair peeked out of her cap and fell untidily to her shoulders. The small, triangular face was dominated by big blue eyes that seemed to hold jokes all of their own. But it was the smile, the one that said, isn't this fun? that caught him by the throat. Shaken, he stepped back while the girl dusted herself off and studied him.

"I've never seen you before."

He slipped his hands into his pockets. *But I've seen you,* he thought. "No. Do you live here?"

"Yeah, but the shop's around the side." A snowball landed with a plop at her feet. She lifted a brow in a sophisticated manner. "That's Jimmy," she said in the tone of a woman barely tolerating a suitor. "His aim's lousy. The shop's around the side," she repeated as she bent to ball more snow. "Just walk right in."

She raced off holding a ball in each hand. Jason figured Jimmy was in for a surprise.

Faith's daughter. He hadn't asked her name and nearly called her back. It didn't matter, he told himself. He'd only be in town a few days before he took the next assignment. Just passing through, he thought. Just cleaning the slate.

He backtracked to walk around the side of the house. Though he couldn't imagine what sort of shop Tom could have, he thought it might be best to see him first. He almost relished it.

The little workshop he'd half expected turned out to be a miniature of a Victorian cottage. The sleigh out in front held two life-size dolls dressed in top hats and bonnets, cloaks and top boots. Above the door was a fancy hand-painted sign that read Doll House. To the accompaniment of bells, Jason pushed the door open.

"I'll be right with you."

Hearing her voice again was like stepping back and finding no solid ground. But he'd deal with it, Jason told himself. He'd deal with it because he had to. Slipping off his glasses, he tucked them into his pocket and looked around.

Child-size furniture was set around the room in the manner of a cozy parlor. Dolls of every shape and size and style occupied chairs, stools, shelves and cabinets. In front of an elf-size fireplace where flames shimmered, sat a grandmother of a doll in lace cap and apron. The illusion was so strong Jason almost expected her to begin rocking.

"I'm sorry to keep you waiting." With a china doll in one

hand and a bridal veil in the other, Faith walked through the doorway. "I was right in the middle of . . ." The veil floated out of her hand as she stopped. It waltzed to the floor with no sound at all. Color rushed away from her face, making the deep-blue eyes nearly violet in contrast. In reaction, or defense, she gripped the doll to her breast. "Jason."

CHAPTER 2

Framed in the doorway with the thin winter light creeping through the tiny windows she was lovelier than his memory of her. He'd hoped it would be different. He'd hoped his fantasies of her would be exaggerated as so many fantasies are. But she was here, flesh and blood, and so beautiful she took his breath away. Perhaps because of it, his smile was cynical and his voice cool.

"Hello, Faith."

She couldn't move, forward or back. He trapped her now as he had so many years before. He didn't know it then, she couldn't let him know it now. Emotion, locked and kept secret for so long struggled against will and was held back. "How are you?" she managed to ask, her hands like a vise around the doll.

"Fine." He walked toward her. God, how it pleased him to see the nerves jumping in her eyes. God, how it tormented him to learn she smelled the same. Soft, young, innocent. "You look wonderful." He said it carelessly, like a yawn.

"You were the last person I expected to see walk through the door." One she'd learned to stop looking for. Determined to control herself, Faith loosened her grip on the doll. "How long are you in town?"

"Just a few days. I had the urge."

She laughed and hoped it didn't sound hysterical. "You always did. We read a lot about you. You've been able to see all the places you always wanted to see."

"And more."

She turned away, giving herself a moment to close her eyes and pull her emotions together. "They ran it on the front page when you won the Pulitzer. Mr. Beantree strutted around as though he'd been your mentor. 'Fine boy, Jason Law,' he said. 'Always knew he'd amount to something.'"

"I saw your daughter."

That was the biggest fear, the biggest hope, the dream she'd put to rest years ago. She bent casually to pick up the veil. "Clara?"

"Just outside. She was about to mow down some boy named Jimmy."

"Yes, that's Clara." The smile came quickly and just as stunningly as it had on the child. "She's a vicious competitor," she added and wanted to say like her father, but didn't dare.

There was so much to say, so much that couldn't be said. If he had had one wish at that moment, it would have been to reach out and touch her. Just to touch her once and remember the way it had been.

"I see you have your lace curtains."

Regret washed over her. She'd have settled for bare windows, blank walls. "Yes, I have my lace curtains and you your adventures."

"And this place." He turned to look around again. "When did all this start?"

She could deal with it, she promised herself, this hatefully casual small talk. "I opened it nearly eight years ago now."

He picked a rag doll from a bassinet. "So you sell dolls. A hobby?"

Something else came into her eyes now. Strength. "No, it's my business. I sell them, repair them, even make them."

"Business?" He set the doll down and the smile he gave her had nothing to do with humor. "It's hard for me to picture Tom approving of his wife setting up a business."

"Is it?" It hurt, but she set the china doll on a counter and began to arrange the veil on its head. "You always were perceptive, Jason, but you've been away a long time." She looked over her shoulder and her eyes weren't nervous or even strong. They were simply cold. "A very long time. Tom and I were divorced eight years ago. The last time I heard he was living in Los Angeles. You see, he didn't care for small towns either. Or small-town girls."

He couldn't name the things that stirred in him so he pushed them aside. Bitterness was simpler. "Apparently you picked badly, Faith."

She laughed again but the veil crumpled in her hand. "Apparently I did."

"You didn't wait." It was out before he could stop it. He hated himself for it, and her.

"You were gone." She turned back slowly and folded her hands.

"I told you I'd come back. I told you I'd send for you as soon as I could."

"You never called, or wrote. For three months I—"

"Three months?" Furious, he grabbed her arms. "After everything we'd talked about, everything we'd hoped for, three months was all you could give me?"

She would have given him a lifetime, but there hadn't been a choice. Struggling to keep her voice calm, she looked into his eyes. They were the same—intense, impatient. "I didn't know where you were. You wouldn't even give me that." She pulled away from him because the need was as great as it had always been. "I was eighteen and you were gone."

"And Tom was here."

She set her jaw. "And Tom was here. It's been ten years, Jason, you never once wrote. Why now?"

"I've asked myself the same thing," he murmured and left her standing alone.

* * *

Her dreams had always been too fanciful. As a child Faith had envisioned white chargers and glass slippers. Reality was something to be faced daily in a family where money was scarce and pride was not, but dreams weren't just for nighttime.

She'd fallen in love with Jason when she'd been eight and he ten and he'd bravely vanquished three boys who'd tossed her into the snow. It had taken three of them. Faith could still look back on that with a sense of satisfaction. But it had been Jason fiercely coming to her rescue and sending her opponents scattering that she remembered best. He'd been thin, and his coat had been too large and mended at the elbows. She remembered his eyes, deep, deep brown under brows drawn close in annoyance as he'd looked down at her. Snow had coated his pale-blond hair and reddened his face. She'd looked into his eyes and fallen in love. He'd muttered at her, hauled her up and scolded her for getting in trouble. Then he'd stalked off with his ungloved hands thrust into the pockets of his too-big coat.

Through childhood and into adolescence she'd never looked at another boy. Of course she'd pretended to from time to time hoping it might make Jason Law notice her.

Then when she'd been sixteen and her mother had sewn her a dress for the spring dance at the town hall, he'd noticed. So had several other boys, and Faith had flirted outrageously, with one goal in mind:

Jason Law. Sulky and defiant he'd watched her dance with

one boy after another. She'd made sure of it. Just as she'd made sure she looked directly at him before she'd stepped outside to take the air. He'd followed her, just as she'd hoped. She'd pretended to be sophisticated. He'd been rude. And he'd walked her home under a fat full moon.

There'd been other walks after that—spring, summer, fall, winter. They were in love as only the young can be, carelessly, heedlessly, innocently. She told him of her longings for a house and children, for lace curtains and china cups. He told her of his passion to travel, to see everything, and write it down. She knew he'd felt trapped in the small town, hampered by a father who gave him no love and little hope. He knew she dreamed of quiet rooms with flowers in crystal vases. But they were drawn together and tangled all the dreams into one.

Then one night in the summer when the air was sweet with wild grass they stopped being children and their love stopped being innocent.

"Mom, you're dreaming again."

"What?" Up to her elbows in soapy water, Faith turned. Her daughter stood at the doorway to the kitchen, snugly wrapped in a flannel gown that came up to her chin. With her hair freshly brushed and her face scrubbed clean, she looked like an angel. Faith knew better. "I guess I was. You've finished your homework?"

"Yeah. It's dumb having homework when school's nearly out."

"Don't remind me."

"You're grumpy," Clara declared and eyed the cookie jar. "You should go for one of your walks."

"Just one," Faith said, easily outguessing her daughter. "And don't forget to brush your teeth." She waited while Clara rooted through the jar. "Did you see a man this afternoon? A tall man with blond hair?"

"Uh-huh." Mouth full, Clara turned back to her mother. "He was walking up to the house. I sent him to the shop."

"Did he—say anything to you?"

"Not really. He looked at me kind of funny at first, like he'd seen me before. Do you know him?"

While her heart began a slow, dull thud, Faith dried her hands. "Yes. He used to live here a long time ago."

"Oh. Jimmy liked his car." She wondered if she could talk herself into another cookie.

"I think I will take that walk, Clara, but I want you in bed."

Recognizing the tone, she knew the cookie would have to wait. "Can I count the presents under the tree again?"

"You've counted them ten times."

"Maybe there's a new one."

Laughing, Faith gathered her up. "Not a chance." Then she grinned and carried Clara into the living room. "But it won't hurt to count them one more time."

The air was brittle when she stepped outside and it smelled of snow. There was no reason to lock the doors in a town where she knew everyone. Bundling her coat closer, she glanced back at the second-story window where her daughter slept. Clara was the reason why the house wasn't cold, why her life wasn't empty when both things could easily have been true.

She'd left the tree burning and the lights around the door sent out festive color. Four days until Christmas, she thought, and the wonder of it came home again. From where she stood, the town looked as pretty as a postcard with the strings of lights, the tree with its star in the town square, the street lamps burning. She could smell smoke from the chimneys and the bursting scent of pine.

Some might find it too settled, others would find it dull. But Faith had made it a home for herself and her daughter. She'd altered her life to suit her, and it fitted her well.

No regrets, she promised with one last glance at her daughter's window. No regrets at all.

The wind picked up a bit as she walked. There'd be snow for Christmas. She could feel it. She'd look forward to that, not back any longer.

"Still fond of walking?"

CHAPTER 3

Had she known he'd find her? Perhaps she had. Perhaps she'd needed him to. "Some things don't change," she said simply as Jason fell into step beside her.

"I've found that out in one afternoon." He thought of the town that had stayed so much the same. And of his feelings for the woman beside him. "Where's your daughter?"

"She's sleeping."

He was calmer than he'd been that afternoon, and determined to stay that way. "I didn't ask you if you had other children."

"No." He heard the wistfulness in her voice, just a sigh of it. "There's only Clara."

"How did you pick the name?"

She smiled. It was so like him to ask questions no one else would think of. "From the Nutcracker. I wanted her to be able to dream." As she had. Dropping her hands in her pockets she told herself they were simply two old friends walking through a quiet town. "Are you staying at the inn?"

"Yeah." Amused, Jason rubbed a hand over his chin. "Beantree took my bags up himself."

"Local boy makes good." She turned to look at him. It was easier somehow walking like this. Odd, she realized, she'd seen the boy when she'd looked at him the first time. Now she saw the man. His hair had darkened a bit but was still very blond. It was no longer unkempt, but cut in a carelessly attractive style that had it falling over his brow. His face was still thin, hollow at the cheeks in the way that had always fascinated her. And his mouth was still full, but there was a hardness around it that hadn't been there once. "You did make good, didn't you? You made everything you wanted happen."

"Most everything." When his eyes met hers, she felt all the old longings come back. "What about you, Faith?"

She shook her head, watching the sky as she walked. "I never wanted as much as you, Jason."

"Are you happy?"

"If a person isn't, it's their own fault."

"That's too simple."

"I haven't seen the things you've seen. I haven't had to deal with what you've had to deal with. I am simple, Jason. That was the problem, wasn't it?"

"No." He turned her to face him and slid his hands up to her face. He wore no gloves, and his fingers warmed against her skin. "God, you haven't changed." As she stood very still he combed his fingers up through her hair, then down to where the tips brushed her shoulders. "I've thought about the way you look in the moonlight countless times. It was just like this."

"I've changed, Jason." But her voice was breathless. "So have you."

"Some things don't," he reminded her and gave in to the need.

When his mouth touched hers, he knew that he'd come home. Everything he remembered, everything he thought he'd lost was his again. She was soft and smelled of springtime even when snow dusted the ground around them. Her mouth was willing, even as it had been the first time he'd tasted it. He couldn't explain, even to himself, that every other woman he'd held had been nothing but a shadow of his memory of her. Now she was real, wrapped in his arms and giving him everything he'd forgotten he could have.

Just once, she promised herself as she melted against him. Just once more. How could she have known her life had such a void in it? She'd tried to close the door on the part of her life that included Jason, though she'd known it wasn't possible. She'd tried to tell herself it was only youthful passion and girlish fancy but she'd known that was a lie. There'd been no other men, only memories of one, and wishes, half-forgotten dreams.

She was holding no memory now but Jason, as real and urgent as he'd always been. Everything about him was so familiar, the taste of his lips on hers, the feel of his hair as her fingers raked through it, the scent of man, rough and rugged, that he'd always carried with him even as a boy. He murmured her name and drew her closer, as if the years were trying to separate them again.

She wrapped her arms around him, as willing, as eager, and as in love as she'd been the last time he'd held her. The wind whipped around their ankles, puffing up clouds of snow while the moonlight held them close.

But it wasn't yesterday, she reminded herself as she stepped back. It wasn't tomorrow. It was today, and today had to be faced. She wasn't a child any longer without responsibilities and a love so big it overshadowed anything else. She was a woman with a child to raise and a home to make. He was a wanderer. He'd never pretended to be anything else.

"It's over for us, Jason." But she held his hand a moment longer. "It's been over for a long time."

"No." He caught her before she could turn away. "It isn't. I told myself it was, and that I'd come back and prove it.

You've been eating at me half my life, Faith. It's never going to be over."

"You left me." The tears she promised herself she wouldn't shed spilled over. "You broke my heart. It's barely had time to mend, Jason. You won't break it again."

"You know I had to leave. If you'd waited—"

"It doesn't matter now." With a shake of her head she backed away. She would never be able to explain to him why it hadn't been possible to wait. "It doesn't matter because in a few days you'll be gone again. I won't let you whirl in and out of my life and leave my emotions in chaos. We both made our choices, Jason."

"Damn it, I missed you."

She closed her eyes. When she opened them again, they were dry. "I had to stop missing you. Please leave me alone, Jason. If I thought we could be friends—"

"We always were."

"Always is gone." Nonetheless she held out both hands and took his. "Oh, Jason, you were my best friend, but I can't welcome you home because you scare the hell out of me."

"Faith." He curled his fingers around hers. "We need more time, to talk."

Looking at him she let out a long breath. "You know where to find me, Jason. You always did."

"Let me walk you home."

"No." Calmer, she smiled. "Not this time."

* * *

From the window of his room, Jason could see most of Main Street. He could, if he chose, watch the flow of business in Porterfield's Five and Dime or the collection of people who walked through and loitered in the town square. Too often he found the direction of his gaze wandering to the white house near the end of the street. Because he'd been restless, Jason had been up and at the window when Faith had walked outside with Clara to see her off to school with a group of other children. He'd seen her crouch down to adjust the collar of her daughter's coat. And he'd seen her stand, hatless, her back to him, as she'd watched the children drag themselves off for a day of books. She'd stood there a long time with the wind pulling and tugging at her hair, and he'd waited for her to turn, to look at the inn, to acknowledge somehow that she knew he was there. But she'd walked around the side of the house to her shop without looking back.

Now, hours later, he was at the window again, still restless. From the number of people he could see walk back to the Doll House, her business was thriving. She was working, busy, while he was standing unshaven at a window with his portable typewriter sitting silent on the desk beside him.

He'd planned to work on his novel for a few days—the novel he'd promised himself he'd write. It was just one more promise he'd never been able to keep because of the demands of travel and reporting. He'd expected to be able to work here, in the quiet, settled town of his youth away from the demands of journalism and the fast pace he'd set for himself. He'd expected a lot of things. What he hadn't expected was to find himself just as wildly in love with Faith as he'd been at twenty.

Jason turned away from the window and stared at his typewriter. The papers were there, notes bulging in manila envelopes, the half-finished manuscript pages. He could sit down and make himself work through the day into the night. He had the discipline for it. But in his life there was more than a book that was half finished. He was just coming to realize it.

By the time he'd shaved and dressed, it was past noon. He thought briefly about walking across the street to Mindy's to see if she still served the best homemade soup in town. But he didn't feel like chatty counter talk. Deliberately he turned south, away from Faith. He wouldn't make a fool of himself by chasing after her.

As he walked, he passed a half a dozen people he knew. He was greeted with thumps on the back, handshakes and avid curiosity. He'd strolled down the Left Bank, up Carnaby Street and along the narrow streets of Venice. After a decade of absence he found the walk down Main Street just as fascinating. There was a barber pole that swirled up and around and back into itself. A life-size cardboard Santa stood outside a dress shop gesturing passersby inside.

Spotting a display of poinsettias, Jason slipped into the store and bought the biggest one he could carry. The saleswoman had been in his graduating class and detained him for ten minutes before he could escape. He'd expected questions, but he hadn't guessed that he'd become the town celebrity. Amused, he made his way down the street as he had countless times before. When he reached the Widow Marchant's, he didn't bother with the front door. Following an old habit, he went around the back and knocked on the storm door. It still rattled. It was a small thing that pleased him enormously.

When the widow opened the door, and her little bird's eyes peered through the bright-red leaves of the flowers, he found himself grinning like a ten-year-old.

"It's about time," she said as she let him in. "Wipe your feet."

"Yes, ma'am." Jason scrubbed his boots against the rough mat before he set down the poinsettia on her kitchen table.

No more than five feet tall, the widow stood with her hands on her hips. She was bent a bit with age and her face was a melody of lines and wrinkles. The bib apron she wore was covered with flour. Jason smelled cookies in the oven and heard the majestic sound of classical music from the living-room speakers. The widow nodded at the flowers.

"You always went for the big statement." When she turned to look him up and down, Jason found himself automatically standing tall. "Put on a few pounds I see, but more wouldn't hurt. Come, give me a kiss."

He bent to peck her cheek dutifully, then found himself gathering her close. She felt frail; he hadn't realized it by looking at her, but she still smelled of all the good things he remembered—soap and powder and warm sugar.

"You don't seem surprised to see me," he murmured as he straightened up.

"I knew you were here." She turned to fuss at the oven because her eyes had filled. "I knew before the ink dried where you signed the registration at the inn. Sit down and take off your coat. I have to get these cookies out."

He sat quietly while she worked and absorbed the feeling of home. It was here he'd always been able to come as a child and feel safe. While he watched, she began to heat chocolate in a dented little pan on the stove.

"How long you staying?"

"I don't know. I'm supposed to be in Hong Kong in a couple of weeks."

"Hong Kong." The widow pursed her lips as she arranged cookies on a plate. "You've been to all your places, Jason. Were they as exciting as you thought?"

"Some were." He stretched out his legs. He'd forgotten what it was to relax, body, soul and mind. "Some weren't."

"Now you've come home." She walked over to put the cookies on the table. "Why?"

He could be evasive with anyone else. He could even lie to himself. But with her there could only be the truth. "Faith."

"It always was." Back at the stove, she stirred the chocolate.

He'd been a troubled boy, now he was a troubled man. "You heard she married Tom."

And with her, he didn't have to hide the bitterness. "Six months after I left I called. I'd landed a job with *Today's News*. They were sending me to a hole in the wall in Chicago, but it was something. I called Faith, but I got her mother. She was very kind, even sympathetic when she told me that Faith was married, had been married for three months and was going to have a baby. I hung up, I got drunk. In the morning I went to Chicago." He plucked a cookie from the plate and shrugged. "Life goes on, right?"

"It does, whether it tows us along with it or rolls right over us. And now that you know she's divorced?"

"We promised each other something. She married someone else."

She made a sound like steam escaping from a kettle. "You're a man now from the looks of you, not a bullheaded boy. Faith Kirkpatrick—"

"Faith Monroe," he reminded her.

"All right then." Patiently, she poured heated chocolate into mugs. After she set them on the table, she seated herself with a quiet wheeze. "Faith is a strong, beautiful woman inside and out. She's raising that little girl all alone and doing a good job of it. She's started a business and she's making it work. Alone. I know something about being alone."

"If she'd waited—"

"Well, she didn't. Whatever thoughts I have about her reasons I'm keeping to myself."

"Why did she divorce Tom?"

The old woman sat back, resting her elbows on the worn arms of her chair. "He left her and the baby when Clara was six months old."

His fingers tightened around the handle of the mug. "What do you mean, he left her?"

"You should know the meaning. You did so yourself." She picked up her chocolate and held it in both hands. "I mean he packed his bags and left. She had the house—and the bills. He cleaned out the bank account and headed west."

"But he has a daughter."

"He hasn't laid eyes on the girl since she was in diapers. Faith pulled herself out. She had the child to think of after all if not herself. Her parents stood behind her. They're good people. She took a loan and started the doll business. We're proud to have her here."

He stared out the window to where the boughs of an old sycamore spread, dripping with snow and ice. "So I left, she married Tom, then he left. Seems Faith has a habit of picking the wrong men."

"Think so?"

He'd forgotten how dry her voice could be and nearly smiled. "Clara looks like Faith."

"Hmm. She favors her mother." The widow smiled into her mug. "I've always been able to see her father in her. Your chocolate's getting cold, Jason."

Absently, he sipped. With the taste came floods of memories. "I hadn't expected to feel at home here again. It's funny. I don't think I felt at home when I lived here, but now . . ."

"You haven't been by your old place yet?"

"No."

"There's a nice couple in there now. They put a porch on the back."

It meant nothing to him. "It was never home." He set the chocolate down and took her hand. "This was. I never knew any mother but you."

Her hand, thin, dry as paper, gripped his. "Your father was a hard man, harder maybe because he lost your mother so young."

"I only felt relief when he died. I can't even be sorry for

it. Maybe that's why I left when I did. With him gone, the
house gone, it seemed the time was right."

"Maybe it was, for you. Maybe the time's right to come
back again. You weren't a good boy, Jason. But you weren't
so bad either. Give yourself some of that time you were always so desperate to beat ten years ago."

"And Faith?"

She sat back again. "As I recall, you never did much court-
ing. Seems to me the girl chased after you with her eyes
wide open. A man who's been all the places you been oughta
know how to court a woman. Probably picked up some of
those fancy languages."

He picked up a cookie and bit into it. "A phrase or two."

"Never knew a woman who wouldn't flutter a bit with
some fancy language."

Leaning over he kissed both her hands. "I missed you."

"I knew you'd come back. At my age, you know how to
wait. Go find your girl."

"I think I might." Rising, he slipped into his coat. "I'll
come back and visit again."

"See that you do." She waited until he opened the door.
"Jason—button your coat." She didn't pull out her handkerchief until she heard the door close behind him.

CHAPTER 4

The sun was high and bright when he stepped outside. Across the street a snowman was rapidly losing weight. He found the streets as he'd found them yesterday on his drive in—full of children fresh out of school. He felt the surge of freedom himself. As he headed north, he saw a girl break away from a group of children and come toward him. Even bundled in hat and scarf he recognized Clara.

"'Scuse me. Did you use to live here?"

"That's right." He wanted to tuck her hair into her cap but stopped himself.

"My mother said you did. Today in school, the teacher said you went away and got famous."

He couldn't stop the grin. "Well, I went away."

"And you won a prize. Like Marcie's brother won a trophy for bowling."

He thought of his Pulitzer and managed, barely, not to laugh. "Something like that."

To Clara he looked like a regular person, not someone who bounded around the world on adventures. Her eyes narrowed. "Did you really go to all those places like they said?"

"That depends on what they said." In tacit agreement they began to walk together. "I've been to some places."

"Like Tokyo? That's the capital of Japan, we learned that in school."

"Like Tokyo."

"Did you eat raw fish?"

"Now and again."

"That's really disgusting." But she seemed pleased all the same. She bent and scooped up snow without breaking rhythm. "Do they squish grapes with their feet in France?"

"I can't say I ever saw it for myself, but I've heard tell."

"I sure wouldn't drink it after that. Did you ever ride a camel?"

He watched her bullet the snowball into the base of a tree. "As a matter of fact, I did."

"What was it like?"

"Uncomfortable."

It was a description she readily accepted because she'd already figured it out for herself. "The teacher read one of your stories today. The one about this tomb they found in China. Did you see the statues?"

"Yes, I did."

"Was it like *Raiders?*"

"Like what?"

"You know, the movie with Indiana Jones."

It took him a minute, then he laughed. Without thinking he tipped her cap over her eyes. "I guess it was, a little."

"You write good."

"Thank you."

They were standing on the sidewalk in front of her house. Jason glanced up, surprised. He hadn't realized they'd come so far and found himself regretting he hadn't slowed his pace a bit. "We have to do this report on Africa." Clara wrinkled her nose. "It has to be five whole pages long. Miss Jenkins wants it in right after Christmas vacation."

"How long have you had the assignment?" It hadn't been that long since his school days.

Clara drew a circle in the snow at the edge of her lawn. "Couple of weeks."

No, he realized with some pleasure, it hadn't been so very long. "I guess you've started on it."

"Well, sort of." Then she turned that quick, beautiful smile on him. "You've been to Africa, haven't you?"

"A couple of times."

"I guess you know all kinds of things about climate and culture and stuff like that."

He grinned down at her. "Enough."

"Maybe you should stay for dinner tonight." Without giving him a chance to answer, she took his hand and led him around to the shop.

When they walked in, Faith was boxing a doll. Her hair was pinned up in the back, and she wore a baggy sweatshirt over jeans. She was laughing at something her customer had said. "Lorna, you know you wouldn't have it any other way."

"Bah, humbug." The woman put a hand on her enormous stomach and sighed. "I really wanted this baby to make an appearance before Christmas."

"You still have four days."

"Hi, Mom!"

Faith turned to smile at her daughter. As she spotted Jason the spool of ribbon in her hand spun in a red stream to the floor. "Clara, you didn't wipe your feet," she managed to say, but kept her eyes on Jason.

"Jason! Jason Law." The woman rushed over and grabbed him by both arms. "It's Lorna—Lorna McBee."

He looked down into the pretty round face of his longtime neighbor. "Hello, Lorna." His gaze drifted down, then back up. "Congratulations."

With a hand on her stomach she laughed. "Thanks, but it's my third."

He thought of the scrawny, bad-tempered girl next door. "Three? You work fast."

"So does Bill. You remember Bill Easterday, don't you?"

"You married Bill?" He remembered a boy who had hung out in the town square looking for trouble. A few times Jason had helped him find it.

"I reformed him." When she smiled, he believed it. "He runs the bank." His expression had her giggling. "I'm serious, stop in sometime. Well, I've got to be moving along. This box has to go into a locked closet before my oldest girl sees it. Thanks, Faith, it's just lovely."

"I hope she likes it."

To keep her hands busy, Faith began to rewind the spool of ribbon. A puff of cold air came in, then was cut off as Lorna breezed out.

"Was that the bride doll?" Clara wanted to know.

"Yes, it was."

"Too fussy. Can I go over to Marcie's?"

"What about homework?"

"I don't have any except that dumb Africa report. He's going to help me." Jason met her smile with a lifted brow. "Aren't you?"

Jason would have dared any man within a hundred miles to resist that look. "Yes, I am."

"Clara, you can't—"

"It's okay 'cause I asked him to dinner." She beamed, almost sure her mother would be trapped by the good manners she was always talking about. "There's no school now for ten whole days so I can do the report after dinner, can't I?"

Jason decided it wouldn't hurt to apply a little pressure from his side. "I spent six weeks in Africa once. Clara might just get an A."

"She could use it," Faith muttered. They stood together, looking at her. Her heart already belonged to both of them. "I guess I'd better start dinner."

Clara was already racing across the yard next door before Faith pulled the door of the Doll House shut and turned the sign around to read Closed.

"I'm sorry if she was a nuisance, Jason. She has a habit of badgering people with questions."

"I like her," he said simply and watched Faith fumble with the latch.

"That's nice of you, but you don't have to feel obliged to help her with this report."

"I said I would. I keep my word, Faith." He touched a pin in her hair. "Sooner or later."

She had to look at him then. It was impossible not to. "You're welcome to dinner, of course." Her fingers worried the buttons of her coat as she spoke. "I was just going to fry chicken."

"I'll give you a hand."

"No, that's not—"

He cut her off when he closed his fingers over hers. "I never used to make you nervous."

With an effort, she steadied herself. "No, you didn't." He'd be gone again in a few days, she reminded herself. Out of her life. Maybe she should take whatever time she was given. "All right then, you can help."

He took her arm as they crossed the lawn. Though he felt her initial resistance, he ignored it. "I went to see Widow Marchant. I had cookies right from the oven."

Faith relaxed as she pushed open the door of her own kitchen. "She has every word you've ever written."

The kitchen was twice the size of the one he'd just left and there were signs of a child in the pictures hanging on the front of the refrigerator and a pair of fuzzy slippers kicked into a corner. Moving with habit, Faith switched on the burner under the kettle before she slipped out of her coat. She hung it on a peg by the door, then turned to take his. His hands closed over hers.

"You didn't tell me Tom left you."

She'd known it wouldn't take him long to hear it, or long to question. "It's not something I think about on a daily basis. Coffee?"

She draped his coat over a hook and turned to find him blocking her way. "What happened, Faith?"

"We made a mistake." She said it calmly, even coolly. It was a tone he'd never heard from her before.

"But there was Clara."

"Don't." Fury came into her eyes quickly and simmered there. "Leave it alone, Jason, I mean it. Clara's my business. My marriage and divorce are my business. You can't expect to come back now and have all the answers."

They stood a moment, facing each other in silence. When the kettle let out a whistle, she seemed to breathe again. "If you want to help, you can peel some potatoes. They're in the pantry over there."

She worked systematically, he thought angrily, as she poured oil to heat in a skillet and coated chicken. Her temper was nothing new to him. He'd felt the brunt of it before, sometimes deflecting it, sometimes meeting it head-on. He also knew how to soothe it. He began talking, almost to himself at first, about some of the places he'd been. When he told her about waking with a snake curled next to his head while he'd been camping in South America, she laughed.

"I didn't find it too funny at the time. I was out of the tent in five seconds flat, buck naked. My photographer got a very interesting roll of pictures. I had to pay him fifty to get the negatives."

"I'm sure they were worth more. You didn't mention the snake in your series on San Salvador."

"No." Interested, he put down his paring knife. "You read it?"

She arranged chicken in the hot oil. "Of course. I've read all your stories."

He took the potatoes to the sink to wash them. "All of them?"

She smiled at the tone but kept her back to him. "Don't let your ego loose, Jason. It was always your biggest problem. I'd estimate that ninety percent of the people in Quiet Valley have read all your stories. You might say we all feel we have a stake in you." She adjusted the flame. "After all, no one else around here's had dinner at the White House."

"The soup was thin."

Chuckling, she put a pan of water on the stove and dumped in the potatoes. "I guess you just have to take the good with the bad—so to speak. I saw a picture of you a couple of years ago." She adjusted a pin in her hair and her voice was bland. "I think it was taken in New York, at some glitzy charity function. You had a half-naked woman on your arm."

He rocked back on his heels. "Did I?"

"Well, she wasn't actually half-naked," Faith temporized. "I suppose it just seemed that way because she had so much more hair than dress. Blond—very blond if my memory serves me. And let's say—top-heavy."

He ran his tongue around his teeth. "You meet a lot of interesting people in my business."

"Obviously." With the efficiency born of habit she turned the chicken. Oil hissed. "I'm sure you find it very stimulating."

"Not as stimulating as this conversation."

"If you can't stand the heat," she murmured.

"Yeah. It's getting dark. Shouldn't Clara be home?"

"She's right next door. She knows to be home by five-thirty."

He went to the window anyway and glanced at the house next door. Faith studied his profile. It was stronger now, tougher. She supposed he was, too, had had to be. How much was left of the boy she'd loved so desperately? Maybe it was something neither of them could be sure of.

"I thought of you a lot, Faith." Though his back was to her she could almost feel the words brush over her skin. "But especially at this time of year. I could usually block you out when I had work to do, deadlines to meet, but at Christmas you wouldn't let go. I remember every one we spent together, the way you'd drag me through the shops. Those few years with you made up for all the times as a kid I woke up to nothing."

The old sympathy welled up. "Your father couldn't face the holidays, Jason. He just couldn't handle it without your mother."

"I understand that better now. After losing you." He turned back. She wasn't looking at him now but bent industriously over the stove. "You've been spending Christmas alone, too."

"No, I have Clara."

She tensed as he walked to her. "No one to fill the stockings with you, or share secrets about what's under the tree."

"I manage. You have to alter life to suit yourself."

"Yeah." He took her chin in his hand. "I'm beginning to believe it."

The door slammed open. Wet and beaming, Clara stood dripping on the mat. "We made angels in the snow."

Faith raised a brow. "So I see. Well, you've got fifteen minutes to get out of those wet things and set the table."

She struggled out of her coat. "Can I turn on the tree?"

"Go ahead."

"Come on." Clara held out a hand for Jason. "It's the best one on the block."

Emotions humming, Faith watched them walk out together.

CHAPTER 5

They were still humming when the meal was over. She knew her daughter was a friendly, sometimes outrageously open child, but Clara had taken to Jason like a long-lost friend. She chattered away at him as though she'd known him for years.

It's so obvious, Faith thought as she watched Clara stack dishes. Neither of them noticed. What would she do if they did? She didn't believe in lies, yet she'd been forced to live one.

The other two paid little attention to her as they settled down with Clara's books. In the easy, flowing style he'd been born with, Jason began to tell her stories about Africa—the desert, the mountains, the thick green jungle that teemed with its own life and its own dangers.

As their heads bent together over a picture in Clara's book Faith felt a flood of panic. "I'm going to go next door," she said on impulse. "I have a lot of work backed up."

"Mm-hmm." With that, Jason dismissed her. A laugh bubbled in her throat until it ached. Grabbing her coat, Faith escaped.

They were more than toys to her. They were certainly more than a business. To Faith the dolls who filled her shop were the symbol of youth, of innocence, of believing in miracles.

She'd wanted to open the shop soon after Clara had been born, but Tom had been adamantly set against it. Because she'd felt indebted, she'd let it pass, as she'd let so many other things pass. Then when she'd found herself alone, with a child to support, it had seemed the natural thing.

She worked long hours there, to ease the void that even the love for her daughter couldn't fill.

In her workroom behind the store were shelves filled with pieces and parts of dolls. There were china heads, plastic legs and torsos. In another section lay the ones she called the sick and injured. Dolls with broken arms or battered bodies were brought to her for repair. Though she enjoyed selling and found a great creative thrill in making her own dolls, nothing satisfied her quite so much as taking a broken toy that was loved and making it whole again. She turned on the light and her radio and set to work.

It soothed her. As time passed, her nerves drained away. With crochet hook and rubber bands, with glue and painstaking care she replaced broken limbs. With a bit of paint and patience she brought smiles back to faceless dolls. Some were given new clothes or a fresh hairstyle, while others only needed a needle and thread plied by clever fingers.

By the time she picked up a battered rag doll she was humming.

"Are you going to fix that?"

Startled, she nearly stabbed herself with the needle. Jason stood in the doorway, hands in pockets, watching her. "Yes, that's what I do. Where's Clara?"

"She nearly fell asleep in her book. I put her to bed."

She started to rise. "Oh, well I—"

"She's asleep, Faith, with some green ball of hair she called Bernardo."

Determined to relax, Faith sat down again. "Yes, that's her favorite. Clara isn't much on ordinary dolls."

"Not like her mother?" Interested, he began to prowl the workroom. "I always thought when a toy broke or wore out it got tossed away."

"Too often. I've always thought that showed a tremendous lack of appreciation for something that's given you pleasure."

He picked up a soft plastic head, bald and smooth, that grinned at him. "Maybe you're right, but I don't see what can be done about that pile of rags in your hand."

"Quite a lot."

"Still believe in magic, Faith?"

She glanced up and for the first time her smile was completely open, her eyes warm. "Yes, of course I do. Especially at Christmastime."

Unable to help himself he reached down to run a hand over her cheek. "I said before that I'd missed you. I don't think I realized how much."

She felt the need shimmer and the longing plead inside her. Denying both, she concentrated on the doll. "I appreciate you helping Clara, Jason. I don't want to keep you."

"Does it bother you to have someone watch you work?"

"No." She began to replace stuffing. "Sometimes a concerned mother will stay here while I doctor a patient."

He leaned a hip against the counter. "I imagined a lot of things when I was coming back. I never imagined this."

"What?"

"That I'd be standing here watching you stuff life back into a rag. You may not have noticed, but it doesn't even have a face."

"It will. How did the report go?"

"She needs to do the final draft."

Faith glanced up from her work. Her eyes were wide with the joke. "Clara?"

"She had the same reaction." Then he smiled as he leaned

back. The room smelled of her. He wondered if she knew. "She's a bright kid, Faith."

"Sometimes uncomfortably so."

"You're lucky."

"I know." With quick skillful movements, she pushed the stuffing into place.

"Kids love you no matter what, don't they?"

"No." She looked at him again. "You have to earn it." With needle and thread she began to secure the seams.

"You know, she was out on her feet, but she insisted on stopping at the tree to count the presents. She tells me she had this feeling there's going to be one more."

"I'm afraid she's doomed to disappointment. Her list looked like an army requisition. I had to draw the line." Putting down the thread, she picked up her paintbrush. "My parents already spoil her."

"They still live in town?"

"Mmm-hmm." She'd already gotten a sense of the doll's personality as she'd worked with it. Now, she began to paint it on. "They mumble about Florida from time to time, but I don't know if they'll ever go. It's Clara. They just adore her. You might go by and see them, Jason. You know my mother was always fond of you."

He examined a slinky red dress no bigger than his palm. "Your father wasn't."

She grinned at that. "He just didn't quite trust you." She sent him a quick, saucy smile. "What father would have?"

"He had good reason." As he walked toward her, he saw the doll she held. "I'll be damned." Charmed, he took it, holding it under the light. What had been a misshapen pile of rags was now a plump, sassy doll. Exaggerated lashes spiked out from wide eyes. Curls had been sewn back into place so that they fell teasingly over the brow. It was soft, friendly and pretty as a picture. Even a full grown man could recognize what would make a small girl smile.

She felt a ridiculous sense of accomplishment at seeing him smile at her work. "You approve?"

"I'm impressed. How much do you sell something like this for?"

"This one's not for sale." Faith set it in a large box at the back of the room. "There are about a dozen little girls in town whose families can't afford much of a Christmas. There are boys, too, of course, but Jake over at the five-and-dime and I worked a deal a few years back. On Christmas Eve, a box is left on the doorstep. The girls get a doll, the boys a truck or a ball or whatever."

He should have known. It was so typical of her, so much what she was. "Santa lives."

She turned to smile at him. "He does in Quiet Valley."

It was the smile that did it. It was so open, so familiar. Jason closed the distance between them before either of them realized it.

"What about you? Do you get what you want for Christmas?"

"I have everything I need."

"Everything?" His hands cupped her face. "Aren't you the one who used to dream? Who always believed in wishes?"

"I've grown up. Jason, you should go now."

"I don't believe that. I don't believe you've stopped dreaming, Faith. Just being with you makes me start again."

"Jason." She pressed her hands to his chest, knowing she had to stop what could never be finished. "You know we can't always have what we want. You'll leave in a few days. You can walk away and go on to a hundred other things, a hundred other places."

"What does that have to do with right now? It's always right now, Faith." He drew his hands through her hair so that pins scattered. Rich warm sable tumbled over his fingers. He'd always loved the feel of it, the smell of it. "You're the only one," he murmured. "You've always been the only one."

She closed her eyes before he could draw her close. "You'll go. I have to stay here. Once before I stood and watched you walk away. I don't think I can bear it if I let you in again. Can't you understand?"

"I don't know. I know I understand I want you so much more now than I ever did. I'm not sure you can keep me out, Faith." But he backed away, for both of them. "Not for long anyway. You said before I didn't have a right to all the answers. Maybe that's true. But I need one."

It was a reprieve, it was space to think. She let out a long breath and nodded. "All right. But you promise that you'll go now if I answer?"

"I'll go. Did you love him?"

She couldn't lie. It wasn't in her. So her eyes were direct and pride kept her chin high. "I never loved anyone but you."

It came into his eyes—triumph, fury. He reached for her but she pulled away. "You said you'd go, Jason. I trusted your word."

She had him trapped. She had him aching. "You should've trusted it ten years ago." He swung from the workroom and into the frigid night.

CHAPTER 6

Quiet Valley bustled with Christmas energy. From a jerry-rigged loudspeaker on top of the hardware store roof carols rang out. An enterprising young man from a neighboring farm got a permit and gave buggy rides up and down Main Street. Kids, keyed up with lack of school and anticipation, shouted and raced on every corner. The skies had clouded over, but the snow held off.

Jason sat at the counter in the diner and sipped coffee while he listened to town gossip. Word was the Hennessys' oldest had the chicken pox and would be scratching himself through the holidays. Carlotta's was selling Christmas trees at half price and the hardware store had a sale on ten-speeds.

Ten years before Jason would have found the conversations mundane. Now he sat content, sipping his coffee and listening. Maybe this was what had been missing from the novel he'd been trying to write for so long. He'd been around the world, but everything had always been so fast paced, so urgent. There had been times when his life as well as his story had been on the line. You didn't think about it when it was happening. You couldn't. But now, sitting in the warm diner with the scent of coffee and frying bacon he could look back.

He'd taken assignments, a great many of them dangerous, because he hadn't given a damn. He'd already lost the part of himself he'd valued. It was true that over the years he'd built something back, inch by gritty inch, but he'd never found the whole—because he'd left it here, where he'd grown up. Now he just had to figure out what the hell to do with it.

"Guess they serve almost anybody in here."

Jason glanced up idly then grinned. "Paul. Paul Tydings." His hand was gripped by two enormous ones.

"Damn it, Jas, you're as good-looking and skinny as ever."

Jason took a long look at his oldest friend. Paul's hair was thick and curly around a full, ruddy face offset now by a bushy moustache. His bull-like frame had assured him a starting place on the offensive line. Over the years, it had thickened into what was politely termed a successful build. "Well," Jason decided. "You're as good-looking."

With a roar of laughter, Paul slapped him on the back. "I never expected to see you back here."

"Nor I you. I thought you were in Boston."

"Was. Made myself some money, got married."

"No kidding? How long?"

"Seven years come spring. Five kids."

Jason choked on his coffee. "Five?"

"Three and a set of twins. Anyway, I brought my wife back for a visit six years ago and she fell in love. Had a jewelry store in Manchester, so I opened one here, too. I guess I've got you to thank for a lot of it."

"Me? Why?"

"You were always filling my head with ideas. Then you took off. It made me think I should try my hand at seeing a few places. In about a year I was working in this jewelry

store in Boston and in walks the prettiest little thing I ever
laid eyes on. I was so flustered I never imprinted her credit
card. She came back the next day with the blank receipt and
saved my job. Then she saved my life and married me. Never
even would have met her if it hadn't been for you talking
about all the places there were to see." Paul nodded as his
coffee was served. "Guess you've seen Faith."

"Yeah, I've seen her."

"Throw a lot of business her way being as three of my kids
are girls and all of 'em are brats." He grinned and added two
packages of sugar to his coffee. "She's as pretty as she was
when she was sixteen and dancing in the town hall. Settling
in this time, Jason?"

With a half laugh he pushed his cooling coffee aside.
"Maybe."

"Come by the house and meet the family, will you? We're
just south of town, the two-story stone place."

"I saw it driving in."

"Then don't go out again without coming in. A man doesn't
have many friends who go back to red wagons with him, Jason. You know—" he glanced at his watch "—seems to me
Faith breaks for lunch about now. I've got to get back." With
a last slap on the back, Paul left him at the counter.

Thoughtfully, Jason sipped at his coffee. He'd been away
ten years, a long time by any standard, yet everyone in town
he ran into saw him and Faith as a couple. It seemed it was
easy to blink away a decade. Easy for everyone, he added,
but for himself and Faith. Maybe he could brush away the
years, the time lost, but how could he ignore her marriage
and her child?

He still wanted her. That hadn't changed. He still hurt. That
hadn't eased. But how did she feel? She'd told him the night
before that she'd never loved another man. Did that mean she

still loved him? Jason dropped a bill on the counter and rose. There was only one way to find out. He'd ask her.

* * *

The Doll House was crowded with children. Noisy children. When Jason walked in, shouts and laughter bounced off the walls. Helium-filled balloons hugged the ceiling and cookie crumbs littered the floor. In the doorway of the workroom was a tall cardboard castle. Just in front of a shiny white curtain stood a puppet of Santa Claus and a green-suited elf. With a lot of chatter and exaggerated effort, they loaded a glittering golden sleigh with colorful boxes. Twice the elf fell on his face while lifting a box and sent the children into peals of laughter. After a great deal of confusion, all the presents were loaded. With a belly-bursting *Ho-ho-ho!* Santa climbed into the sleigh. Bells jingling, it rocked its way through the curtain.

To the clatter of applause, a series of puppets crossed the stage for bows. Jason saw Mrs. Claus, two elves and a reindeer with a telltale red nose before Santa took the stage with a ringing *Merry Christmas!* He didn't even realize he was leaning back against the door and grinning when Faith popped around the castle for a bow of her own.

But she saw him. Feeling foolish, she took another bow as the children clambered up. With the ease of a veteran kindergarten teacher, she maneuvered them toward the punch and cookies.

"Very impressive," Jason murmured in her ear. "I'm sorry I missed most of the show."

"It's not much." She combed her fingers through her hair. "I've been doing it for years now without much variation." She glanced over at the group of children. "It doesn't seem to matter."

"I'd say it does." He took her hand and brought it to his lips while a group of girls giggled. "Very much."

"Mrs. Monroe." A little boy with carrot-red hair and a face full of freckles tugged on her slacks. "When's Santa coming?"

Faith crouched down and smoothed at his hair. "You know, Bobby, I heard he was awfully busy this year."

His bottom lip poked out. "But he always comes."

"Well, I'm sure he'll find a way to get the presents here. I'm going to go in the back in a minute and see."

"But I have to talk to him."

The pout nearly did her in. "If he doesn't make it, you can give me a letter for him. I'll make sure he gets it."

"Problem?" Jason murmured when she straightened up again.

"Jake always plays Santa after the puppet show. We give out a few little things, it's nothing really, but the kids depend on it."

"Jake can't make it this year?"

"He caught the chicken pox from the Hennessy boy."

"I see." He hadn't celebrated Christmas in years, not since . . . since he'd left Faith. "I'll do it," he told her and surprised himself.

"You?"

Something in her expression made him determined to be the best St. Nick since the original. "Yeah, me. Where's the suit?"

"It's in the little room off the back, but—"

"I hope you remembered the pillows," he said before he sauntered away.

She didn't think he'd pull it off. In fact, five minutes after he walked away, Faith was sure he'd changed his mind altogether and continued out the back door. No one, including the group of kids with mouths full of cookies was more enchanted than she when Santa walked in the front door with a bag over his shoulder.

He had the chance for one booming *Merry Christmas* before he was surrounded. Too stunned to move, she watched the children bounce and jump and tug.

"Santa needs a chair." Jason sent her a long, intense look that had her swallowing before her feet could move. Dashing into the back room, she brought out a high-backed chair and set it in the center of the room.

"Now you have to line up," she began, scooting children around. "Everyone gets a turn." Grabbing a bowl of candy canes, she set them on a table beside the chair. One by one, the children climbed up on Jason's knee. Faith needn't have worried. She'd had to school Jake to make the right responses, and most importantly, not to promise and risk disappointing. After the third child had climbed down, Faith relaxed. Jason was wonderful.

And having the time of his life. He'd done it just to help her out, perhaps even to impress her, but he got a great deal more. He'd never had a child sit on his lap and look at him with complete faith and love. He listened to their wishes, their confessions and complaints. Each one was allowed to reach in the sack he carried and pull out one gift.

He was hugged, kissed with sticky mouths and poked. One enterprising boy had a good grip on his beard before Jason managed to distract him. Happy, they began to file out of the shop with their parents or in groups.

"You were great." Faith turned her sign around after the last child had left to give herself a chance to catch her breath.

"Want to sit on my lap?"

Laughing, she walked to him. "I mean it, Jason, you were. I can't tell you how much I appreciate it."

"Then show me." He pulled her down onto his lap where

she sank into pillows. She laughed again and kissed his nose.

"I've always been crazy about men in red suits. I wish Clara could have been here."

"Why wasn't she?"

With a little sigh, Faith let herself relax against him. "She's too old for all this now—so she tells me. She went shopping with Marcie."

"Nine's too old?"

She didn't speak for a minute, then moved her shoulders. "Kids grow up fast." She turned her head so she could look at him. "You made a lot of them happy today."

"I'd like to make you happy." Reaching up, he stroked her hair. "There was a time when I could."

"Do you ever wish we could go back?" Content, she let herself be cradled in his arms. "When we were teenagers, everything seemed so simple. Then you close your eyes for a minute and you're an adult. Oh, Jason, I wanted you to carry me away, to a castle, to a mountaintop. I was so full of romance."

He continued to stroke her hair as they sat, surrounded by dolls and the echo of children's laughter. "I didn't have enough of it, did I?"

"You had your feet on the ground, I had my head in the clouds."

"And now?"

"Now, I have a daughter to raise. It's terrifying sometimes to realize you're responsible for another life. Did you . . . ?" She hesitated, knowing the ground was dangerous. "Did you ever want kids?"

"I haven't thought about it. Sometimes I have to go into places where it's tough enough being responsible for your own life."

She'd thought of that—had nightmares about it. "It still excites you."

He thought of some of the things he'd seen, the cruelty, the misery. "It stopped exciting me a long time ago. But I'm good at what I do."

"I suppose I always knew you would be. Jason." She shifted again so that her eyes were level with his. "I am glad you came back."

His fingers tightened when she rested her cheek against his. "You had to wait until I was stuffed like a walrus to tell me that."

With a laugh, she wrapped her arms around his neck. "It seems to be the safest time."

"Don't bet your life on it." He pressed his lips to hers and felt hers tremble. "What's so funny?"

Choking back the laugh, she drew away. "Oh nothing, nothing at all. I've always dreamed of being kissed by a man in a beard wearing a red hat and bells. I've got to clean up this mess."

When she rose, he hauled himself up. "The timing has to click sooner or later." She said nothing as she gathered up bits of colored paper. Jason picked up his sack and glanced inside. "There's one more box in here."

"It's for Luke Hennessy. Chicken pox."

He looked at the box, then back at her. Her hair curtained her face as she pulled a sticky candy cane from the carpet. "Where does he live?"

Still holding the candy, she stood up. Some might say he looked foolish, padded from chest to hips, wrapped in red and with his face half concealed by a curly white beard. Faith thought he'd never looked more wonderful. She walked to him to pull the beard down to his chin. Her arms went around him, her mouth found his.

Her kiss was warm as it always was, full of hope and simple goodness. Desire raced through him and settled into sweet contentment. "Thank you." She kissed him again in friendship. "He lives on the corner of Elm and Sweetbriar."

He waited a moment until he was steady. "Can I get a cup of coffee when I get back?"

"Yeah." She adjusted his beard again. "I'll be next door."

CHAPTER 7

He had to admit, it had given him a kick to walk through town. Kids flocked after him. Adults called out and waved. He was offered uncountable cookies. The biggest satisfaction had been the awe on the young Hennessy boy's face. That had topped the wide-eyed shock of his mother when she'd opened the door to S. Claus.

Jason took his time walking back, strolling through the square. It was strange, he discovered, how easy it was to take on the personality of a set of clothes. He felt . . . well, benevolent. If anyone he'd ever worked with had seen him now, they'd have fallen into the snow in a dead faint. Jason Law had a reputation for being impatient, brutally frank and quick-tempered. He hadn't won the Pulitzer for benevolence. Yet somehow, at the moment, he felt more satisfaction in the polyester beard and dime store bells than he did with all the awards he'd ever earned.

He was ho-hoing his way along when Clara stepped out of the five-and-dime. She and the little brunette at her side went off in peals of giggles.

"But you're—"

One narrow-eyed stare from Jason did the trick. Cutting

herself off, Clara cleared her throat and offered her hand. "How do you do, Santa?"

"I do very well, Clara."

"That's not Jake," Marcie informed Clara. She stepped closer to try to recognize the face behind the puffs of white.

Enjoying himself, Jason sent her a wink. "Hello, Marcie."

The brunette's eyes widened. "How'd he know my name?" she whispered to her friend.

Clara covered another giggle with her hand. "Santa knows everything, don't you, Santa?"

"I have my sources."

"There isn't any Santa really." But Marcie's grown-up sophistication was wavering.

Jason leaned over and flicked at the fluffy ball on top of her cap. "There is in Quiet Valley," he told her and nearly believed it himself. He saw Marcie stop looking beyond the beard and accept the magic. Deciding against pressing his luck, he continued on down the street.

It wasn't easy for a fat man in a red suit to slip into a door inconspicuously, but Jason had had some experience. Once he was in the back room of Faith's shop, he shed the Santa clothes. He wanted to do it again. As Jason slipped into his own slim slacks, he realized he hadn't had so much fun in years. Part of it had been the look in Faith's eyes, the way she'd warmed to him, if only briefly. Part had been the simple act of giving pleasure. How long had it been since he'd done something without an angle? On an assignment there was constant bargaining. You give me this, I'll give you that. He'd had to toughen himself against sympathy, against compassion to find the truth and report it. If his style had a hard edge, it was because he'd always gone for the story that demanded it. It had helped him forget. Now that he'd come home it was impossible not to remember.

What kind of man was he really? He wasn't sure anymore,

but he knew there was one woman who could make or break him. Leaving the suit in the closet, he went to find her.

She had been waiting for him. She was ready to admit she'd been waiting for him for ten years. Throughout the rest of the afternoon, Faith had made her own decisions. She'd made a success of her life. Though the search hadn't always been easy, she'd found contentment. Confidence had come with the years and she knew she could go on alone. It was time to stop being afraid of what her life would be like when Jason left again and to accept the gift she'd been offered. He was here, now, and she loved him.

When he came into the house, he found her curled in a chair by the tree, her cheek resting on the arm. She waited until he came to her. "Sometimes at night I sit like this. Clara's asleep upstairs and the house is quiet. I can think about little things, enormous things, just as I did as a child. The lights all blend together and the tree smells like heaven. You can go anywhere, sitting just like this."

He picked her up, felt her yield, then settled in the chair with her on his lap. "I remember sitting like this with you at Christmastime in your parents' house. Your father grumbled."

She snuggled close. There was no padding now, just the long, lean body she knew so well. "My mother dragged him into the kitchen so we could be alone for a little while. She knew you didn't have a tree at home."

"Or anything else."

"I never asked where you live now, Jason, whether you found a place that makes you happy."

"I move around a lot. I have a base in New York."

"A base?"

"An apartment."

"It doesn't sound like a home," she murmured. "Do you put a tree in the window at Christmas?"

"I guess I have once or twice, when I've been around."

It broke her heart, but she said nothing. "My mother always said you had wanderlust. Some people are born with it."

"I had to prove myself, Faith."

"To whom?"

"To myself." He rested his cheek on top of her head. "Damn it, to you."

She breathed in the scent of pine while the lights danced on the tree. They'd sat like this before, so long ago. The memories were nearly as sweet as the reality. "I never needed you to prove anything to me, Jason."

"Maybe that's one of the reasons I had to. You were too good for me."

"That's ridiculous." She would have shifted, but he held her still.

"You were, and still are." He too stared at the tree. The tinsel shimmered in the lights like the magic he'd always wanted to give her. "Maybe that's why I had to leave when I did—maybe it's why I came back. You're all the good things, Faith. Just being with you brings out the best parts of me. God knows, there aren't many."

"You were always too hard on yourself. I don't like it." This time she did shift so that her hands were on his shoulders and her eyes were directly on his. "I fell in love with you. There were reasons for it. You were kind though you pretended not to be. You wanted to be considered tough and a troublemaker because you felt safer that way."

He smiled and ran a finger down her cheek. "I was a troublemaker."

"Maybe I liked that, too. You didn't just accept things, you weren't afraid to question."

"I nearly got kicked out of school twice because I questioned."

The old anger stirred. Had no one understood him but herself? Had no one else been able to see what had been racing and straining inside him? "You were smarter than anyone else. You've proved that if you needed to."

"You spent a lot of time defending me, didn't you?"

"I believed in you. I loved you."

He reached for her face in an old gesture that melted her heart. "And now?"

She had too much to say and not enough ways to say it. "Do you remember that night in June, after my Senior Prom? We drove out of town. The moon was full and the air was so sweet with summer."

"You wore a blue dress that made your eyes look like sapphires. You were so beautiful I was afraid to touch you."

"So I seduced you."

She looked so pleased with herself he laughed. "You did not."

"I certainly did. You would never have made love with me." She touched her lips to his. "Do I have to seduce you again?"

"Faith—"

"Clara's having dinner next door at Marcie's. She's going to spend the night. Come to bed with me, Jason."

Her quiet voice raced along his skin. The touch of her hand to his cheek seared like fire. But tangled with his need for her was a love that had never grown old. "You know I want you, Faith, but we're not children now."

"We're not children." She turned her face to press her lips into his palm. "And I want you. No promises, no questions. Love me the way you did on that one beautiful night we had together." Rising, she held out her hand. "I want something for the next ten years."

With their hands linked they walked up the stairs. He

pushed away all thought of the other man she'd chosen, of the other life she'd lived. He, too, would block out ten years of loss and take what was offered.

Night came early in the winter so the light was dim. In silence she lit candles so that the room glowed gold and shifted with shadows. When she turned back to him, she was smiling, with all the confidence and knowledge of a woman in her eyes. Saying nothing, she came to him, lifted her mouth and offered everything.

Her fingers were steady as she reached for the buttons of his shirt. His trembled as he reached for hers. Murmuring, she waited for the brush of his hands against her skin, then sighed from the sheer glory of it. They undressed each other slowly, not tentatively, but with the quiet understanding that every moment, every instant would be treasured.

When he saw her, as slim, as lovely, as unexplainably innocent as she'd been the first time, his head spun with needs, with doubts, with desires. But she stepped to him, pressed her body against his and dissolved all choices. She was stronger than she'd been. He could feel it, not in muscle but in spirit. Perhaps she had changed, but the longings that were racing through him were the same as they'd been in the boy on the brink of manhood. As heedlessly as the children they'd once been, they tumbled onto the bed.

They didn't relive the experience. It was as fresh, as wildly thrilling as the first time. But they were man and woman now, more demanding, hungrier. She drew him closer, running her hands over him with an urgency just discovered, with a turbulence just released. She'd waited so long, so very long and wouldn't wait a moment longer.

But he took her hand and brought it to his lips. He quieted her tumbling breath with his mouth.

"I hardly knew what to do with you the first time." Gently

he nuzzled at her throat until she moaned in frenzied anticipation. Raising his head, he smiled at her. "Now I do."

Then he took her places she'd never been. Higher, still
higher he drew her, then just as suddenly plunged her deep
where the air was thick and dark. Trapped in the whirlwind,
she clung. She'd wanted to give, but he left her helpless. Tender, soft, easy, his fingers caressed until her body shuddered.
He drank in her sigh with lips abruptly urgent, ruthlessly
demanding, then patiently soothed her again. Sensations
rocketed inside her, leaving no room for thought, for reason
or even for memories.

When they came together, it was everything for both of
them. Time didn't slip back but trapped them and held them
close in the here and now.

He kept his arms tightly around her and they were quiet.
With her eyes closed, she absorbed the unity. She loved, and
for the moment there was nothing else. For him both ecstasy
and contentment were troubled with questions. She was so
warm, so free with her emotions. She loved him. He needed
no words to know it and never had. But the loyalty he'd always understood as an intrinsic part of her had been broken.
How could he rest without knowing why?

"I have to know why we lost ten years, Faith." When she
said nothing, he turned her head toward him. Her eyes glis-
tened in the shifting light but the tears didn't fall. "Now
more than ever I have to know."

"No questions, Jason. Not tonight."

"I've waited long enough. We've waited long enough."

On a long breath, she sat up. Bringing her knees to her
chest, she wrapped her arms around them. Her hair cascaded
down her back. He couldn't resist taking a handful. She'd
been his once, completely. No one else had ever touched her
as he had. He knew he had to accept her marriage, and that

her child belonged to another man, but he needed to understand first why she had turned to someone else so soon after he'd gone away.

"Give me something, Faith. Anything."

"We loved each other, Jason, but we wanted different things." She turned her head to look at him. "We still want different things." She took his hand and brought it to her cheek. "If you had let me, I would have gone anywhere with you. I would have left my home, my family and never looked back. You needed to go alone."

"I didn't have anything for you," he began. She stopped him with a look.

"You never gave me a choice."

He reached for her once more. "If I gave you one now?"

She closed her eyes and let her forehead rest on his. "Now I have a child, and she has a home I can't take away from her. What I want doesn't come first." She drew back far enough to look at him. "What you want can't come first. Before somehow I never thought you'd really go. This time I know you will. Let's just take what we have, give each other this one Christmas. Please."

She closed her mouth over his and stopped all questions.

CHAPTER 8

Christmas Eve was magic. Faith had always believed it. When she awoke with Jason beside her, it was more than magic. For a while, she simply lay there, watching him sleep. She'd imagined it before, as a girl, as a woman, but now she didn't need the dreams. He was here beside her, warm, quiet, and outside an early morning snow was falling. Careful not to wake him, Faith slipped out of bed.

When he rolled over, he smelled her—the springtime scent her hair had left on the pillowcase. For a few minutes, he lay still and let it seep into his system. Content, he lay back and looked at the room he hadn't been able to see in the dark.

The walls were papered, ivory, with little sprigs of violets. At the windows were fussy priscillas. There was an antique rosewood bureau cluttered with colored bottles and boxes. On a vanity was an old-fashioned silver-handled brush and comb. He watched the snow fall and smelled the potpourri on the stand beside the bed. The room was so like her—charming, fresh, and very, very feminine. A man could relax there even knowing he might find stockings draped over a chair or a blouse mixed with his shirts. He could relax there. And he wasn't letting her go again.

He smelled the coffee before he was halfway down the

stairs. She had Christmas music on the stereo and bacon frying. He hadn't known it would feel so good just to walk into a kitchen and find your woman cooking for you.

"So you're up." She was wrapped from head to foot in a bright flannel robe. Desire dragged quietly at his stomach muscles. "There's coffee."

"I could smell it." He went to her. "I could smell you the moment I woke."

She rested her head on his shoulder, trying not to think that this was the way it might have been—if only. "You look as though you could have slept for hours. It's a good thing you didn't or the bacon would be cold."

"If you'd stayed in bed a few more minutes, we might have—"

"Mom! Mom! It's snowing!" Clara burst through the door and danced around the kitchen. "We're going to go caroling tonight in the hay wagon and there's snow all over the place." She stopped in front of Jason and grinned. "Hi."

"Hi yourself."

"Mom and I are going to build a snowman. She says Christmas snowmen are the best. You can help."

She hadn't known just what reaction Clara would have to finding Jason at the breakfast table. With a shake of her head, Faith began to beat eggs. She should have known Clara would be willing to accept anyone she'd decided to like. "You have to have some breakfast."

Clara fingered the plastic Santa on her lapel, tugging on the string so that the nose lit up. It never failed to please her. "I had cereal at Marcie's."

"Did you thank her mother for having you?"

"Yeah." She stopped a minute. "I think I did. Anyway we're going to build two of them and have a wedding and everything. Marcie wanted the wedding," she added to Jason.

"Clara would prefer a war."

"I figured we could have that after. Maybe I should have some hot chocolate first." She eyed the cookie jar and calculated her chances. Slim at best.

"I'll fix it. And you can have a cookie after the snowman," Faith told her without bothering to turn. "Hang your things by the door."

Scrambling out of her coat, she chattered at Jason. "You're not going back to Africa, are you? I don't think Africa would be much fun at Christmas. Marcie's mother said you'd probably be going to some other neat place."

"I'm supposed to go to Hong Kong in a few weeks." He glanced at Faith. She didn't turn. "But I'll be around for Christmas."

"Do you have a tree in your room?"

"No."

She gave him a wide-eyed look. "Well, where do you put your presents? It's not Christmas without a tree, is it, Mom?"

Faith thought of the years Jason had grown up without one. She remembered how hard he'd tried to pretend it didn't matter. "A tree's only so that we can show other people it's Christmas."

Unconvinced, Clara plopped into a chair. "Well, maybe."

"She used to say the same thing to me," Jason told Clara. "In any case, I don't think Mr. Beantree would like it if I left pine needles all over the floor."

"We've got a tree, so you can have dinner with us," Clara declared. "Mom makes this big turkey and Grandma and Grandpa come over. Grandma brings pies and we eat till we're sick."

"Sounds great." Amused, he looked over as Faith scooped eggs onto a plate. "I had Christmas dinner with your grandparents a couple of times."

"Yeah?" Interested, Clara studied him. "I guess I heard

somewhere that you used to be Mom's boyfriend. How come you didn't get married?"

"Here's your hot chocolate, Clara." Faith set it down. "You'd better hurry, Marcie's waiting."

"Are you coming out?"

"Soon." Grateful that her daughter was easily distracted, she set the platter of bacon and eggs on the table. Ignoring the half-amused lift of brow from Jason, she took her seat.

"We need carrots and scarves and stuff."

"I'll take care of it."

With a grin Clara gulped down chocolate. "And hats?"

"And hats."

A snowball hit the kitchen window. Clara was up like a shot. "There she is. Gotta go. Come soon, Mom, you make the best."

"Soon as I'm dressed. Don't forget your top button."

Clara hesitated at the back door. "I've got a little plastic tree in my room. You can have it if you want."

Moved, he only stared at her. Just like her mother, he thought, and fell in love a second time. "Thanks."

"'Sokay. Bye."

"She's quite a kid," Jason commented as the door slammed behind her.

"I like her."

"I'll give her a hand with the snowman."

"You don't have to, Jason."

"I want to, then I've got some things to take care of." He checked his watch. It was only Christmas Eve for so long. When a man was being offered a second chance, it wasn't wise to waste time. "Can I get an invitation for tonight?"

Faith smiled but simply pushed the food around on her plate. "You've never needed one."

"Don't cook, I'll bring something."

"It's okay, I—"

"Don't cook," he repeated, rising. He bent to kiss her, then lingered over it. "I'll be back."

He took his coat from the hook where it had hung beside Clara's. When he was gone, Faith looked down at the toast she'd crumbled in her hand. Hong Kong. At least this time she knew where he was going.

* * *

The snow people in the side yard grinned at him as he struggled past. Boxes balanced, Jason knocked on the back door with the toe of his boot. The snow hadn't let up a whit.

"Jason." Speechless, Faith stepped back as he teetered inside.

"Where's Clara?"

"Clara?" Still staring, she pushed back her hair. "She's upstairs getting ready for the hayride."

"Good. Take the top box."

"Jason, what in the world have you got here?"

"Just take the top box unless you want pizza all over the floor."

"All right, but . . ." As the enormous box in his arms shifted, she laughed. "Jason, what have you done?"

"Wait a minute."

Holding the pizza, she watched him drag the box into the living room. "Jason, what is that thing?"

"It's a present." He started to set it under the tree then discovered there wasn't enough room. With a bit of rearranging, he managed to lean the box against the wall beside the tree. He was grinning when he turned to her. If he'd ever felt better in his life, he couldn't remember it. "Merry Christmas."

"Same to you. Jason, what is that box?"

"Damn, it's cold out there." Though he rubbed his hands

together now, he hadn't even noticed the biting wind. "Got any coffee?"

"Jason."

"It's for Clara." He discovered that feeling a bit foolish didn't dim the warmth.

"You didn't have to get her a present," Faith began, but her curiosity got the better of her. "What is it?"

"This?" Jason patted the six-foot box. "Oh, it's nothing."

"If you don't tell me, you don't get any coffee." She smiled. "And I keep the pizza."

"Spoilsport. It's a toboggan." He took Faith's arm to lead her out of the room. "She happened to mention when we were building the snowman that some kid had this toboggan and it went down Red Hill like a spitfire."

"Spitfire," Faith murmured.

"And snow like this is just made for going down Red Hill like a spitfire, so . . ."

"Sucker," Faith accused and kissed him hard.

"Put that pizza down and call me that again."

She laughed and kept it between them.

"Wow!"

Faith raised a brow at the noise from the living room. "I think she saw the box."

At full speed, Clara barreled into the kitchen. "Did you see? I knew there'd be one more, I just knew. It's as tall as you are," she told Jason. "Did you see?" She grabbed his hand to drag him back. "It has my name on it."

"Imagine that." Jason picked her up and kissed both cheeks. "Merry Christmas."

"I can't wait." She threw her arms around his neck and squeezed. "I just can't wait."

Watching them, Faith felt her emotions tangle and knot until her bones ached with it. What should she do? What could she do? When Jason turned with Clara, the lights from the tree fell like wishes over their faces.

"Faith?" He didn't need words to recognize distress, pain, turmoil. "What is it?"

Her hands were digging into the cardboard of the box. "Nothing. I'm going to dish out this pizza before it's cold."

"Pizza?" Delighted, Clara bounced down. "Can I have two pieces? It's Christmas."

"Monkey," Faith scolded gently, tousling her hair. "Set the table."

"What is it, Faith?" Jason took her arm before she could follow her daughter into the kitchen. "Something's wrong."

"No." She had to control herself. She'd managed everything for so long. "You overwhelmed me." With a smile she touched his face. "It's happened before. Come on, let's eat."

Because she seemed to need to keep her thoughts to herself, he let it go and followed her into the kitchen where Clara was already peeking into the cardboard box. He'd never seen a child plow through food with such unrestrained glee. He'd never known Christmas Eve could be special simply because there was someone beside him.

Clara swallowed the last of her second piece. "Maybe if I opened one present tonight there'd be less confusion in the morning."

Faith seemed to consider. "I like confusion," she decided and Jason realized the conversation was an old tradition.

"Maybe if I opened just one present tonight, I could get right to sleep. Then you wouldn't have to wait so long to creep around and fill the stockings."

"Hmm." Faith pushed aside her empty plate and enjoyed the wine Jason had brought. "I like creeping around late at night."

"If I opened—"

"Not a chance."

"If I—"

"Nope."

"But Christmas is just hours and hours away."

"Awful, isn't it?" Faith smiled at her. "And you're going caroling in ten minutes, so you'd better get your coat."

Clara walked over to tug on her boots. "Maybe when I get back, there'll be just one present that you'll figure isn't really important enough to wait until morning."

"All the presents under the tree are absolutely vital." Faith rose to help her on with her coat. "And so are the following instructions. Stay with the group. Keep your mittens on, I want you to keep all your fingers. Don't lose your hat. Remember that Mr. and Mrs. Easterday are in charge."

"Mom." Clara shifted her feet and sighed. "You treat me like a baby."

"You are my baby." Faith gave her a smacking kiss. "So there."

"Jeez, I'll be ten years old in February. That's practically tomorrow."

"And you'll still be my baby in February. Have a good time."

Clara sighed, long-suffering and misunderstood. "Okay."

"Okay," Faith mimicked. "Say good-night."

Clara peeked around her mother. "Are you going to stay until I get back?"

"Yeah."

Satisfied, she grinned and pulled open the door. "Bye."

"Monster," Faith declared and began to stack plates.

"She's terrific." Standing, Jason helped clear the clutter. "Little for her age, I guess. I didn't realize she was almost ten. It's hard to—" He stopped as Faith clattered dishes in the sink. "She'll be ten in February."

"Umm. I can't believe it myself. Sometimes it seems

like yesterday, and then again . . ." She trailed off, abruptly breathless. With studied care, she began to fill the sink with soapy water. "I'll just be a minute here if you'd like to take your wine into the living room."

"In February." Jason took her arm. When he turned her, he saw the blood drain from her face. His fingers tightened, bruising without either of them noticing. "Ten years in February. We made love that June. God, I don't know how many times that night. I never touched you again, we never had the chance to be alone like that again before I left, just a few weeks later. You must have married Tom in September."

Her throat was dry as bone. She couldn't even swallow, but stared at him.

"She's mine," he whispered and it vibrated through the room. "Clara's mine."

She opened her mouth to speak, but there seemed to be nothing she could say. Lips trembling, eyes drenched, she nodded.

"God!" He had her by both arms, nearly lifting her off her feet before he backed her into the counter. The fury in his eyes would have made her cringe if she hadn't been willing to accept it. "How could you? Damn you, she's ours and you never told me. You married another man and had our baby. Did you lie to him, too? Did you make him think she was his so you could have your cozy house and lace curtains?"

"Jason, please—"

"I had a right." He thrust her away before he could give into the violence that pushed him on. "I had a right to her. Ten years. You stole that from me."

"No! No it wasn't like that. Jason, please! You have to listen!"

"The hell with you." He said it calmly, so calmly she stepped back as though she'd been slapped. The anger she could argue with, even reason with. Quiet rage left her help-less.

"Please, let me try to explain."

"There's nothing you can say that could make up for it. Nothing." He yanked his coat from the wall and stormed out.

* * *

You're a damn fool, Jason Law." The Widow Marchant sat in her kitchen rocker and scowled.

"She lied to me. She's been lying for years."

"Hogwash." She fiddled with the tinsel on the little tree on the stand by the window. Cheerful strains from the Nut-cracker floated in from the living room. "She did what she had to do, nothing more, nothing less."

He prowled around the room. He still wasn't sure why he'd come there instead of heading for Clancy's Bar. He'd walked in the snow for an hour, maybe more, then found himself standing on the widow's doorstep. "You knew, didn't you? You knew I was Clara's father."

"I had my ideas." The rocker squeaked gently as she moved. "She had the look of you."

That brought a peculiar thrill, one he didn't know what to do with. "She's the image of Faith."

"True enough if you don't look hard. The eyebrows are you, and the mouth. The sweet Lord knows the temperament is. Jason, if you'd known you were to be a father ten years back, what would you have done?"

"I'd have come back for her." He turned, dragging a hand through his hair. "I'd have panicked," he said more calmly. "But I'd have come back."

"I always thought so. But it—well, it's Faith's story to tell. You'd best go on back and hear it."

"It doesn't matter."

"Can't stand a martyr," she muttered.

He started to snap, then sighed instead. "It hurts. It really hurts."

"That's life for you," she said not unsympathetically. "Want to lose them both again?"

"No. God, no. But I don't know how much I can forgive."

The old woman raised both brows. "Fair enough. Give Faith the same courtesy."

Before he could speak again, the kitchen door burst open. In the doorway stood Faith, covered with snow, face washed with tears. Ignoring the wet she brought in with her, she ran to Jason. "Clara," she managed to stammer.

When he took her arms, he felt the shudders. Terror flowed from her into him. "What's happened?"

"She's missing."

CHAPTER 9

They're going to find her." Jason held her arm as they both stumbled through the snow to her car. "They probably have already."

"One of the kids said he thought she and Marcie went behind this farmhouse to look at the horses in the barn. But when they went back, they weren't there. It's dark." Faith fumbled with her keys.

"Let me drive."

She gave him no argument as she climbed in the passenger side. "Lorna and Bill called the sheriff from the farmhouse. Half the town's out there looking for them. But there's so much snow, and they're just little girls. Jason—"

He took her face in his hands, firmly. "We're going to find them."

"Yes." She wiped away tears with the heels of her hands. "Let's hurry."

He couldn't risk more than thirty miles an hour. They crept down the snow-covered road, searching the landscape for any sign. The hills and fields lay pristine and undisturbed. To Faith they looked unrelenting. But while fear still overwhelmed her, she'd conquered the tears.

Ten miles out of town the fields were lit up like noonday.

Groups of cars crisscrossed the road and men and women tramped through the snow calling. Jason had barely stopped when Faith was out and running toward the sheriff.

"We haven't found them yet, Faith, but we will. They won't have gone far."

"You've searched the barn and the outbuildings?"

The sheriff nodded at Jason. "Every inch."

"How about in the other direction?"

"I'm going to send some men that way."

"We'll go now."

The snow was blinding as he weaved through the other cars. He slackened his speed even more and started to pray. He'd been on a search party once in the Rockies. He hadn't forgotten what a few hours in the wind and snow could do.

"I should have made her wear another sweater." Faith gripped her hands together in her lap as she strained to see out the window. In her hurry she'd forgotten her gloves but didn't notice her numb fingers. "She hates it so when I fuss and I didn't want to spoil the evening for her. Christmas is so special for Clara. She's been so excited." Her voice broke as a ripple of fear became a wave. "I should have made her wear another sweater. She'll be— *Stop!*"

The car fishtailed as he hit the brakes. It took every ounce of control for him to deal with the swerve. Faith pushed open the door and stumbled out. "Over there, it's—"

"It's a dog." He had her by the arms before she could run across the empty field. "It's a dog, Faith."

"Oh, God." Beyond control, she collapsed against him. "She's just a little girl. Where could she be? Oh, Jason, where is she? I should have gone with her. If I'd been there she—"

"Stop it!"

"She's cold and she must be frightened."

"And she needs you." He gave her a quick shake. "She needs you."

Struggling for control, she pressed a hand to her mouth. "Yes. Yes, I'm all right. Let's go. Let's go a little further."

"You wait in the car. I'm going to walk across this field for a bit and see if I spot something."

"I'll go with you."

"I can move faster alone. I'll only be a few minutes." He started to urge her toward the car when a flash of red caught his eye. "Over there."

He gripped her arm as he tried to see through the snow. Just at the edge of the field, he saw it again.

"It's Clara." Faith was already struggling away. "She has a red coat." Snow kicked up around her as she ran. It fell cold and wet to mix with the tears that blinded her vision. With all the breath she had she called out. Arms spread wide, she caught both girls to her. "Oh God, Clara, I've been so scared. Here, here now, you're frozen, both of you. We'll get to the car. Everything's going to be fine. Everything's all right now."

"Is my mom mad?" Shivering, Marcie wept against her shoulder.

"No, no, she's just worried. Everyone is."

"Up you go." Jason hauled Clara up in his arms. For one brief minute he gave himself the luxury of nuzzling his daughter. Looking back, he saw Faith gathering up Marcie. "Can you manage?"

She smiled, holding the still weeping girl close. "No problem."

"Then let's go home."

"We didn't mean to get lost." Clara's tears ran down his collar.

"Of course you didn't."

"We just went to look at the horses and we got all turned around. We couldn't find anybody. I wasn't scared." Her breath hitched as she pressed against him. "Just Marcie."

His child. He felt his own vision blur as he wrapped his arms tighter around her. "You're both safe now."

"Mom was crying."

"She's okay, too." He stopped at the car. "Can you handle them both on your lap in the front? They'll be warmer."

"Absolutely." After Faith had settled in with Marcie, Jason handed her Clara. For one long moment, their gazes held over her head.

"We couldn't find the lights of the house with all the snow," Clara murmured as she held on to her mother. "Then we couldn't find the road for the longest time. It was so cold. I didn't lose my hat."

"I know, baby. Here, get your wet mittens off. You, too, Marcie. Jason has the heater turned all the way up. You'll be cooked before you know it." She ran kisses over two cold faces and fought the need to break down. "What Christmas carols did you sing?"

"'Jingle Bells,'" Marcie said with a sniffle.

"Ah, one of my favorites."

"And 'Joy to the World,'" Clara put in. The heater was pumping warm air over her hands and face. "You like that one better."

"So I do but I can't remember just how it starts. How does it start, Marcie?" She smiled at Clara and snuggled her closer.

In a thin, piping voice still wavery with tears Marcie started to sing. She was nearly through the first verse when they came to the rest of the search party.

"It's my dad!" Bouncing on Faith's lap, Marcie started to wave. "He doesn't look mad."

With a half laugh, Faith kissed the top of her head. "Merry Christmas, Marcie."

"Merry Christmas, Mrs. Monroe. See you tomorrow, Clara." Marcie barely had time to open the door before she was scooped up.

"What a night." There were waves and cheers as the car weaved through the crowd.

"It's Christmas Eve," Clara reminded her mother. The world was safe and warm again. "Maybe I should open that one big present tonight."

"Not a chance," Jason told her and tugged at her hair.

Faith turned Clara in her arms and squeezed tight.

"Don't cry, Mom."

"I have to, for just a minute." True to her word, her eyes were dry when they arrived home. An exhausted Clara dozed on Jason's shoulder as he carried her inside. "I'll take her up, Jason."

"We'll take her up."

She let her arms fall back to her sides and nodded.

They pulled off boots and socks and sweaters and wrapped Clara in warm flannel. She murmured a bit and tried to stay awake but the adventures of the evening took their toll. "It's Christmas Eve," she mumbled. "I'm going to get up real early in the morning."

"As early as you like," Faith told her as she pressed a kiss to her cheek.

"Can I have cookies for breakfast?"

"Half a dozen," Faith agreed recklessly. She smiled and was asleep before Faith pulled the blankets around her.

"I was afraid . . ." She let her hand linger on her daughter's cheek. "I was afraid I'd never see her like this again. Safe, warm. Jason, I don't know how to thank you for just being there. If I'd been alone—" She broke off and shook her head.

"I think we should go downstairs, Faith."

The tone made her press her lips together. She'd be ready, she promised herself, to handle the accusations, the bitterness, the resentment. "I think I'd like a drink," she said as they walked downstairs. "Some brandy. It looks like the fire's gone out."

"I'll take care of it. You get the brandy. There are some things I have to say."

"All right." She left him to go to the little cabinet in the dining room. When she came back, the fire was just catching. He straightened from it and took a snifter.

"Do you want to sit down?"

"No, I can't." She sipped, but it would have taken more than brandy to steady her nerves. "Whatever you have to say, Jason, you should say it."

CHAPTER 10

She stood looking at him, her back straight, her eyes burning with emotion, her hands clasping the snifter tightly. Part of him wanted to go to her, gather her close and just hold on. He'd found a child and nearly lost her in the same night. Did anything else matter? But inside was a void that had to be filled. Questions, demands, accusations had to be answered. There had to be an accounting before there could be understanding, and understanding before there could be forgiveness. But where did he start?

He walked to the tree. There was a star on top that shed silver light over all the other colors. "I'm not sure I know what to say. It isn't every day a man turns around and finds himself with a half-grown daughter. I feel cheated out of watching her learn to walk, hearing her talk, Faith. Nothing you can do or say can ever give that back to me, can it?"

"No."

He turned to see her holding the brandy at waist level. Her face was very pale and calm. Whatever emotions she was feeling she managed to restrain. Yes, this was a different Faith than the one he'd left. The girl would never have been able to exert the self-control the woman did. "No excuses, Faith?"

"I guess I thought I had them, then tonight when I thought I'd lost her . . ." Her voice trailed off and she shook her head. "No excuses, Jason."

"She thinks Tom's her father."

"No!" Her eyes weren't calm now but brilliant. "Do you think I'd let her believe her father had deserted her, that he didn't care enough even to write? What she knows is basically the truth. I never lied to her."

"What is the truth?"

She took a steadying breath. When she looked at him, her face was still pale but her voice was calm again. "That I loved her father, and he loved me, but he had to go away before he even knew about her and he wasn't able to come back."

"He would have."

Something rushed into her eyes but she turned away. "I told her that, too."

"Why?" The fury came back and he fought against it. "I have to know why you did what you did. I lost all those years."

"*You?*" Her temper was less easily controlled than her grief. Years of holding back bubbled inside her and burst out. "*You* lost?" she repeated as she whirled around. "You were gone and I was eighteen years old, pregnant and alone."

Guilt flared. He hadn't expected it. "I wouldn't have left if you'd told me."

"I didn't know." She put the brandy down and pushed back her hair with both hands. "It was just a week after you'd gone that I found out I was carrying our baby. I was thrilled." With a laugh, she wrapped her arms around her chest. For a moment she looked heartbreakingly young and innocent. "I was so happy. I waited every day, every night for you to call so I could tell you." Her eyes sobered. The smile faded. "But you never called, Jason."

"I needed time to set things up—a steady job, a place I could ask you to live in."

"You never understood it didn't matter where I lived, as long as it was with you." She shook her head before he could speak. "It doesn't matter now. That part's over. A week passed, then two, then a month. I got ill, just tension, morning sickness, but I began to realize you weren't going to call. You weren't coming back. I was angry for a while, acknowledging you just hadn't wanted me enough. Small-town girl."

"That's not true. That was never true."

She studied him a moment, almost dispassionately. The lights of the tree fell over his dark-blond hair, glimmered in the deep, deep eyes that had always held their own secrets. Restlessness. "Wasn't it?" she murmured. "It was certainly true that you wanted out. I was part of Quiet Valley and you wanted out."

"I wanted you with me."

"But not enough to let me go with you." She shook her head when he started to speak. "Not enough to let me come to you until you'd proved the things you needed to prove. I didn't always understand that, Jason, but I began to when you came back."

"You weren't ever going to tell me about Clara, were you?"

She heard the bitterness again and closed her eyes against it. "I don't know. I honestly don't."

He drank, hoping it would warm the ice in his veins. "Tell me the rest."

"I wanted the baby, but I was scared, too scared even to tell my mother."

She picked up the brandy again but merely warmed her hands with it. "I should have of course, but I wasn't thinking clearly."

"Why did you marry Tom?" But even as he asked, he

realized the old jealousies were fading. He only wanted to understand.

"Tom would come by almost every night. We'd talk. He didn't seem to mind me talking about you and God knows I needed to. Then one night we were sitting on the porch and I just broke down. I was three months pregnant and my body was changing. That morning I hadn't been able to snap my jeans." With a shaky laugh, she ran a hand over her face. "It sounds so silly, but I hadn't been able to snap my jeans and it was terrifying. It made me realize there was no going back. Everything just poured out while we sat there. He said he'd marry me. Of course I said no, but he began to reason it all out. You weren't coming back and I was pregnant. He loved me and wanted to marry me. The baby would have a name, a home, a family. It sounded so right the way he said it and I wanted the baby to be safe. I wanted to be safe."

She drank now because her throat ached. "It was wrong, right from the beginning. He knew I didn't love him, but he just wanted me, or thought he did. The first few months he tried, we both really tried. But after Clara came, he couldn't handle it. I could see every time he looked at her he thought of you. There was nothing I could do to change the fact that she was yours." She paused and found it easier to say it all. "There was nothing I would have done to change that. As long as I had her, I had part of you. Tom knew it, no matter how much I tried to be what he wanted. He started drinking, picking fights, staying out. It was as though he wanted me to ask for a divorce."

"But you didn't."

"I didn't because I . . . well, I felt I owed him. Then one day I came home from taking Clara out and he was gone. Divorce papers came in the mail, and that was that."

"Why didn't you ever try to contact me, Faith, through one of the magazines or newspapers?"

"And say what? Jason, remember me? By the way, you have a daughter back here in Quiet Valley. Drop in some time."

"One word—one word from you and I'd have left everything and come back. I never stopped loving you."

She closed her eyes. "I watched you walk away from me. I watched you get on the bus and leave me without a trace. I stood there for hours, half believing you'd get off at the next stop and come back. I was the one who had to stay behind, Jason."

"I called. Damn it, Faith, it only took me six months to get something started."

She smiled. "And when you called I was seven months pregnant. My mother didn't tell me for a long time, not until after Tom had left. She said you made her promise."

"I needed my pride."

"I know."

That she didn't question. He saw the way she smiled as she said it, as if she'd always understood. "You must have been terrified."

Her smile softened. "There were moments."

"You must have hated me."

"Never. How could I? You went away but you left me with the most beautiful thing in my life. Maybe you were right, maybe I was. Maybe we were both wrong, but there was Clara. Every time I looked at her, I could remember how much I loved you."

"How do you feel now?"

"Shaky." She laughed a little, then folded her hands, determined to do what was right. "Clara should be told. I'd prefer doing it myself."

The idea made him reach for the brandy again. "How do you think she'll take it?"

"She's learned to get along without a father. It doesn't mean she hasn't needed one." She sat up straight and raised her chin. "You have a right, of course, to see her whenever you like, but I won't have her bounced around. I also realize you can't be here for her all the time because of your work, but don't think you can just pop into her life and out again. You'll have to make an effort to keep in touch with her, Jason."

So this was another fear she'd lived with, he realized. Maybe he deserved it. "You don't trust me, do you?"

"Clara's too important." She let out a little sigh. "So are you."

"If I told you I fell for her before I knew, would it make a difference?"

She thought of the toboggan, of the way he'd looked when Clara had thrown her arms around his neck. "She needs all the love she can get. We all do. She's so much like you, I—" She broke off when her eyes filled. "Damn, I don't want to do this." Impatient, she brushed tears away. "I'll tell her tomorrow, Jason. On Christmas. You and I can work out the arrangements. I know you're leaving soon, but if you could stay a few more days, give her some time, it would make it easier for all of us."

He rubbed at the tension at the back of his neck. "You never asked me for much of anything, did you?"

She smiled. "I asked you for everything. We were both too young to realize it."

"You always believed in magic, Faith." He pulled a box out of his pocket. "It's nearly midnight. Open it now."

"Jason." She pushed her hands through her hair. How could he think of presents now? "I don't think this is the time."

"It's ten years past time."

When he thrust the box at her she found herself gripping it with both hands. "I don't have anything to give you."

He touched her face, almost hesitantly. "You've just given me a daughter."

Relief poured through her. Instead of bitterness, she heard gratitude. Love, never dimmed, shimmered in her eyes. "Jason—"

"Please, open it."

She pulled off the glossy red paper and revealed the black velvet box beneath. With fingers not quite steady she opened it. The ring was a teardrop, frozen in place, glorious with the reflected lights from the tree.

"Paul told me it was the best he had."

"You bought this before you knew—"

"Yeah, before I knew I was going to ask the mother of my child to marry me. We'll be legal, the three of us." He took her hand and waited. "How about a second chance? I won't let you down, Faith."

"You never did." Close to tears again, she reached out her hand to his cheek. "It wasn't you, it wasn't me, it was life. Oh, Jason, I want this. Understand, all I've ever really wanted was to be married to you, have a family with you."

"Then let me put the ring on."

"Jason, it's not just me. If it were, I'd leave with you this instant. We'd go to Hong Kong, Siberia, Peking. Anywhere. But it's not just me; I have to stay."

"It's not just you," he repeated. He took the ring and tossed the box aside. "And *I* have to stay. Do you think I'd leave you again? Do you think I could leave what's upstairs or the chance to have more that I can watch grow up? I'm not going anywhere."

"But you said—Hong Kong."

"I quit." When he grinned, he felt the pressure of years melt away. "Today. That was one of the things I took care of this afternoon. I'm going to write a book." He took her by the shoulders. "I'm out of a job, I'm living in a room at the inn and asking you to marry me."

The breath backed up in her lungs. Her heart was pounding. Yes, she'd always believed in magic. It was standing in front of her. "Ten years ago, I thought I loved you as much as it was possible to love. You were a boy. In the last few days I've learned that loving a man is something quite different." She paused and saw the ring in his hand explode with the joyful lights on the tree. "If you'd asked me ten years ago, I'd have said yes."

"Faith—"

With a laugh, she threw her arms around his neck. "You're going to get the same answer now. Oh, I love you, Jason, more than ever."

"We've got years to make up for."

"Yes." She met his mouth with equal hunger, equal hope. "We will. The three of us."

"The three of us." He let his forehead rest against hers. "I want more."

"We've more than enough time to give Clara a baby brother or sister for next Christmas." Her lips sought his again. "We've got more than enough time for everything."

They both heard the bells peal out from the town hall. Midnight.

"Merry Christmas, Faith."

She felt the ring slide onto her finger. All wishes were granted. "Welcome home, Jason."